Furnished Room

For my father
MAURICE DEL-RIVO

and the memory of my mother
NAOMI DEL-RIVO
with love and gratitude

The
Furnished
Room

Laura Del-Rivo

New London Editions

The Furnished Room
by Laura Del-Rivo

Published in 2011
by Five Leaves Publications,
PO Box 8786, Nottingham NG1 9AW
www.fiveleaves.co.uk

The Furnished Room
was first published in 1961
by Hutchinson & Co.

ISBN 9781907869143

Five Leaves acknowledges
financial support from
Arts Council England

Typeset and designed by
Four Sheets Design and Print
Printed in Great Britain

Chapter 1

WHEN HE WOKE it was evening but the air in the room was still heavy with heat. He lay on the bed, on top of the grey ex-army blankets, fully dressed except for his shoes.

As he became more awake he knew that it was still there: the pain circuit inside his head. It was not caused, it simply existed; it was part of him.

Rivulets of sweat felt like flies. The window was wide open but no air was coming in.

The objects in the room had an oppressive life of their own, like the atmosphere before a thunderstorm. His suedette zipper jacket hung from the door. It seemed to swell, as if the appearance of the jacket had come forward from the jacket itself. He tried looking at the wall, and the wall expanded and loomed towards him. He thought that it was wrong that objects should intrude so much. They were inescapable; great lumps of matter.

He felt in his pocket for the cigarettes, because the act of striking a match and lighting the cigarette would knock a few seconds off the boredom. Then he lay smoking and flicking ash into the Watney's Ales ashtray.

The alarm clock had a cheap, loud tick. It limited his consciousness like a wall. Thought became the clock noise, so that he thought: *Trk* trk, *trk* trk, *trk* trk — 'No!' he said aloud, covering his ears with his hands. Then he relaxed the pressure of his hands, unable to stop listening to the clock which now sounded different, going: Trk *trk,* trk *trk,* trk *trk.*

Once, as a child, he had knelt at the back of an empty church. There had been a statue beside the altar, and a bush of flowering candles. He had held his breath to make himself feel dizzy. The candles had seemed to shoot skywards. He had concentrated all his energies in the effort to distort his vision, because he had willed that, at the climax, the statue of Christ would move and speak to him.

At fifteen he had decided to become a priest. He had spent his last year at school in the surety of his vocation. His whole life had been based on the assumption that he would take Holy Orders.

Then he lost belief in religion. One memory served for the many Sundays spent at home in the family's terrace house, Homelea. He had been lying in bed, smoking, and listening to his mother in the next room preparing for church. Her noise and bustle had been designed to shame him, and in this he had taken a perverse pleasure. He had thought: It's absurd to expect me to believe that Christ, whom I've never met, died to redeem me from the sin of Adam, whom I've also never met. He had read the *News of the World*. If his mother came in the paper and his rumpled pyjamas would show his indifference. Through the wall he had recognized every sound she made. That closing drawer was for her best hat, the hard straw with the brooch pinned in front. Another drawer for the black cotton gloves. Then the missal, with pious pictures between the pages. Let her make all the noise she likes. She won't succeed in making me feel ashamed. I am utterly indifferent. I am reading my paper.

Then she had come into his room, with her worn face and loving eyes. 'Well, dear, I must go.' Pause. 'It's Palm Sunday.'

He had turned a page. ''Bye, then.'

'You're not going to stay in bed all day, are you, Joe? It's such a waste of time.'

'Shouldn't think so.'

'I'll pray for you. I always pray for you at Mass.'

He had felt nauseated and resentful. Because he coldly knew that he did not love her or anyone he had felt like an adult in a world of children. He had taken to long, solitary walks at night. Sometimes he had gone to the all-night transport café on the arterial road near his home and fed coins into the juke-box. He had enjoyed walking the deserted streets; he was the only living, active being in the sleeping town. Returning home, he had fried eggs and bacon and sat up reading in the kitchen for most of the night. Consequently, he was always half asleep at his job the next day. His behaviour led to trouble at home and at work, and finally he left home and hitchhiked to London with a suitcase containing clothes and books.

In London he lived in various furnished rooms. He changed addresses from time to time, but all the rooms were much the same. One overlooked the railway near Paddington Station; that had been pleasant.

His present room was in Tewkesbury Road, W11. It was furnished with a bed, an armchair, and a folding card-table with a scarred, green-felt top. The wardrobe, with its newspaper-lined drawer, was too large for the room. On top of the wardrobe he had stowed his suitcase and the fringed shade he had removed from the light. The grate was not used except as an ashtray, as there was a gas fire and a greasy ring on a tin tray. The gas meter, beside the fireplace, was fixed so that the tenant did not get the full value of the shillings. On the wash-stand was a rose-patterned china bowl, his toilet things, a bottle of Daddy's Favourite Sauce, and a regiment of unwashed milk bottles. Beside it was a plastic slop bucket. He used the cupboard part of the wash-stand as a larder, and stacked his books along the window-ledge.

He stubbed out his cigarette, then got up. He stood without moving in the centre of the room, as if his feet were welded to the floor. He was paralysed by boredom and the heaviness of the room. Looking at the rumpled blankets, he wanted to straighten them, but could not do so because they existed more strongly than he did.

The unreality was bad. Finding everything unreal led logically to thinking that there was no point in doing anything. Every attempt was undermined by insight into the futility of its end. Therefore every action, from getting up in the morning and on through-out the day, had become an effort. Often he stayed up, doing nothing, until two or three in the morning because he was too bored and lethargic to go to bed. He was in a desert. Others believed in the mirages; only he was condemned to the clarity of sight which knew them to be unreal.

He went to the window and looked down at the square of back yard. A woman's vest hung from the clothes-line.

He suddenly wanted to smash the window. He foresaw the dark star in the pane and the broken glass in the yard below. The upper sash was lowered so there were two thicknesses of glass to break. He would cut his hand, which would be interesting.

Then he knew he would not do it. His mind had come between the impulse and the action, making the action impossible. He often had such urges to violence. They were occasioned by seeing, for instance, the bald head of a baby or of an old man. Once, seeing a bald baby, the impulse to smash its skull had been so strong that he had clenched his fists in fear of giving way to it. He had imagined the horror of the parents, and had sweated with fear that he might be unable to combat the compulsion.

Sooner or later he would commit a violent crime. He was certain of it. It was only a matter of time.

He went downstairs to the bathroom to fetch hot water, then washed in the rose-patterned bowl. He washed his face and hands and armpits. He had not closed the door properly and the sound of somebody's radio floated up. The jazz music was pleasant.

He took the towel from the back of the armchair and walked round the room as he dried himself. As usual he felt slight surprise when he saw his face in the mirror. He was surprised that he looked like anything. His name was Joseph Ignatius Beckett and they called him Joe.

The tune on the radio changed: a celestial choir was rendering the theme-song of a film. He put the bowl on the floor to wash his feet, soaping between his toes with his fingers. His stretch-nylon grip-top socks had made a pattern on his feet. He sniffed the socks to ensure they were still wearable, before putting them on again.

Before leaving, he checked his pockets. One contained the green notebook. From time to time he wrote in it. He entered his disbelief in God and in everything, his sensations of unreality and lack of meaning, and his inability to love or feel. Essentially, the book stated that he believed in nothing. It was his declaration of spiritual bankruptcy.

He flipped through it and found a pencil sketch on one of the pages. It was signed: *From your own Ilsa Barnes with tons of love. XXXX*. The sketch was of him but bore little resemblance. None of Ilsa's work was any good; it was both technically bad and uninspired. She was a little blonde bitch, a phony art student. She had been his girlfriend once, and they had been on such intimate terms that it had no longer been necessary to make love every time they slept together. Ilsa belonged to the days of the Paddington room overlooking the railway. Together they had watched the trains from the window, her hair spilled on her shoulders, and, in the dingy, grimy city, summer had been the blonde tendrils of her hair. Suddenly he had heard himself asking her to go away with him and live in Cornwall. He hadn't known why he had asked her. He didn't love her and her company rather bored him. She had refused, he had pleaded and she had refused again. When she had left him for another man he had felt miserable on one level but on another level utterly indifferent.

He shut the door of his room behind him. The stairs and passage had the odour of loneliness and soup which is peculiar to bedsitter-land. It impregnated the orange flowers on the wallpaper and the strips of beige linoleum that led to the front door. Without being actually impolite, Beckett generally avoided contact with the other tenants. He disliked intrusions on his privacy.

He walked from Tewkesbury Road to Paradine Street. Some giggling schoolgirls passed, returning from Porchester Hall Public Baths with rolled towels and meagre hair flattened to their scalps.

An old man shuffled along the gutter. The placard safety-pinned to his coat said:

HELL FIRE AWAITS SINNERS.

He had close-set fanatic's eyes; his mouth was lipless.

Beckett thought angrily: Fool! Hell isn't a place you go to after death. Hell is a state of mind. The nothingness is hell, the emptiness, the desert. Disbelief in the mirages is hell, pain without anaesthetic, the price of knowledge.

The old man passed, his feet shuffling slowly in unlaced plimsolls.

The Paradine Café snack bar had wiped-over tables, and a counter with urns and a glass case of buns. The advertisements on the walls were for Coca-Cola, Aspro, and Senior Service. It was the place where he always ate, for he had a conservative nature. Three workmen, who were also regulars, exchanged nods of greeting with him.

The menu slate listed egg, peas, and chips; sausage, peas, and chips; shepherd's pie, peas, and chips; rice pudding with jam; jam roll with custard; tea; coffee; ice cream.

Beckett chose the Vienna steak and a coffee.

The proprietor held a fistful of cups under the nozzle of the tea urn. 'Another hot day.'

'Isn't it.'

'Still, makes up for last summer.'

'Doesn't it.' Beckett had no remembrance of what last summer had been like.

'I'll bring your meal over.'

He sat down at his usual table in the corner. When the food came he ate hungrily. The peas were the tinned sort, and swam in bright-green juice. The radio was relaying a variety show, which emerged at intervals from the noise of cutlery, conversation, and hissing steam. *'Well, my mother-in-law; you know my mother-in-law...'* The laughter of the studio audience switched on and off like a buzzer.

A girl in a short, tight skirt sat at the table opposite. She swung her slim, nyloned leg, regarding her shoe, tapping her cigarette on the edge of the ashtray.

'I only live a stone's throw away from my mother-in-law.' 'You only live a stone's throw away from your mother-in-law?' 'Yes; so help me to pick up some more stones.' The vase of cutlery on top of the radio rattled.

His gaze travelled up the girl's leg to the edge of her slip and the darkness beyond it. He felt half-desire mixed with the fragments of remembered past desires.

He had images of a girl with inelegantly opened legs against a wall, or on the back seat of a car. Then there had been another girl, the first. One autumn day in a glade she had lain on her back, waiting for him, with her skirt drawn up showing her suspenders, her knickers round one ankle, and her plastic handbag among the fallen leaves.

The girl opposite stroked her hair. For a second her gaze met Beckett's. Her eyes were untrustworthy, and as cool as fishes, and he felt that she was one woman promising all women.

Then a man sat down beside her, and she remarked: 'Mustn't be long, eh? or we'll miss the big picture.'

Beckett turned away. He was not disappointed because she had an escort, but because he knew there was no universal woman; only individuals. He did not want individuals. He wanted everything and nothing.

He knew that although the woman had excited him across the café, if she had come and sat on his knee he would not have wanted her. Many of his desires were like that: threads stretched to strangers across cafés or Tube compartments or night streets. They were the mark of the lonely; not unpleasant.

On the way home he noticed a small boy squatting on the pavement outside the house where Gash lived.

As Beckett got nearer, he saw that the boy was writing with chalk on the pavement.

The boy stood up defensively, and Beckett read the words:

MISTER GASH IS A SILLY FOOL. TRUE.

'Why did you write that?'

The boy said nothing. He took used bus tickets from his pockets and counted them.

'Why did you write that?'

The boy still did not answer, so Beckett started to rub out the words with his shoe.

The boy watched in silence for a while, then asked: 'You a friend of his, then?'

'Yes.'

'He cuts children up inter pieces, and makes them inter pies.'

'Who told you that?'

'My mum.' The boy continued to watch for a few seconds, then dropped his collection of bus tickets, yelled: 'You're daft...' and ran away.

The writing could not be entirely obliterated. Beckett looked at the blurred chalk-marks and scattered tickets, then walked home. He did not know why he had bothered to remove the insulting words. They would not have worried Gash.

Chapter 2

THE PARTY WAS in Fulham, in somebody's flat. People were sitting on the divan or on the floor; a few were dancing. On the mantelpiece were a stolen "Gents" sign, a child's dish of soggy cornflakes, and a photograph of an ex-wife fondling an Alsatian in a back garden. The top of the radiogram served as a bar, and the babble of voices rose above the LP of the latest American musical.

'...he always does it in telephone kiosks. ...'

'...I go to Private Views for the free drink... .'

'...darling, your shoulder-strap's showing. ...'

'...why are Bob and George such ages at the off licence? ...'

Beckett was jammed on the edge of the divan. A woman, aged about thirty-five, was sitting heavily on his knee. He did not know who she was, except that someone had introduced her as Georgia. She was drinking gin-and-orange. When she held out her cup for a refill he noticed the coin-shaped vaccination mark on her plump upper arm, and wanted to bite her arm.

He and Georgia talked nonsense and kissed. She had a tilted nose; her sexy suggestive eyes were experienced in double beds and saloon bars and in being combined mistress and mother to many men.

'Have a cigarette, love,' she said, groping in her handbag among makeup, letters, and Kleenex tissues. He saw down her dress.

When there was more room on the divan they sat side by side, their arms uncomfortably round each other. He was kissing her again when somebody said: 'Oh look, there's Ilsa Barnes...' Ilsa, just arrived, stood in the doorway. He noticed that she had given up her arty garb of shirt-tails and paint-smeared jeans, and was dressed in a smart, sophisticated manner in a scarlet dress that matched her lipstick. Otherwise she was unchanged, with her brittle body and dissatisfied, avaricious eyes. The habitual cigarette smouldered between her fingers.

He wondered what he felt, then realized that he felt nothing.

'That girl Ilsa is a friend of mine,' Georgia said. 'Do you know her?'

'I used to, yes.'

'She was at St Martin's Art School, wasn't she? I thought it was such a pity when she left.'

He said: 'She decided she couldn't paint, and anyway didn't want to, and that it would be better to break off completely and start something new.'

'What a pity.' Georgia regarded the tip of her cigarette. 'She was very keen; she was going to take her Teacher's Diploma and get a job teaching art in a school. Well, I must say I wish I had the talent to do drawing or something. What a crime to throw it away!'

'Oh, well.'

'Did you know her well, then?'

'Fairly. I spent a weekend at her parents' farm once. They have a farm in Sussex. Pleasant people.'

'I think she drinks too much. It's wrong in a young girl. Different for me...' She raised her glass. 'Mother's ruin.'

As usual, Ilsa seemed to know everyone. Her loud, bad-mannered voice rose above the general clamour as she rushed about greeting people. As she talked, she pushed her hair back from her forehead with abrupt, nervous movements.

There was something strained about her gaiety and pale, taut face. She was like a woman in wartime, living it up in order to forget that she might die tomorrow.

She saw him at last and energetically waved her arm, shouting across the room: 'Hello! I *must* come and talk to you later!' Then she dashed off to greet somebody else. She was very popular.

'Oh dear,' Georgia said, 'she's too busy to talk to us. Nobody loves us. Still, never mind, we love each other.'

'That's right, we love each other.'

She pushed against him. 'Do you know, all this drink has gone to my head rather.'

'Mine too.'

'Drink takes away all my powers of resistance, which aren't very strong at the best of times.' Suggestive giggle. 'You could do anything with me now, Joe. Anything at all, if you wanted to.'

He stared at her. Then kissed her mouth hard and unlovingly and forced her down on to the divan.

The room was not there. There was only Georgia's body, lying half across him, as heavy and inevitable as a sandbag. Her mouth was glued to his; the curtain of her hair was rung down against escape.

Then, inevitably, he was saying that the room was too noisy, too crowded, that the party was a bore anyway, and that it would be a good idea if they left and went back to his place.

She sat up. Her lipstick was smudged; her face was sensual with surrender. 'All right, Joe.'

'Now?'

'Yes, now if you like.'

They were both embarrassed by the mechanics of seduction. He said: 'Well, let's go, then.'

'I must just get my jacket. I left it in the other room. Will you wait?'

'Yes, of course. Don't be long.'

As she got up, her dress brushed his knees. He felt quick surprise that she was now a stranger, and tonight he was going to sleep with her. Already the element of disappointment was there.

He knew he must be drunk, because when he put his glass down on the table the table was not there and the glass fell to the floor. He watched the wetness darkening the carpet; and then he was not there but in another corner of the room, talking to strangers. He did not know how he came to be talking to them.

Discomfort made him lurch off in search of the lavatory. Going down the stairs, he thought: Tonight I shall sleep with an auburn-haired tart... Soon he and Georgia would be on the Tube, sitting with their thighs touching, and he would be thinking to the rattle of the train: I'm going to sleep with an auburn-haired tart; I'm going to sleep with an auburn-haired tart...

His mouth was thick with the metallic taste of wine. He could hear the noise of the party. The flat was full of drunken extroverts. He had only to let go to be as drunk as they were. But he could not let go. He remained unbending, thinking of Georgia with adult loveless lust. He felt immeasurably older than the others.

When he returned to the room Ilsa and a young man were giving an exhibition of jiving. It was the sort of situation Ilsa adored; she loved being the centre of attention. Her skirt flame-swirled as she danced.

Suddenly she stopped, and shouted in her rude voice to one of the watching men: 'Go on, stare! I've got nice legs, haven't I?'

Everybody was silent. Ilsa's partner stood with his arm extended, like a statue.

The man whom she had insulted backed, embarrassed. 'I wasn't staring at you... I wasn't doing any harm... I was only watching.'

'Oh yes, I know the way you watch. Would you like me to take my dress off, so that you can watch better?'

'No, no, really...'

Ilsa had worked herself up into a pitch of insolence. 'Go on, tell me to and I will. That's what you want, isn't it?' Beckett felt jealousy because of her showing-off, and because none of the people here knew that Ilsa had belonged to him.

Then the incident was over. More couples took the floor, and the dancing began again.

Beckett went and stood by the window. He drew back the curtain and looked down at the garden. The noise of the party seemed distant, as if he was shut off from it. That was a relief. He didn't want anything to do with the party or with that bloody little bitch Ilsa Barnes.

After a while she came and stood beside him. 'I say, give me a fag, will you?'

He offered her the packet and then took one himself.

She bent her head for the match, her blonde hair falling in separate strands to her shoulders. She smiled at him. Then she looked out of the window. 'Joe-Joe.'

'Ilse-Ilse.'

'I'm glad to see you.'

'I'm glad to see *you*.'

She said: 'You keeping all right?'

'Not bad. And you?'

'Oh, marvellous. On the whole.' She switched to her hard bright voice. 'Have you been to Tony's Club? They've got a new guitarist.'

'No, I haven't.'

'To the Jazz Cellar?'

'No.'

'To the Saturday-night parties at Cliff and Una's, then?'

'No.'

'Christ,' she said, 'you don't go anywhere, do you? No wonder I've looked out for you in vain.'

'Have you?'

'Well of course I have, hon. You don't think I'm so unfriendly, do you?'

He said: 'I've always tended to spend most of my time in my room, reading. As if it was a monastic cell. By the way, I've moved from the Paddington room. I'm in Notting Hill now.'

'Nice room?'

'No, hideous. You know, the typical bedsitter.'

They were silent for a while. He watched her as she smoked. Her bare arms were thin, like the broken stalks of flowers. Suddenly she exclaimed: 'I say, wasn't it funny when I went for that chap! He was staring at me with his eyes popping out of his head, the fool. He was scared stiff I'd really take my dress off.'

'I wouldn't have let you do that.'

'Oh, really? And what would you have done to stop me?'

'Hit you or something, probably.'

She said rudely: 'How caveman.'

'Oh, shut up.' Then he asked: 'Who was the man, anyway?'

'Just somebody I went out with once or twice. He's in love with me, I think. But I got sick of him.' She crushed out her unfinished cigarette. 'You know how it is.'

'Yes, I know.'

'I enjoy making a man fall in love with me. Especially if he doesn't want to; if he doesn't like me or if he belongs to somebody else. I make him fall in love with me but when he does I lose interest. And the more of a devoted spaniel he becomes the more he irritates me. And finally I ditch him, and the girl I took him off can have him back. Only generally he doesn't want her. He still wants me.'

'I see.'

She regarded him with her anxious, untrustworthy eyes. 'I suppose I was an awful bitch to you, wasn't I?'

'No, not really, love.'

'I bet I was. I always am. But you were just as unpleasant in your way as I was in mine. You always despised me, didn't you, Joe? You didn't really love me; you only gave an imitation of it. You wanted my body, and tolerated my company for the sake of that. The other men I've had were spaniels, and I always ended by kicking them, but you and I parted just about quits. And I am honest with you, Joe, aren't I?'

'Oh yes.'

'Even if it's only to tell you that it's no good.' She strummed her fingers on the window-ledge. 'I say, give me another cigarette, will you?'

He gave her one.

'Thanks. Do you think they've got any Bugs Bugloss records here?'

'I don't know. Who is he?'

'Haven't you heard of him? He's my latest craze. Vocal and clarinet. He was guest artiste at the Cellar Club last week, and I spent the last of my wages on entrance money. Here, I've got the photographs...'

The first three showed a band playing, and people jiving in a dimly lit club. Ilsa was in the foreground in all of them; a thin girl with a hard, young face, showing off for the cameras. The other photographs were an assortment of snaps, nearly all signed with some sentimental message. *To Ilsa, with tons of love; Ilsa, always a pal; To Ilsa, with fond remembrance.*

'I collect snaps,' she said, taking them back and returning them to her handbag.

'And friends, it would seem.'

'Oh yes, I like lots of people, lots of excitement. Otherwise I get bored. By the way, why were you in such a huddle with Georgia? She's years older than you, and she's fat.'

'Don't you like her? She seemed to like you.'

'Oh yes,' Ilsa jeered, 'I can just imagine her saying it. "Poor Ilsa, she is so sweet, what a pity she had to leave the art school." Bloody fool! Everybody seems to think I must be upset at leaving St Martin's. Well, as a matter of fact I never gave a damn about painting. I only went there to escape from home, and because I thought there would be lots of attractive male students. And I left because I was sick of dressing like a student, and never having any money, and because I wanted to buy some smart clothes. Does that shock you? Too bad.' She pushed her hair abruptly back from her forehead. 'Well, I must go and talk to somebody. Bye-bye, see you later.'

Alone, Beckett looked at the cigarette-ends, smeared with lipstick, that she had trodden into the carpet. She chucked everything away like that, like unfinished cigarettes. She chucked away her smart social manner, her trite remarks: 'Bye-bye.' 'Marvellous to see you.' 'Like to buy me a drink?' 'Christ, how I hate rain.' And men scrambled for these chuck-outs as if they were pearls.

There was another drink in his hand. He could not remember how he had got it, and he had lost count of the number he had drunk. '... but, I mean, Cornwall is terribly bogus, isn't it?...'

'... so this American goes into this chemist shop, you see, and asks for ...'

'... surely all the white wine hasn't gone...'

'... and her husband put a tape-recorder under the bed...'

A boy called Michael, who at seventeen was a cross between a juvenile delinquent and a poet, was dancing

in an ecstatic frenzy. The jazz was in demonic posses-
sion of him; he yipped and screamed.

'Joe!' Georgia slipped her hand through Beckett's
arm. 'Are we going?' She was wearing a jacket of pale-
blue nylon fur, which cast a soft shadow on her
powdered cheek.

'Of course. Right away. I was waiting for you.'

'I'm sorry I was such a long time, but I was talking to
a man who hasn't got anywhere to stay the night. Oh,
here he is...'

'Dyce,' the man said, gripping Beckett's hand.
'Captain Dick Dyce.'

He was in a garden, talking to the dark, well-dressed
man with the decisive features who had introduced
himself as Dyce. He felt his drunkenness recede. A
shape floated beside him; he concentrated on the
shape, and it became static and turned into a rose
bush. He thought it strange that there should be a rose
bush in the middle of a party night.

Dyce said: 'Well, I'm glad we've got out of that dreary
gathering upstairs. Who's giving the party, anyway?
You got any idea?'

Beckett frowned, trying to collect his thoughts.
'Where's Georgia?'

'Oh, she's all right. She said she'd wait.'

'Wait. She'd wait.' He rubbed his brow, and the
drunkenness receded further. He was almost sober. He
answered Dyce: 'I think the hostess is the woman in
leopard-skin trousers. Not sure, though.'

'The leopard-skin female, by God. It's always as well
to know who one's hostess is. Otherwise I might have
told her what a bloody hideous flat she's got. Although
I suspect she would have taken it as a compliment.
Most women like being insulted. Well, tell me, what
brought you here tonight?'

'I wanted to pick up a girl.'

Dyce grinned, showing the good teeth. 'Quite, old boy. But none of the girls here are worth picking up.'

'Not even the little blonde one, Ilsa?'

'Ah yes. Now she has something. A natural style. But she's too rowdy, with that strident voice of hers, and the way she has to call attention to herself all the time. But spend some time and money training that girl and she could be made into quite a stunner. Unfortunately, life's too short. I don't have that much time to spend on one woman; there are too many other apples waiting to be picked.'

Annoyed, Beckett said nothing.

'How old is the Ilsa girl?' Dyce asked. 'Twenty-two or something?'

'Nineteen.'

'Oh well, I'll have another look at her in a few years' time, when she's had the corners knocked off her.'

'What makes you think she'll like you?'

'When I'm drunk, old boy, everything happens right,' Dyce said. He added: 'I'm drunk now.'

'You don't seem it.'

'I know; I never do. Strange, isn't it?'

'I'm much the same.'

'By the way, are you and Georgia fixed up?'

Beckett said: 'She's coming home with me, if that's what you mean.'

'Well, look, I wonder if you could do me a favour. I don't particularly care for Georgia. The good-hearted-barmaid type, not my style at all. But I'm out of a place to stay the night, and I wondered if Georgia could put me up. Unless it means a lot to you, of course.'

Beckett felt slightly disgusted by his own conduct and by the false heartiness in Dyce's voice. Dyce evoked the fake major in the Tudor roadhouse who slaps you on the back and asks you to cash his cheque. He said:

'I'm not particularly interested in her. If you think you can get her to put you up for the night, go ahead. It's all right by me.'

'Oh, I can get her all right. She's a nympho, that girl. Go with any man who snapped his fingers for her.'

'Go ahead, then.'

'I like you,' Dyce said. 'You're a decent type. Know what my philosophy is? Like people but never trust them. What do you do for a living?'

'I'm a clerk in an office.'

'An office? That's death from suffocation. I tried it once. Hopeless lot of old fuddy-duddies. Terrified of change, progress, the new man with bright ideas. Try to speed things up a bit, and they gasp and flounder like landed fish. Miserable until they get back into their safe tank again.' Dyce offered his cigarette-case, then flicked the lighter. When he smoked he slit his eyes as if he were mapping out a plan of campaign. 'We'll have to get you out of that office, my lad.'

'Don't worry, I never keep any job for long. I generally get sacked for lateness. In the mornings the thought of the office depresses me so much that I stay in bed instead. Sometimes I'm so late that I decide to take the whole day off. One day stretches to three, and by the time I've been away for a week I know I shall never return. I've left innumerable jobs that way.'

Dyce nodded, blowing out smoke. 'Offices are the end. My God, what a life. End up at fifty living in some hideous semi-detached villa in the suburbs, which you can't leave because of the mortgage. Sleeping with some fat, ugly woman because you were stupid enough to marry her when she was young and pretty. That's no life for anyone with any guts.'

'I get lousy jobs deliberately. I prefer to have a lousy job, and keep sight of the fact that I detest it and regard it as a stupid waste of time, rather than have a better job and the risk of compromising with it.'

'I don't agree with you there. You've got to comp-romise if you're going to succeed in life. But always make sure that you get the best side of the compromise. Only make treaties when they're in your favour. That's the way to get on in life, to get money and the other things you want.'

Beckett said: 'You're an ambitious man, then?'

'Ambitious? If wanting to get my share of the good things is ambitious, yes, I am.' Dyce pointed to the lit windows of the party flat. 'That flat up there, for instance. It's ugly, it's depressing, it's cheap. And I'll lay a fiver that you live in a place practically identical to it.'

'Worse. I only have a room, not a flat.'

'Of course you do. And millions like you do. A poky, furnished room, or a house in some dull suburb. And do you know why? It's because they haven't the guts to seize life by the throat and take what they want from it.'

Beckett felt angry, not only at Dyce's last remark but at his whole patronizing attitude, his irritating 'old boys'. Dyce could not be more than twenty years older than he. He said: 'It's easy to talk, but if you've got so much money why do you need Georgia to put you up for the night? Why can't you afford a hotel?'

'I admit it, I admit it freely. I'm skint at the moment. But, by Christ, I don't intend to stay skint for long. I've got plenty of possibilities lined up, and I guarantee that within a few days some of them will have materialized, and I'll have plenty of loot. Listen, I've been around all over the world, and I've seen life. Life in high society and life in the gutter. If it suits me to live like a tramp for a bit I can sleep in ditches and it won't affect me. But if I've got money it's got to be big money. I'll have the best hotel, and the best service, and a genuine high-class haughty girl to hang on my arm. And when I've spent the money I'll change again. Either I'll return to being a tramp for a bit or else I'll pit all my wits into getting some more money.' Dyce spun his cigarette into the roses. 'You've got to adapt in this world, old boy. Adapt and compromise. But do it when it suits you, not when it suits other people.'

'If you make money so fast, you must have a racket, not a job.'

'So what if I have? Any disapproval?'

'No, not at all,' Beckett said. 'It's no concern of mine how you get your money.'

Dyce grinned. 'I like you. I like you more and more.' He pointed to the sky. 'Look at that. All those stars. Sky looks like a suspended snowstorm. Hey, not bad, that. I should be a poet.' He turned to Beckett again. 'My life has taught me a bit, anyway. Taught me that I've got to make my body as efficient and controlled as a machine. A machine which is always ready, which only has to be triggered off to react correctly, automatically, at a moment's notice. I've trained myself to do the right thing automatically in situations when I don't have time to think but only to act. Reflex action, like pressing a switch.and the red light comes on. And I'll tell you, I can take care of myself anywhere, in an East End pub or a Riviera casino, and I'll win out no matter how much bigger and stronger the other guy is.' Dyce rubbed his right fist on his left palm. 'How old would you say I was?'

Beckett said with bored politeness: 'Late thirties?'

'Forty-five. And never felt fitter. Look, I'll show you...'

Dyce took off his jacket and hung it on the rose bush. He tapped himself on the solar plexus. 'Come on, hit me. Hit me here, hard.'

'Don't be daft, I'd hurt you.'

'You couldn't hurt me. This is hard muscle; real hard muscle. No fat or flabbiness on me.'

'All right, I believe you. You don't have to prove it.'

'But I want to prove it. You wouldn't hurt me. Come on.'

'No,' Beckett said, 'I'm not going to, so you might as well stop wasting time and put your coat on.'

'Come on. It's my risk, you've got nothing to lose.'

'No.'

'I'll lay a fiver you can't hurt me.'

'This is absurd,' Beckett said. 'No.'

'Why are you so scared? I've told you, it's my risk.'

Beckett was angry. His impulse was to conquer Dyce by taking him at his word. He wanted to see the handsome patronizing face distorted with pain. Perversely, his obstinacy had pledged him against the very thing he wanted to do.

Dyce's face was rigid as steel. The same rigid quality was in his voice. 'You will do it. I have been trained to command. You don't know it yet, but if I give an order, a real order, you will find yourself obeying automatically.'

Surprise at this took Beckett aback. He realized that it was a battle of wills. He said: 'You think you're strong-willed, but you're not, because strength involves having a purpose. And you have no purpose, except to senselessly try to boss me around. You just want to prove to yourself what a tough guy you are. You're nothing but a moron.'

'I am, hey?'

'Yes, you bloody well are.'

For a moment they stood facing each other, with violence and mutual antagonism like a bond between them. Then Dyce threw his head back and laughed in great shouts. When he had stopped laughing, he said in a normal voice: 'Never mind. Skip it for now.' Beckett relaxed also, and shrugged.

27

'I like you, old boy. Like people but never trust them. Only trust myself to keep a grip on the other fellow so he won't have a chance to do me down.' Dyce lay down on the grass, on his back, and clasped his hands under his head. 'You know what?'

Beckett sprawled on the grass also. It smelled fresh and earthy. The trees above him had silver leaves.

'You know what?' Dyce said. 'I was in the Army. Sometimes I wish I had stayed in, but Christ! I had a nice little racket going. Sale of equipment. Not just knocking off a few cans of stuff; any fool can do that. But in a big way. I had it all lined up: organization, contacts, men working for me. I was raking in a tidy bit on the side. Then somebody tumbled to it. The fuss that was made was bloody ridiculous. I mean, everybody in the Army works a fiddle of one kind or another. They'd want their heads testing if they didn't. Selling equipment is something that goes on all the time. A recognized thing. Officially it's illegal, but everybody knows about it and the authorities just turn a blind eye. That's why it was ridiculous to make such a fuss in my case. All I'd done was to show a bit more enterprise than usual. They should have been glad to find somebody with some sense and enterprise.'

Beckett laughed. 'I like your reasoning!'

'I wish they had. Result was I resigned my commission.' Dyce's shrewd eyes looked at him too straight: the too-straight eyes of a liar. 'Damned if I was going to crawl and grovel to a lot of bloody little clerks.'

Beckett suspected that Dyce had really been chucked out, but his natural politeness prevented him from voicing his suspicion.

'Anyway, I was out, and I had to reorganize my life. Decided to sponge off my relations for a bit. I've got an old trout of an aunt who has more money than use for it, and there was no reason why she shouldn't spend some on her blue-eyed nephew. But, Christ, I couldn't stand her for long. She handed out mean little sums as if they were charity soup, and accompanied each quid with a pious prayer that I wouldn't squander it in riotous living. Putting up with her lectures meant that I earned every penny I managed to squeeze out of her. She's supposed to have a weak heart, and I was hoping she'd pop off and leave me her money. But I soon decided that the weak-heart business was just an act, and as I didn't have time to hang about waiting for her to die, I cleared out. Did a bunk. Put some ads in the Personal Ad columns of newspapers. "Officer, ex-public school, do anything, go anywhere." You know the sort of thing. You ought to try it yourself. Were you an officer or public school?'

'No, neither.'

'Doesn't matter. They expect you to lie. Want you to, in fact. They want a man who knows how to bluff. I got some pretty interesting jobs that way. Some fairly legal. Others...' Dyce winked. 'Oh yes, the world is full of rich cowards who are willing to pay somebody else to do their living for them.'

Beckett offered his cigarettes and they both lit up.

Dyce lay back, grinning, his eyes narrowed. 'Shocked you, hey? The life of crime.'

'No, not at all. Crime interests me. I think that today it mainly springs from boredom. A deprived man wants the object he is deprived of: food, work, political liberty. But the man who has no pressing material needs can suffer instead from spiritual sickness. He realizes he lives in a system of lies, and consequently believes in nothing.' Beckett sat up suddenly. 'Well, look, I mean, what is nihilism? Inability to believe, inability to feel, a sort of paralysing insight into the meaninglessness of existence. Boredom. The nihilist is constantly undermined by his sense of absurdity and lack of meaning.

Nihilism is a claustrophobic state; a prison. I think crime can be an attempt to break out of the prison; a dynamite to blast the walls.'

'Carry on.'

'The nihilist wants to feel, so he strikes at life in order that life may strike him back.'

Dyce said: 'By putting him in prison?'

'No, by making him feel sin, danger, or anything. Anything is better than nothing.'

'Oh yes, I agree with you there.'

Beckett said: 'Of course murder is the only absolute crime, qualitatively different from every other crime.'

'Yes. Well, I hadn't thought along those lines myself. Probably because I'm seldom bored, I play life like a poker game, and it seems fun to me. It doesn't worry me that I live in a system of lies as long as my lies are more successful than the other fellow's.'

Beckett laughed, liking Dyce's frankness.

Dyce said: 'But you over-glamorize the criminal. The blasé youths, the Teddy-boy types, probably don't believe in anything. But they wouldn't put it into the sort of words you use. And with the older ones it's mostly laziness.'

'Oh yes. Most criminals, I suppose, drift into crime through laziness or through lack of free will.'

'You believe in free will?'

'I don't think we have as much as we should like to suppose.'

'But a murderer might have it? You said murder was qualitative....'

Beckett said: 'He might.' The grass was damp, and he stood up. 'Let's go back inside.'

'And collect our nympho, who probably thinks we've both deserted her. Well, which of us is going to stagger over the bridal threshold with that not inconsiderable weight?'

'You are.'

'Thanks, old boy. Sheer necessity, you know. Must have somewhere to sleep, and plug my electric razor. With any luck I might get her to wash my drip-dry shirt as well.' Dyce stood up, and collected his jacket from the rose bush.

At that moment Michael bounded into the garden, with his arms flung wide in ecstatic love for all humanity. Seeing Beckett and Dyce, he twined an arm round the neck of each, and swung his feet off the ground. 'Darlings, are you gay? Let's all be gay!'

They staggered under his weight. Then Dyce disengaged himself and pushed the boy away. He exclaimed to Beckett: 'That brat needs a few well-placed kicks.'

'Oh, I rather like him.'

'I can't stand queers. They give me the creeps.' Dyce returned indoors.

Beckett went to assist Michael, who was now being sick into the roses.

When Beckett rejoined the party, noise and brightness were like a wall. He inspected everybody to see whether they were Dyce and Georgia, but they were not.

There were some men wearing the rosettes and striped scarves of football-team supporters. They carried rattles and cardboard trumpets. Nobody seemed to know how they had got there. They all stood together, with their raincoat pockets stuffed with beer-bottles, blowing raspberries down their trumpets.

He found Ilsa and said: 'Hello.'

'I'm drunk. I'm bloody drunk.'

'You are a bit.'

'Am I? Does it show?'

'It doesn't matter.'

Her face was pale and strained; the skin was taut over the sharp cheekbones. She pushed her hair back with the hand that held the habitual cigarette, then squashed the cigarette out. 'Don't know why I bother to get cigarettes,' she said. 'Never finish the damn things. Never finish anything. Unfinished conversations, unfinished love-affairs. I get bored.' The cigarette had broken where she had squashed it, spilling tobacco. 'See, I spoil things.'

He said: 'You don't belong here.'

'Don't belong where?'

'To this party. To all these stupid drunks.'

'You're crazy! Of course I belong. I love them all; they're my sort of people.'

'You don't belong,' he repeated. He knew she was right, but wanted to convince her and himself.

'Oh, you're making a big mistake. I'm like them; absolutely like them. They spoil things too, they never finish anything. That's why I'm at home here. That's why I'm happy. That's why I'm drunk. Are you drunk?'

'No. I was, but I got sober again.'

'Do you know, I was in a pub once, and they had some stuffed owls in a glass case. It was funny somehow; I can't explain. None of us could stop looking at them. We all sat looking at the owls and roaring with laughter.'

'Ilsa —' he began.

'Oh, listen! Is that a Bugloss record?' She pointed to the radiogram.

Irritated, he said: 'Can't you stay in one place for a minute?'

'Gotta keep moving, gotta keep moving.'

He followed her over to the radiogram. When she listened to the record her body tensed, and she tapped her foot as if the jazz was jerking her like a marionette. He felt annoyed that it should have such a hold on her. Looking at her thin arm with its golden down, he felt a sudden desire to seize her, to bend her physically and morally to his will.

'Ilsa, let's get out of here,' he said.

'Oh, but the party's only just started. It's going on all night. Loads more people are coming.'

'All night?'

'The parties here always do. We just flop on the floor when we're exhausted. In the morning we grab whatever food we can find from the larder. Then we all rave off to the Tube and go round to somebody's place for a coffee-and-record session.'

'No, come on, let's go now.'

She concentrated, peering at him suspiciously. 'Us? We going together, then?'

'Yes.'

'Well, I dunno about that.'

'I can't go with anyone else, love.'

'What about old fat cow Georgia?'

'She's nothing to me.'

'Old fat cow. I'll pull her hair out. She dyes it, anyway. That red colour's never natural. You can see the roots. Ugh! How disgusting!'

He took her hand, drawing her closer. 'Come on, love, get your things. Or let me get them. Where are they?'

'No, I've got to fix my face. Won't be long.'

On her way out she was taken up by the football supporters. She called them all 'Darlings!' and blew down their cardboard trumpets.

When he had waited some time and she had not returned, he went to look for her. He tried a door, and found two children asleep in a cot, amid a rumple of toys and blankets. The next door disclosed a half-naked couple embracing on the bed.

Beckett said: 'Oh, excuse me...'

The man asked: 'Are you the host?'

'No.'

'Well, if you know him ask him if he minds us going to bed in his bed.'

'All right.'

The third door he tried was the bathroom. He switched on the light, and saw Ilsa lying on the floor, asleep. The brave scarlet dress was crumpled around her. She had kicked off her shoes; the soles of her nyloned feet were slightly soiled. He touched her shoulder. 'Ilsa...'

She shuddered and woke. 'Oh, I feel awful. I feel sick.' She sat up, pushing the damp blonde hair from her face with both hands.

'Poor love. You'll be all right; we're going now.'

'Don't want to go anywhere. Want to stay here.'

He helped her up, putting his arm round her shoulders. She seemed very small without her high-heeled shoes. There was a brittle quality about her, as if she might snap.

'I'm a bloody nuisance to you,' she said.

'No, of course you're not.'

'I'm a bloody nuisance to everybody.'

In the taxi Ilsa slept. The illness of her ashen face, with adult shadows under the cheekbones, was accentuated by the scarlet beret she wore.

He was glad she was asleep, because that removed the necessity for conversation. They had little in common. He could not speak to her of the ideas which preoccupied him, and her smart social small-talk bored him on the whole. In the past he had often told her he loved her because they had run out of other conversation.

The taxi sped through Fulham towards Earls Court. Ilsa's nearness was almost unbearable. He groaned inwardly with desire. Her thigh was touching his, making him turn to gold.

He thought: Physically, I adore her. She is the altar at which I worship. And I will go in unto the altar of God, to God, who giveth joy to my youth. With my body

I thee worship. Her company bores me, but I want it. Her voice talking commonplaces is better than music.'

She moaned occasionally, and he wondered if she were going to be sick. He hoped so. He wanted to hold her while she was being sick, and kiss the side of her neck and her damp hair. The idea excited him so much that he was in agony.

The taxi drew up outside her house in Earls Court. He got out and paid the driver, then woke Ilsa and helped her out.

Ilsa shared a basement flat with a girl named Katey. The décor of the flat included glass tumblers with a playing-card design, bowls of peanuts, a wooden dachshund with a corkscrew for a tail, and a doll dressed in bra and pants. The red curtains, through which a light now showed, were patterned with drink labels: Martini, Cinzano, Dubonnet. Ilsa's soul delighted in the sort of furnishings that she considered smart or novel. The girls used one room as a double bedroom and the other as a living room. This arrangement meant that Beckett was unable to spend the night at Ilsa's, but on the whole he was glad of it. He disliked sleeping away from his room.

Ilsa was leaning against the railings beside the area steps. 'Christ, I feel awful. Do you want to come in and have coffee with us?'

'No, I don't think I will. I like Katey, but I'm too tired to sit on the sofa being amiable tonight.'

'Oh well, then. Thanks for bringing me home. I say, did we come in a taxi?'

'Yes.'

'I thought we did, but I wasn't sure.' She said again: 'Oh well, thanks.'

'When shall I see you again?'

Her eyes evaded his. 'It's difficult to say, really. I'm busy.'

'Well, what days aren't you busy?'

The easy promise: 'I'll ring you.'

He wrote his number and gave it to her.

She said conciliatorily: 'Anyway, I'm glad we can still be friends although not lovers. Platonic friendship's a great thing, isn't it?'

'Yes.'

'I'm glad we're on good terms again. I don't want to quarrel with you. In fact we'll probably get on better now that we don't have the strain of a love-affair.'

'Yes.'

She nodded coolly. 'Oh well. Bye.'

'Bye-bye.' Then he put his arms round her and kissed her, pushing her back against the iron railings. They stood with the length of their bodies pressed together, like lovers.

Soon she said: 'Don't, Joe.'

'Why not?'

'As I said, I'd rather be platonic.'

'But you were furious when you thought I was after Georgia.'

'Oh, that. Well, I was drunk, and I just said anything.'

'You want everything your own way, don't you?'

'That's right.' She turned and tottered down the steps. 'Oops... steady, Barnes...' In the doorway she yelled: 'Hi, Katey, I've had a marvellous time...' in a voice pitched to wake the entire street.

Later, walking home alone, he thought of Ilsa, Georgia, and Dyce. He felt a long way removed from all of them.

Chapter 3

Messrs Union Cartons & Packaging (Great Britain) Ltd occupied the ground floor of a building in Holborn. Beckett walked down the corridor to the Invoice Department. He was, as usual, late for work.

The office smelled of dust, radiators, disinfectant, and tea. One corner was partitioned to make a glass tank for Mr Presgate, the departmental manager. The remainder was equipped with green steel desks for the eight clerks. Over each desk hung a light with a metal shade. Beckett's light was held in position by means of a length of string from the flex to the window frame. The lights were permanently on, because two windows were of frosted glass and the other two were dirty. The little light admitted by the windows was further blocked by the dusty files and folders stacked along the ledges. The walls were bi-coloured; the lower half was chocolate brown and the top half yellow. There was a pin-up girl calendar, with August's girl wearing powder-puffs and high heels. Other calendars advertised the firms with whom Union Cartons did business.

Beckett sat down at his desk without greeting any of the other clerks. He knew that he should apologize to Mr Presgate for his lateness, but could not be bothered. He was not afraid of Mr Presgate; he was merely disinclined to invent an excuse, disinclined to pretend sorrow for his lateness and inefficiency and all the other things which were nothing to do with him.

He started the morning's work. There was a heap of invoices and statements which had to be date-stamped and separated into two piles.

The upper floors of the building were occupied by a hotel. Union Cartons was directly below the hotel bathrooms. The hot-water pipes ran through the office, which was consequently hot as a desert noon. The clerks all suffered from the enervating heat. Beckett felt the sweat trickling down his back and the insides of his legs. He wondered why he had imposed on himself the penance of working in such an unpleasant place. He had hardly started work, but already his shoulders ached with boredom.

The clack of keys came from the next room, where four princesses touch-typed and read their horoscopes in women's magazines and ate sandwiches from their desk drawers and patted one another's hair.

A bar of sunlight crept across his desk. He worked on, finishing the stamping and starting the ledger work. Occasionally he looked up at TONS & PAC written in mirror-writing across the windows.

Syd leaned across from the next desk. 'Got a fagarette for us?'

Beckett held out his packet.

'Ta. Got a match?'

Beckett threw the box. 'Sure there's nothing else you'd like, while you're about it? How are you off for five-pound notes?'

'Don't be like that.'

Mr Presgate emerged from his glass compartment. He was a little man with wizened, saurian skin. Behind his wire-framed spectacles his eyes darted around as if he were constantly engaged in totting up petty-cash columns on the walls.

He stopped beside Beckett's, and stood munching his silent sums. Finally he barked: 'Well, well, what was it today? Central Line break down again?'

'No.'

'Won't do, you know. Won't do.'

Presgate's hand was resting on his desk. Beckett had a close-up of the skin that was dry as if it had been dusted with chalk, and the shiny cuff with one button sewn on with unmatching thread. His stomach contracted in sudden revulsion.

When Presgate had gone, Syd told him: 'Do you know that Presgate complained to Mr Glegg about you being late this morning?'

'Did he?'

'He's trying to get in good with Mr Glegg. He's hoping for a rise.'

'Yes, I suppose so.'

'Aren't you mad?'

'No,' Beckett said. 'He's quite justified in complaining.'

'Oh well, if you look at it like that...'

Beckett picked up his phone and asked for a line. He dialled the number. It rang once and then the efficient switchboard voice said: 'Jamieson and McBride.'

'Typing pool, please.'

'Engaged. Will you hold?'

'All right,' Beckett said.

Mrs Little came into the office with the tea-trolley. She put a cup on his desk, and he nodded his thanks.

Syd scraped his chair back. 'Oh, Mrs Little, you ravishing creature, you. What has Brigitte Bardot got that you haven't?'

'Brigitte Bardot, indeed!'

'And give me another spoonful of sugar in my tea, will you?'

'You've got the same as everyone else,' the tea-woman said.

'Oh, go on. You know I'm irresistible.'

'Well, hark at you.' She gave Syd more sugar.

Syd drank, then raised his cup, calling after her: 'Divine, Mrs Little. Better than British Railways'.'

Becket held the phone. The line clicked and another girl's voice said: 'Typing pool.'

'May I speak to Miss Barnes?'

'One moment...'

He waited again, stirring his tea with the red Biro. From the other end of the line he could hear giggles, and the girl's voice saying: 'It's a *man*...'

Finally Ilsa's cool ill-mannered voice came over. 'Hello?'

'Hello, Ilsa, this is Joe. You didn't ring me, so —'

'What?'

'You didn't ring me.'

'Who is that?' she said.

'Joe. You were going to ring me, remember?'

'Oh yes. I didn't recognize your voice. No, you sillies, shut up...'

'What?' he said.

'Sorry, I was talking to the other girls in my office. They keep crowding round me.'

He felt irritated. 'You said you were going to ring me. You didn't, so I thought I'd ring you.'

'Yes, I'm sorry. I meant to ring you, but things happened. You know how it is.'

'I see.' He stirred the tea again without drinking. It was orange-coloured and had a skin. 'Well, anyway, how are you?'

'Oh, not bad. Marvellous in fact. How are you?'

'Not bad.'

Then there was silence. He imagined her tapping her foot impatiently or pushing her hair back from her forehead. He said quickly: 'Look, Ilsa, can I see you tonight?'

'I've got to wash my hair. It's Friday.'

'Can't you wash it some other time?'

'No, I can't. I always wash it on Friday, ready for the party on Saturday.'

His irritation increased. He was jealous of the other girls in her office, who were probably giggling round the phone, and of Ilsa's stupid rigidity in washing her hair on one night only. He almost slammed the phone down, then said: 'Well, what about over the weekend?'

'I don't know, really.'

'We could go out into the country for the day. Go somewhere by coach, then get out and walk. I'd like to go out into Surrey. There are some fine walks there, along the tops of hills, and you can see for miles.'

'Oh, walking. I hate walking, except to pubs. I'm definitely a town mouse.' She had put on a smart-remark voice for the benefit of the other girls.

He gave up, surprised at his former persistence. It was nothing to him, anyway. He had no particular need to see Ilsa. Then, as a convention, he made a final attempt. 'All right. What about Monday, then?'

To his surprise, she said: 'Yes, I suppose Monday would be all right.'

'Good. I leave work at five-thirty. Shall I meet you at six?'

'Okay,' she said for the other girls. 'Six at Mick's Café in Charlotte Street.'

Beckett put the phone down and drank the tepid tea.

Syd asked him: 'A girl?'

'Yes.' He did not want to defile Ilsa for Syd, but could not help adding: 'A blonde. With a smashing little body. Very slim.'

'Smashing. Hey, you know that nurse I was telling you about? I took her on Hampstead Heath last night.'

'I thought it was Streatham Common.'

'No, that was last week, with that Italian girl. Marisa something-or-other. I never could pronounce her beastly name.'

41

'London's parklands must be strewn with your discarded French letters.'

Flattered, Syd said: 'Don't be like that.'

At five-thirty Beckett left the office and boarded the Tube at Holborn. Although it was rush-hour, the compartment was comparatively empty. He sat looking at the advertisements for Heinz 57 Varieties and Amplex. On the brassiere advertisement, somebody had pencilled in the nipples and written: 'Lovely tits.'

Then he began to watch the man in the homburg hat. The man was leaning across the gangway to talk to a friend opposite. Because of the noise of the train Beckett could not hear what was said.

The homburg-man's mouth moved soundlessly. He jabbed his newspaper with a thick, businessman's finger, as if holding forth about some Stock Exchange item.

Beckett thought: He isn't real. Why on earth does this man believe he is real?

He looked round at the other passengers, and none of them seemed real. It struck him as absurd, all these people sitting there and believing they were real.

He left the Tube at Notting Hill Gate and walked home to Tewkesbury Road. The usual gang of snot-nosed, cosmopolitan children was rioting in the street. Then one of the children threw a stone and broke Gash's window.

There was a moment's pause, then the children lifted like a flight of starlings. They ran, circling in vee formation, down the street. Their voices carried back.

'You broke the winder, Jimmy Riley...'

'I never! It wasn't me...'

'The cops'll be after you...'

'Can't catch me for a toffee flea...'

Only two remained. They were youths of about nineteen. They lounged on the street corner, smoking cigarettes in a knowing way, like Apaches.

Gash padded barefoot out of the house. He was an old man wearing shabby striped trousers and a cardigan. He had no shirt, and his vest was safety-pinned at the neck. A white rime of stubble edged his jaw and the strings of his throat.

Gash inspected the damage done to his window; the hole radiating cracks. Then he looked at the two youths.

They returned his gaze, lounging insolently. Then they strolled towards him. One of them combed his Ted-style hairdo as he walked. They came so close that Gash was forced to back a few steps.

Finally one of them spoke: 'Those naughty kids have broken the gentleman's window.'

'T's t's!...' The other clicked his tongue in mock concern. 'What a nasty thing to do.'

'It's of no account,' Gash said courteously. 'I'm sure it was an accident.'

'The gentleman says it was an accident.'

'That's all he knows.'

'I assure you —' Gash began.

The youths had him hemmed against the wall. They stood in front of him, their postures male and suggestive, with their fists in their trousers pockets. They blew out smoke.

'We'll have to take him inside,' the first one said. 'It's not safe for a feeble old fellow like him to be alone in this nasty rough neighbourhood.'

'That's right,' the second one said. 'Me and my mate will look after him.'

'See that no harm comes to him.'

'Like a couple of nursemaids.'

Gash was still mildly protesting. 'I assure you, there's no need —'

They edged him backwards into the house. 'Come on, Grandpa, we're doing you a favour.'

Beckett judged that it was high time for him to intervene. He walked straight up to the youths, and ordered them, 'Let this man alone. Go on, fuck off.'

They turned towards him slowly. Then turned back to each other. The first one said: 'Funnyman here.'

'Looking for trouble.'

The first one turned to Beckett again. His eyes were slitted beneath the pimply boxer forehead. 'We're a bit hard of hearing, Dad. What was it you just said?'

Beckett had a sensation of weightlessness, as if he and his two opponents were suspended in space. As always in such circumstances, he was hindered by his own lack of conviction, his disbelief in the situation. He said with as much force and anger as he could muster: 'I told you to fuck off. Now get going, straight away.'

They hesitated. Then the second one said: 'Oh, come on. It isn't worth bothering about.' They both walked away. When they had gone a little way they started to shove each other and shout with laughter.

Beckett turned to the old man. 'Hello, Mr Gash.'

'Hello, Joe. Come in.'

He followed Gash indoors. His own behaviour made him feel proud and grateful. He was sorry that Gash had been the sole spectator. The old man was too daft to have followed the events. He also regretted that his exhilaration and need for admiration had made him go indoors with Gash. Age, sickness, and senility bored and rather disgusted him.

Gash's room smelled fetid. There was the yellowish smell of insanity that Beckett had noticed in mental wards. There was no bed, because Gash, to the despair of his landlady, insisted on sleeping on the floor. Beside the heap of unsavoury blankets there was a kitchen chair on which were an asthma inhaler, a book entitled

The Bible of the World, and a bowl covered by a cloth.

A frugal meal, consisting of vegetable stew and a hunk of bread, was waiting on the table.

Beckett squatted on his heels to inspect the books on the shelves. He took out *Practical Aids to Contemplation* and flipped through the pages.

Gash said: 'I don't mind about the broken window. It's good to have fresh air in summer.'

Beckett nodded abstractedly. He read a paragraph which recommended the novice to concentrate on any object, such as a dish or a clump of grass, until it seemed to change in appearance and reveal its true nature. He said: 'Don't let me stop you eating your meal.' Returning his attention to the book, it occurred to him that this was the sort of exercise which painters did as a matter of course. He replaced the book on the shelf. 'You shouldn't have talked to those lads, you know, Mr Gash.'

'Why not?'

'They were having you on, and it might have developed into something unpleasant.'

'I don't think they'd want to harm me. I've done nothing to them.'

Beckett said vaguely: 'Oh well, you know what these Teds are like....'

'You're like my landlady. Both of you think that I'm incapable of living alone and taking care of myself.'

'Oh no. Not really. I didn't mean to give that impression.'

'You live alone yourself, don't you, Joe?' As he spoke, Gash fetched another dish and prepared to divide the food. 'You'll give me the pleasure of sharing my meal, won't you?'

'Oh no. No thanks. I've got some food at home.'

'It's only a humble meal.'

'No, really, it isn't that. But I do have food at home.

Don't let me stop you eating though.' Beckett looked at his watch. 'I must be going, anyway.'

'Stay a little longer.'

Gash began to eat, and Beckett answered his earlier question. 'Yes, I live alone. Pretty much in isolation, shut up in my room most of the time.'

'That is good. It's only when a man is alone that he can experience the moments of assent. When he understands such experiences, he will know them to be timeless moments of union with God, imminent and transcendent. And, understanding, he will centre his whole life round the experience. His sole desire will be to contain such energy as would cause an ordinary man to explode.'

Beckett shifted his weight from one foot to the other. He didn't understand Gash. He noticed that Gash's trouser leg was ripped from the knee down, showing the skin that was discoloured in patches. The flesh was hairless as a baby's; an old man's flesh.

Gash said: 'I know what you want, Joe.'

'What is that?'

'You want freedom.'

Surprised at the accuracy, Beckett admitted: 'Yes, that's true. But I'm a disbeliever, and disbelief is the opposite of freedom, because it paralyses action at the root.'

'Nevertheless, in spite of your disbelief, you seek freedom. You have a religious temperament and seek God.'

'No,' Beckett said. 'You're wrong. I've rejected religion and there is no God.'

'Perhaps I understand you better than you understand yourself.'

Beckett felt a spasm of disgust at the old man with his milky, unfocused eyes. The stale smell of mania in the room also disgusted him. He resented Gash's claim to understand him.

Before leaving, he gave Gash's landlady some money for the repair of the window. She thanked him profusely and told him that he was very kind.

He knew that he was not really kind. He performed various acts of kindness more as a duty to himself than as genuine liking for others.

As he left the house, he could hear Gash coughing. It was worse than ordinary coughing.

He returned to his lodging. On the hall table were a Vernons Pools envelope, a religious tract headed AWAKE!, and a letter addressed to him. It was in his mother's writing. He had a sinking feeling of guilt. He pocketed the letter, unread.

He was starting up the stairs when his landlady's door opened. 'Oh, Mr Beckett...'

He said in the tired, polite voice he used for keeping her at a distance: 'Good evening, Mrs Ackley.'

'That shouting in the street. What was the meaning of it?'

'Oh, nothing. Just a couple of our local bright lads trying to make trouble.'

'Indeed. Well, I won't have any dirty words shouted outside this house. It makes the house seem like a common place. What would the neighbours think if they heard those disgusting words you use so freely?' She wore a skirt with a broken zipper. The brooch that skewered the neck of her blouse was made in the shape of a vase of flowers.

He said coldly: 'I neither know nor care what the neighbours think. Most of them are incapable of thinking at all.'

'Oh, very high and mighty, aren't you? Well, let me tell you, I don't want any bad habits here. It gives the house a bad name, that sort of thing. Shouting words like that! Next thing is, I suppose, you'll be starting a brawl on the doorstep.'

His temper rose. He was infuriated by her pettiness, and by the knowledge that, if he gave way to his temper, he would have all the bother of finding another lodging. He started to mount the stairs again, but she followed him, asking: 'And what were they trying to make trouble about?'

'The lads? Oh, just some harmless old man.'

'What old man?'

'His name is Gash. Is that all you want to know? If so, if you'll excuse me, I'm busy.'

'One minute. If that old man Gash is a friend of yours, well, I know it's none of my business, but I should advise you to keep away from him.'

'You're right; it is none of your business.'

'I saw you leave his house.'

He realized, with distaste, that her previous questions had been moves in a complicated plan to get him to talk about Gash. He said: 'Since you've obviously been watching me from behind your net curtains you must have known that the quarrel was about Gash. Why didn't you come straight to the point, instead of twisting and turning?'

'Yes, well, no need to take that tone.' She hesitated, then said: 'Come in for a few minutes, Mr Beckett.'

Her room smelled of furniture polish and soup. The table was covered by a green chenille cloth with a fringe. The centrepiece was a cut-glass bowl containing wax fruit and a half-darned stocking. She said: 'I'll tell you something about your friend Mr Gash. He was in a mental home.'

He said indifferently: 'Was he?'

'A mental home!'

'Yes, I heard you.'

'They came and took him away. And he should never have been allowed back, in my opinion. In fact I shouldn't be surprised if he escaped or something. After all, these lunatics are supposed to be ten times more cunning than normal people, aren't they? Anyway, he was certainly in no state to mix with ordinary decent people. And they say he's even worse now.'

'Whom do you mean by They?'

'Well, I don't know exactly who. Everybody. Everybody says it. They say he had to be put away because... well... because he interfered with little girls.'

'Have you proof?'

'Well, not proof exactly, but that's what they say he did.'

'You keep referring to the mysterious They. Can't you be more specific?'

'Well, they, everybody. Anyway, it stands to reason he was one of those nasty old men like you read about in the papers. All those men who have to be taken away, it's because they're nasty and dirty. That's what that Freud said, isn't it? Not that I've ever read his books myself, of course. I don't want to read a lot of gloomy books about those nasty twisted people, thanks all the same. And I don't want them roaming the streets, either.' She flicked a minute speck of dust from the tablecloth; a gesture of finality.

Beckett left her room, seething with rage. The argument had been pointless because his liking for Gash, or for any of his acquaintances, would not have been diminished by learning that the acquaintance in question was a rapist.

On the stairs he met the Irish tenant, who was returning from the bathroom in a towelling robe and black socks.

Beckett's anger overcame his habitual aloofness. He exclaimed: 'She's an insect, a petty-minded insect! Crawling behind net curtains and up noses and over the Sunday scandal papers.'

'Could it be Ma Ackley to whom you're referring?'

'Yes, her. The worst thing about her is that she's petty. She expends my time and temper with her constant petty nagging.'

'Ah,' the Irishman said. 'Join me in some Guinness.' He led the way into his room. Beside the door were three paper carrier-bags, filled with empty bottles. On the chest of drawers were clothes brushes, shoe polish, a pound of sausages, and a *New Testament*. The bed had ex-army blankets, like Beckett's bed. The Irishman poured out two glasses of Guinness.

'I detest landladies.' Beckett assumed a squeaky voice in imitation: 'You walk up and down, you've blocked the toilet, you're running your radio from the light, your bedsprings creaked, your visitors stay after ten, well it just isn't good enough, this is a respectable house.' He reverted to his normal voice. 'They cover the walls with their illiterate little notices, forbidding you to do practically everything except breathe. And they probably grudge you even that privilege. If only they would keep the thing as a business transaction, whereby you pay the rent and they let you alone. But no; they can't let you alone. They must be perpetually prying and nagging.'

The Irishman's dark marsh eyes beamed. 'Now that was an interesting point you made; that she wastes your time and temper. Now I myself consider all human beings to be worthy of consideration, and all human activities too. And if you refuse to acknowledge certain people; if you say they are nothing to do with you, it means that you are cutting yourself off from life.'

'Most of my activities, such as my job, and most of the people I know, I refuse to acknowledge as being anything to do with me.'

'Then you're not living properly,' the Irishman said. The vee neck of his robe revealed the black hairs on his chest, and the vest worn back-to-front with the maker's label showing. He smelled of sweat and soap.

'You're probably right.'

The Irishman grinned. 'Anyway, as for Ma Ackley, do you know how her late lamented husband passed away, RIP?'

'No?'

'She mistook him for a speck of dust, and swept him into the ashpan.'

Beckett laughed. He suddenly liked the Irishman, which made him feel happy.

'I'm going to Henekeys later,' the Irishman said. 'Why don't you come too?'

'Thanks, I'd like to, but I'm busy this evening.'

Later, he wondered why he had refused the invitation. He understood why he was disliked by his fellow tenants and Mrs Ackley. They resented his aloof manner with its assumption of superiority. Remembering the priggish, assertive way in which he had stated that the neighbours never thought at all, he understood the landlady's dislike.

He thought: I'm a priggish and thoroughly unbearable young man.

He went to the lavatory, and opened his mother's letter, sitting on the lavatory seat. He disliked receiving letters from her because he felt guilty about not loving her or anyone, and about his failure to be a credit to her.

He read swiftly, skipping words:

Joe dear ... so worried... you hardly ever write and your letters are so short and not at all 'newsy' ... don't go short of food, my darling, or have too many late nights... it's bad to keep food in your room in this hot weather. Has your landlady got a frig? I'm sure she would let you keep your meat and milk and butter there, if you asked her… I haven't been at all well lately. I've had to stay in bed which was a nuisance as I hate being a burden to Dad and Granny Dolan, who were splendid need I say! Anyway I think I am 'on my feet' again now…. Father Hogan came round some time ago, he stayed to supper and I gave him some apple pie made from our own apples from the tree in the garden, which was nice … he asked about you, and told some funny stories about when you children used to serve at Mass. I think he is really 'Mad Irish'! He's been transferred to St Elizabeth's in London, which is a new church that has just been built, which is very exciting! So why don't you go and see him? I told him I was sure you'd like to, I didn't tell him you had left the Faith, and I hope and pray constantly that you will return to it… my darling, be good… must end now and catch the post…. I had a letter from Aunty Ann, she has a cold but is otherwise alright. … Dad and Granny send love…. Ever your own Mum, xxxx.

He replaced the letter in his pocket. On the window-ledge was a bent safety-pin and the newspaper that served as toilet paper. He sat on, idly reading the newspaper which was several days old. The front page had a picture of a man wearing a rosette, descending the steps of an aeroplane. His smile and suit were successful; one hand was raised in a civilian salute.

Farther down the page, Beckett read that a little girl had been found, raped and murdered, in the cellar of an empty house.

He wondered about the murderer. What had been wrong with his life, that he had taken such an extreme remedy? There must have been a wolf inside him, that had been roused by the sight of a little girl playing in a street.

The same society had produced the man with the rosette and the unknown murderer. He was suddenly conscious of millions of lives, millions of reactions to the age of sceptics.

Before leaving, he dropped the envelope of his mother's letter into the lavatory pan. He pulled the chain, but the envelope did not go down. It floated in the pan, with the graceful writing blurred by the flush of water.

In his room there was nothing to do. He tore a page from his notebook, and wrote: *Dear Mum, Thank you for your letter. I'm sorry I haven't written for so long, but...*

Here his inspiration failed. He opened the washstand cupboard and found two biscuits in a paper bag. He was not hungry, but ate them for something to do. Then he ironed the paper bag with his palm, and read the advertising matter on it. Then he yawned like a Sunday afternoon.

He sat for a while looking at the unlit gas fire, and listened to the cars passing in the street below. After a while he got up and closed the window. The sound of the cars was fainter now.

Chapter 4

MICK'S CAFÉ was a basement dive. It was crowded, and smelled of frying oil, cats, and dead cigarette smoke. Over the counter NO CREDIT was written in coloured bottle-caps.

The Greek assistant, who wore trousers and a vest, rang the till and shouted up the service hatch: 'Three Vienna, one Bolognese...' He slapped the counter with a damp cloth.

The mirror advertised cigarettes; Beckett caught sight of his distorted image with WOODBINES printed across the forehead. He found a table and sat down.

The other customers were Soho characters; bums and layabouts dressed like artists. They were different from the smartly dressed teenage set who frequented the coffee bars.

When Beckett had lived at home, in the subtopia of semi-detached houses with net curtains, he had thought that the neighbours wore respectability like an extra suit of clothes. He had come to London and found places, like this café, where at first he had thought that the people were more honest because they did not wear this extra covering. But he had found another sort of dishonesty instead. He had found writers who did not write, painters who did not paint, petty thieves who were so unsuccessful that they were always scrounging the price of a cup of tea, and pretty girls who turned out to be art-school tarts with dirty faces.

He had continued to frequent the cafés because the oddly assorted clientele had one thing in common: they were all misfits of one sort or another. Because of this fact, Baroness Tania, who drank methylated spirit, could share a table with Tom, who was a porter and wore British Railways uniform, with Dutchie, whose face bore the scar of a razor slash, and with an ageing young man named Flora who wore make-up and had tinted hair. And because they were all misfits they had not questioned Beckett.

He had first met Ilsa in one of the cafés. She had gone the rounds of cafés, coffee bars, pubs, and clubs in her student days, and presumably still did. This place, Mick's, was one of her regular haunts. The thought brought disgust like a bad taste in his mouth. He looked at his watch and saw that she was late.

An old man pushed past carrying a cup of tea. The pockets of his tattered raincoat were stuffed with bits of paper: newspaper-cuttings, cigarette-cartons, and paper bags. He sat down and started to count them into piles on the table.

Beckett shifted in his chair. The basement was claustrophobic. The crammed ashtray had overflowed on to the table, which depressed him.

The old man was joined by a younger man in seedy pinstripe. The younger man leaned forward to talk, emphasizing his points by jabbing the table with his forefinger. '... so I told him all he had to do was to be outside Cinerama at seven-thirty.....'

The old man nodded, not listening, slowly sorting his papers.

Beckett thought with a sudden sense of freedom that Ilsa was not coming. Then he went through the loose change in his pockets to see whether he had coins to phone her.

'Who's the three Viennas?' The Greek assistant banged plates on to the counter and wiped his hands down his sides.

A student carried a tea with a bun balanced on the saucer. Trying to shove through the crowd, he knocked the old man's papers off the table.

The old man stooped, patiently retrieving them one by one.

The Baroness Tania entered. She was a shrivelled old crone, wearing a black satin dress hung with fringes and crystal beads. Her feet shuffled in unlaced plimsolls. She clutched a wool-embroidered bag filled with scavengings from dustbins.

Someone shouted: 'A tea for Tania ... Come and have a tea, ducks.'

Beckett caught a scrap of conversation from the next table. The girl: 'Tell me what you are looking for.'

The boy, in beard and duffel coat: 'I don't know. Perhaps I am looking for something to look for.'

'... outside Cinerama, I told him. Just be there, I told him, that's all....'

'... Tania wants a tea....'

The man in the pin-stripe gave up talking of his appointment outside Cinerama. He swivelled his chair round, and tried to sell a camera to Silent.

Silent had a skull-shaped face. His eyes were unmatching, one being set higher than the other. His manner was generally rude and offensive. The other man accepted this because Silent was a cripple. They accepted his rudeness as a peculiarity of speech, like a foreign accent. He was now examining the camera closely, without speaking.

The pin-stripe man said: 'It's a good one...'

Silent took the camera to pieces, putting the component parts on the table with the precision of a surgeon or a jeweller laying out instruments.

'... made in Germany....'

Silent reassembled the camera with the same unhurried precision. He handed it back, and shook his head.

Beckett wondered whether it was true that Silent was a police informer. Everybody said he was. Not that this worried the customers of Mick's café, for they were too small to be worth shopping, and Silent was useful to them as a buyer of pilfered goods.

Silent beckoned him over, and asked in his hoarse voice: 'You got your portable chess?'

'Yes, but I haven't got time for a game now. I'm waiting for someone.'

'Lend me the set, I want to work something out.'

Beckett's chess was in a cardboard box, much battered, and mended with Sellotape. The lid was held on by an elastic band. He lent it to Silent, who gave an ungracious grunt of thanks.

At nearly seven Ilsa arrived. She was wearing dark glasses, and a smart dress that contrasted sharply with the shabby clothes of the other customers. She posed for a moment in front of the Woodbine mirror, then immediately started to greet people. 'Jimmy! How marvellous! It's been simply ages!' Then she went on to three girls in trousers and long, witch hair. 'Hello, you three. Turning Les?'

'Oh, Ilsa!' they chorused in shocked admiration, 'you know we're not! You are awful!'

She passed on to beautiful Michael, who was viciously stabbing the air in the stomach with his flick-knife.

'Hello, Michael, how are you?'

'Fab, dear, but dying for a cigarette. Oh, thanks. I suppose you can't introduce me to a rich Daddy who's a TV producer, can you? I've decided to become a teenage idol.'

'I'll do my best to find one for you,' Ilsa said.

'Or of course I might decide to be a ponce, and get some girl to work for me. Think, dear, I read in the paper about a ponce who made six hundred pounds a week, and lived in a Mayfair luxury flat. I mean, it's a well-known fact they make that amount of money. Would you like to work for me? You could have the flat, and I'd have one room in it. I'd have one wall painted black and the others white. Do you think that would look dramatic?'

'Terribly. But why should I work to support you, you lazy little bastard?'

'Well, *some*one's got to support me, dear. I mean, I don't want to work, or anything depressing like that, do I?'

A man called out: 'Don't listen to him, Ilsa. Come and talk to me instead.'

Jealous, Beckett watched her extravagant gestures, her orange mouth laughing, and the admiration she caused. She had no interests, he thought. Only stimulants. Without excitement and attention she would be lifeless.

When she joined him, she said: 'Sorry I'm late.'

'It doesn't matter.'

'I looked in at the Cellar Club on the way here, and honestly, you've no idea! Bob and George were dancing together, pretending to be queers. God, they were funny. Then we all raved off to the Prince of Wales for a drink.'

He said: 'I don't know your friends.'

'Well, I'll take you to the Cellar Club one evening and introduce you. You'll love them. They're the craziest people.'

'Why are you wearing dark glasses?'

'Because I've got a simply bloody hangover from last night.' She removed the glasses, dangling them by one stem. Without them she was unmasked, pale and ill.

He went to the counter to order. When he returned, she said: 'The other evening a man took me out, and every café we entered I said I didn't like it and demanded to leave. After about the fifth café he was getting terribly embarrassed, and hungry of course. And finally I dragged him all round town to find the one café where I said I'd consider eating, and when we got to the door I said: "What are we doing here?" He said: "Well, we're going to have dinner." "You may be going to have dinner," I said, "but I'm going home. Goodbye." And off I marched.'

'Why do you do things like that?'

'Oh, I don't know. I can't help being nasty to people if they're stupid and take it.' There was an empty American cigarette packet on the table. She pointed to it and said: 'Yanks.'

'Yes.'

'I like Yank cigarettes.'

'So do I.'

Beckett became aware that Silent was croaking angrily to him. He called to Silent: 'What's the matter?'

The unmatching eyes glared. 'The white bishop's broken.'

'I know.'

'Why don't you get a new set? How can you play with a broken piece?'

Beckett said goodhumouredly: 'Yes, I must get a new set.'

Ilsa asked him without interest: 'What was Silent talking about?'

'He borrowed my peg-chess.'

'Oh, I see.'

He asked her: 'What have you been doing since we last met?'

'When was that? Oh, at that mad party. Nothing much. At work, they're going to promote me from the typing pool to a secretarial job.'

He thought: Some man will have her sitting beside his desk, taking down his words on her shorthand pad.

Ilsa flicked ash across the table. 'It'll be more money, which suits me.'

'Yes.'

The food arrived, and they ate in silence. Ilsa, who was bored, demanded: 'What are we going to do tonight?'

'Do you feel like going to the cinema? There's a Western on at my local Odeon.'

'Sounds all right.'

Silent was struggling to his feet between a friend and his crutch. The friend returned Beckett's chess before assisting Silent up the stairs.

Ilsa, watching, said: 'Ugh, he isn't a man, he's only a ruined shell. I hope I commit suicide if ever I get into that state.'

'He was a pilot and his plane crashed. A fate which is not likely to befall you.'

'No, thanks.'

When they had eaten they climbed the stairs and emerged into the dusty heat of Charlotte Street. Ilsa stood on the pavement; a taut, nervous figure in her smart dress. She turned her head to ensure that her nylon seams were straight. 'Well, what did you say we were going to do this evening?'

"The cinema. That's all right, isn't it?'

'Oh yes, I'd forgotten. At least it might be cool there. This heat's exhausting.' In the open air she looked even more pale and drawn than she had done in the café. As they started to walk, she said: 'It's a pity you don't know Bob and George. They're terrific people. Absolutely terrific. They kept us all in fits.'

'Don't you get bored, always being with other people and never having any time by yourself?'

'Heavens, no. I can't stand being alone. It's when I'm alone that I'm bored. I share a flat with Katey because I get the jitters if I'm on my own for more than five minutes.' She took his hand, and demanded: 'What washed Polar white?'

It was their ITV game. He said: 'One of the deter-gents? Bliz or Swiz or something.'

'Snow.'

'Oh yes, Snow.'

'What makes you lyrical, lovable you?'

'I don't know.'

'Sweet Song Shampoo. They have that ad about her being a social outcast; then she uses Sweet Song and a millionaire marries her because she is lyrical and lovable.'

Beckett thought, then asked: 'What do the family jump for?'

'Joy! The scrumpy, scrunchy, mm-m-mm breakfast food.'

'Oh, you're too clever for me. You know them all.'

'Sure. Friends wouldn't come to Mary's house until she switched to...?'

'No?'

'Fairy Godmother fabrics for curtains and loose covers.'

Beckett said: 'I thought it was going to be that one where visitors shun her house because the lavatory smells.'

'No, no. You mean the one where the tin of Kleenlav appears to her in a dream.'

Later, he told her about his conversation with Gash.

She said: 'He sounds insane to me.'

'So everybody says. But insanity isn't an absolute state. You are only insane in relation to the majority of people. For instance, we all hallucinate in our sleep; we call it dreaming. Everybody does it, it's normal, so we can dream and still be considered sane. But if we hal-lucinate when we're awake, we're in a minority and considered mad.'

Bored, Ilsa said: 'Yes, I suppose you're right.'

'It infuriates me when a sane man is defined as one who is perfectly adjusted to society. Suppose the society stinks? Is he supposed to adjust to it then?'

She said smartly: 'Better disinfect it with Kleenlav.' Then she caught his arm. 'A tobacconist! Wait for me, will you? I must get some cigarettes.'

Waiting for her, he continued to think of Gash. Living as a hermit must produce some extreme mental state, even if it's only extreme boredom. Extremes. The human mind under stress, driven to its limits. Like testing an aeroplane under extreme climatic conditions. Normality is uninteresting. I am obsessed by the possibility of extremes.

He walked up and down past the shop window. I do nothing. I am not happy. I am not even particularly unhappy. I am empty. I do nothing. I merely kill time. Killing time is humanity's greatest sin. Boredom means not being in a state of grace.

They took the Tube at Tottenham Court Road. On the next seat was a mother and small child. The child tottered down the gangway on fat, unsteady legs, clutching at his cotton trousers.

The mother said: 'Barry... now don't you be a nuisance.'

The child staggered towards them, his plump starfish hand outstretched.

Ilsa said without interest: 'Cute kid.'

Beckett suddenly knew how she would be in ten years' time. She would no longer be a flame burning itself out. The sharp bone structure of her face would be blurred by softening flesh, and her slim body would have thickened. This hard-drinking, hard-living, desperately young product of the modern age would become a middle-class housewife. She would distract herself with bridge evenings, television evenings, coffee and chat in the High Street Tea Shoppe with women friends, and dances held by her husband's firm. She would cook Italian food because it was smart. From time to time, one of the neighbours would fall in love with her. She would use Family Planning because of buying a car and keeping her figure; but because of her female desire for maternity she would eventually have a child. The child would be as dull and ordinary as she was. This was the girl whom he loved.

When they left the cinema she said: 'By the way, you couldn't do me a great favour, could you?'

'I expect so. What is it?'

She hesitated, then took the plunge. 'I must have two pounds to pay the rent today, and I'm absolutely flat broke. I simply had to buy some new shoes, you see, because I'm going to a twenty-first birthday party tomorrow, and, well, I mean I couldn't possibly go without new shoes. I mean, my other pairs are absolutely falling to pieces, they really are.' Her eyes were anxious and evasive. She combed her fingers through her hair. 'I don't know how I can manage the rent otherwise. I spent the rent money on shoes. You know what I'm like about money.'

'Yes, that's all right. I think I can just about manage two pounds.'

She continued to stare at him. Her face was wan and half ashamed. 'I know it's awful of me, because I still owe you five pounds from way back last year. But I really will pay it all back some day.'

'That's all right.'

She took the money and stuffed it into her bag, quickly snapping the bag shut. 'It's terribly nice of you.'

Embarrassed, he said: 'Well...' They walked a few paces and then stopped again. He said: 'How about coming back to my place for a coffee?'

Oh, she was terribly sorry, she really was. Her gestures were theatrical and her eyes honest-wide as she explained that she couldn't possibly, not tonight, what a pity. She gabbled on, using too many excuses and too much vehemence, until he told her that it didn't matter.

He walked her to the bus-stop. She was still extravagantly protesting her regret when the bus arrived.

Walking home alone, Beckett felt cheated and indignant. He had never considered women as existing in their own right, but only in relation to him. It infuriated him that Ilsa should claim a will of her own, that she should refuse to visit his room when he wanted her to. She should be grateful that he wanted her; she should replace her will with his.

He knew that he would pursue Ilsa determinedly; but that even as he redoubled his efforts to win her, there would be a cold mocking voice inside him telling him that he did not really want her.

He experienced, simultaneously, raging desire for her and the knowledge that he did not really care.

Chapter 5

ST ELIZABETH'S CHURCH was in a suburban-afternoon road of identical dolls' houses.

A young married couple was out walking. The wife pushed the baby's pram, the husband walked beside her, and an older child ran ahead, doing little skips.

Farther up the road, Beckett heard a child screaming in one of the houses. Evidently the child, a girl, was being beaten. The hairs on his scalp prickled. He felt immediate sexual excitement, a sadistic pleasure. He wished he could see the child being beaten.

Then his excitement was replaced by the more creditable emotion of disgust. He felt irritated at being subjected to the screams. Mentally he composed a short essay against beating children. This activity lasted until he reached St Elizabeth's.

The church was a new, yellow-brick building. Builders' materials were in the yard, and there was a wheelbarrow in the porch. The presbytery was next door and was also new and sand-coloured. It was perfectly square, like a child's drawing, with the door in the centre and symmetrical netted windows.

Beckett was about to ring the bell when he happened to glance through the crack in the curtains of the nearest window. Inside, a priest sat alone at a table, his pale, aquiline profile bent over a chess-board. He picked up the red knight. His hawk-like hand holding the piece was beautiful, with long fingers like a medieval carving.

Then two women emerged from the front door. One of them was saying: '... so I told Father Lestrade, the Children of Mary are being run in the hands of the few, with that Mrs Busybody Riordan and her little click,

and all that trouble about the cakes at the social....'
Their feet stabbed righteously down the road; their triumphant voices gossiping into the distance.

He rang the bell, thinking, if things had been different I would have been dealing with complaining women like those. 'Father Beckett, about the cakes for the Children of Mary...' Could I have stood their stupidity and triviality? Yes, I suppose so, if I believed.

The neat housekeeper opened the door. 'Good evening.'

'Good evening. Is it possible to see Father Hogan?'

'Is he expecting you?'

'No, I'm afraid I just called on the off chance.'

She said: 'He's just getting the car out of the garage. He's going out with Father Dominic.'

Beckett felt relieved. 'Oh well, it doesn't matter. I'll come some other time.'

'Why don't you come in and wait? I don't think they'll be long.'

'Thank you.' He followed her into the house. In the passage he met the priest whom he had seen through the window. The priest made a slight bow to him, then asked the housekeeper if the car was ready.

'I think so, Father Dominic.' She showed Beckett into the small parlour. It was plainly furnished, with a table covered by a cloth of Irish linen with a lace border, four hard chairs, and a glass-doored cupboard with books on three shelves and wine glasses on the fourth. The chess-board had been removed.

'Have you seen the new church?' she asked. 'Oh, but I expect you were at the consecration ceremony. We were all very worried in case the building wasn't finished in time, but a number of parishioners lent a hand and between us we got it finished. We were very lucky, it was all completed in time except for the bike-shed, which the workmen are finishing now.'

He said politely: 'Really?'

'Yes. Well, I don't expect Father Hogan will keep you waiting long. He likes to take the car out whenever possible because he's practising for his driving test.'

'Oh, is he?'

'He's taking it next week. I've been saying a decade of the rosary every night that he may pass.'

When she had gone Beckett sat down on one of the hard chairs. There was a vase of gladioli on the table. There were no fallen petals round the vase. The flowers were tidy and sterile, like flowers in an undertaker's window.

He looked around. There was a crucifix on one wall, on another a picture of the Sacred Heart. The picture was a standard reproduction and he had seen it before; Christ parting his robe to display an embarrassing heart which bled crimson glycerine. Even as a child, Beckett had felt nauseated and insulted by that shameless heart, by the idea of drowning in a syrup of love and pity. His pride had revolted at the thought of Christ's embarrassing love; and yet he had been terrified of committing a mortal sin which would cut him off from that love.

The airless parlour made his head ache. He got up and went over to the bookcase, scanning the titles. There was a contrast between insipid lives of saints and similar pious trash, and thick volumes on advanced theology and comparative religion. He wondered who was responsible for the choice. He selected one of the volumes, and sat down to read. The print was small, and the foxed pages had a camphor smell. From time to time he yawned and glanced at the clock.

He had been waiting for three-quarters of an hour when he heard the car returning. He looked out of the window. The black Austin had L plates, and a St Christopher medallion on the windscreen. The violent braking at the kerb amused him. The atrocious driving was typical of Father Hogan.

He watched the two priests alight. Father Hogan had not changed in appearance. He looked as usual as if he had just scrubbed his florid face with a nailbrush and carbolic soap, and flattened the black-bull curls with cold water.

Father Dominic reached the gate first, but waited for Father Hogan to catch up and open the gate for him. He did not appear conceited; he expected others to open gates for him, not because of any personal merit but as part of the order of authority.

Beckett withdrew from the window and waited for the priests' entry.

He could hear Father Hogan's harsh Belfast voice from the hall. 'Who? Who did you say it was?' The housekeeper's answer was indistinct.

Father Dominic entered first. His pale, chiselled features gave the impression that he raised austerity to the level of a passion. He seemed to be a man of great willpower, intellect, and passion, who bent these qualities to the service of the most rigorous discipline he could find: that of the Church. His eyes had the cold fire of a self-imposed ideal.

In comparison Father Hogan looked like a peasant oaf. He pumped Beckett's hand and exclaimed heartily: 'Well, Joe, this is a pleasant surprise. A pleasant surprise indeed. I'd given you up for lost! Your mother and I had a long talk recently. She's a very good woman, Joe, a very pious woman. One of the backbones of the parish. I hope you appreciate her.'

'Yes, Father, she said she'd seen you.'

'Been home, then, have you?'

'No, she wrote to me.'

'Oh, she wrote to you.' Father Hogan turned to the other priest. 'Father Dominic, this is Joe Beckett. Joe's family live in my previous parish; they're old friends of mine.'

'How do you do?' Father Dominic shook hands. 'We met briefly in the passage, earlier.'

'I'm afraid I've called at an inconvenient time. I don't want to interrupt you when you're busy.'

'Not at all. We welcome anyone who calls. Have you seen the new church?'

'From the outside.' Beckett anticipated, with boredom, another long account of the building, but to his relief Father Dominic did not pursue the subject.

'Well, Joe,' Father Hogan said, 'we haven't seen you at home for some years now. What is it? Three? Four?'

'About four, Father.'

'About four. And are you living here now?'

'No, I live in Notting Hill.'

'Ah, Notting Hill. So your church will be...?'

'I'm afraid I don't go to church any more.' As he spoke, dizzy excitement spiralled through Beckett. It was caused by his anticipation of a battle of ideas. The excitement passed off as quickly as it had arisen, leaving his mind clear to deal with the forthcoming argument.

Father Hogan sat down heavily. 'Now, Joe, Joe! What is this?'

'I'm no longer a Catholic, Father.'

'Ah. But! You may be a lapsed Catholic, or an unworthy one, but you are still a Catholic. You are in mortal sin and you had better do something about it.' Then Father Hogan, with crashing lack of tact, confided to the other priest: 'This young renegade here once intended to become a priest, Father.'

'I'm sure Mr Beckett had his reasons for changing his mind.'

Father Hogan agreed: 'Ah, yes, of course, these things can't be forced. Vocations come from God. And sometimes they come to the most unlikely persons. Why, I myself was a holy terror as a boy, and a vocation was farthest from my mind.' He turned to Beckett again. 'However, this business now of mortal sin...'

'Sin is an offence against myself, and therefore I'm the only one to know whether I have sinned.'

'Sin is an offence against God,' Father Hogan contradicted. 'You are disobeying His commandments.'

'Surely it is generally agreed now that the commandments are merely sensible social precepts. If Moses claimed they were God-given, it's probably because he thought that that would be the likeliest way of enforcing them. No laws are absolute; they vary according to the needs of the society they serve.'

'Generally agreed? No it is not generally agreed. Heresies may come and go with the fashion, and the devil may whisper all manner of notions into our ears, but the word of God will always be the truth.'

Father Dominic was sitting like an angular composition in black. He remarked: 'Perhaps we should find out what platform Mr Beckett is speaking from. Is it that of nineteenth-century rationalism?'

'I dunno about platforms, Father.'

Then Beckett burst out: 'But, anyway, enormous advances were made in the nineteenth century. It gave us our awareness of cause and its formative context.'

'Quite so,' Father Dominic said. 'But even the strict determinist will feel, in his daily life, as if he is making choices. He may know theoretically that his actions are determined and that conscience is only a socially conditioned reflex, but nevertheless if he commits a mean action he will, in practice, feel guilty. He arrives, in fact, at a paradox, which could be expressed by saying that man has not got free will, but has the illusion of free will. Do you agree?'

'Yes!' Beckett was enthusiastic. 'Man hasn't got free will, but only the illusion of it. And sometimes the fabric of illusion wears a bit thin, and we glimpse our lack of freedom beneath it.'

'The Church recognizes the same paradox, and expresses it thus: God is timeless, and past, present, and future coexist in His moment. He therefore knows our future actions. Men, living in time, are not affected by His knowledge and have free will.'

The housekeeper entered, bearing a tray of tea-things. There followed the ritual of pouring out from the silver pot, passing cups and offering sugar.

When the woman had gone, Father Dominic enquired: 'Did you say you lived in Notting Hill? I wonder if you know an old friend of mine — Mr Gash?'

'Yes, I know Gash. He lives in the same road as me. Practically opposite. What a coincidence!'

'It's a long time since we've met. Ten years or so. How is he?'

'Well, he's rather a local curiosity. Rumour has it that he was once a rich man, but now he lives like a hermit, dresses in rags, eats scraps, and sleeps on the floor.'

'Oh yes, the Gashes were pretty well off,' Father Dominic said. 'Gash was my parents' friend rather than mine, as I was only a boy at the time. He was a frequent visitor at our house. He was a wealthy socialite, and had a brilliant career, many talents, popularity, good looks, everything. His friends assumed he would climb high in the world. Then he began to suffer from headaches, which were caused, in my opinion, by his self-division. That is, he was divided between his brilliant, successful life and various preoccupations and ideas which tormented him. Finally he disappeared, abandoning his career, his beautiful wife, and their child. He signed over his money to his wife, and kept barely enough to live on. I heard later that he had joined a small religious sect who lived in isolation somewhere in Scotland. I'm sorry to learn from you that he now lives under such squalid conditions. He'd be a welcome visitor here, if he cared to call.'

'I'll tell him, certainly, but I doubt if he'll come. He never leaves his room.'

'As I said, I was only a schoolboy at the time of his visits. But nevertheless he and I used to discuss religion, as at one time he was considering becoming a Catholic. It's a pity he didn't, instead of joining a crank sect.'

Beckett looked at his tea. In its delicate white cup it was transparent, so that he could almost see the sugar through it. He said: 'You are an intelligent man, Father. I once stood on the steps of a church and watched the congregation come out. They were also intelligent men and women, possessed of reason. If the lights went out they knew it was a fuse, not black magic. If they fell ill it was of a classified disease, not witchcraft. Only in religion did they suspend their reason; for every one of those people firmly believed that a couple of characters named Adam and Eve were persuaded, by a talking snake, to eat an apple, which incident condemned the whole of subsequent humanity to damnation. If I had claimed to converse with a cobra they would have given me psychiatric treatment. So why were they so uncritical of the Bible? It seemed absurd.'

'Belief in Adam and Eve may be absurd. But do you consider Adam and Eve themselves to be absurd?'

'Taking them as fictional characters, no. They acted correctly. They were offered two things: the knowledge of good and evil and the power to become gods. I admire them for accepting that offer. They would have been despicable dullards if they had been contented to remain like cabbages in Eden. The Church's condemnation of them always irritates me.'

'You are a seeker after truth, Mr Beckett. It's a pity you despise psychological truth: the externalization, into myth or symbol, of the paradoxes, experiences and aspirations of human nature.'

'I don't despise psychological truth. But what I mean is, I can say with impunity that a thing is relatively true. A scientist or mathematician can also say that a thing is relatively true. But the whole groundwork of the Church is her claim to absolute truth. Destroy that groundwork, and you destroy the whole Church.'

'That would be a pity, for the Church also has practical truth, truth which works for a large number of people. She accommodates the mystic, the intellectual, the respectable householder, the artist, the superstitious peasant. Her doctrines satisfy all these diverse people. Isn't it good, therefore, that her doctrines should persist?'

Beckett said: 'To ensure that they persist the Church has organized inquisitions, slaughtered honest heretics, and terrorized people into submission by threatening them with hell-fire. Is that good?'

'No. It is necessary. The Church cannot exist on a soil of anarchy. Order is necessary to her. Throughout the ages men of willpower have sought to impose order on chaos. And those who believe that order is preferable to chaos will agree that the Church was justified, even at the cost of human lives.' Father Dominic stood up, like the figure of death, with his austere features profiled against the window. 'But I'm afraid I've taken up too much of your time. You wanted to see Father Hogan, and I've interrupted. However, it's been an interesting discussion, and I hope we shall have the opportunity to continue it. If you can persuade Gash to visit us perhaps you will come with him?'

Beckett also rose, clumsily, to say goodbye.

When Father Dominic had gone the other two relaxed, sat back and passed cigarettes. Father Hogan, who had a boisterous manner, told jokes and stories about their mutual acquaintances. Finally he sobered up, wiped his forehead with his large fist, and advised Beckett to mend his ways. He insisted that Mrs Beckett was rightly worried, and that Beckett should try to lead a good Catholic life. 'You have too much conceit in your reason; you lack humility. It is the sin of Satan, *non serviam,* the sin of pride. Renounce your reason and pray instead for faith. Naturally you lose your faith if you stay away from Mass and the sacraments. The sacraments give grace which is the food of the soul. So I want you to make a firm resolution to go regularly to Mass and the sacraments. Will you do that now? Of course you will. Otherwise you see now, Joe, the city is full of dangers, bad companions, who may at first seem adventurous and exciting. Young women, some of them with no moral upbringing, of easy virtue, temptations...' The priest's voice had become low, impersonal, like the monotone from behind the confessional grid.

Beckett left the Presbytery and walked back past the dolls' houses. Clipped trees were spaced at regular intervals along the pavement.

He had made the visit because of guilt feelings towards his mother. By fulfilling one of her requests he could hold off his conscience for a bit. But if she hoped for his reconversion she would be disappointed.

He had once been an ardent Catholic. When his belief and his vocation had been destroyed he had hated the religion as much as he had previously loved it. He had read books; and every disproof of the Church's doctrines, every condemnation of her past villainies, had pleased him. They were like personal knife-thrusts against the Church.

Although in practice he was an individualist, he could share Father Dominic's sympathy for the tyrant with vision, the totalitarian who enforced a social blueprint at the cost of morality and lives. Therefore he could admire the Church which had played power politics as the priest had played chess. His admiration was, however, of a cynical nature. He saw too far behind the scenes to have faith.

He had ceased to believe. He might no longer hate the Church, but he had irretrievably lost belief in the Church or in anything.

His way back to the Tube passed the local common. A fair was in progress, and he walked over to have a look round.

The fairground smelled of trodden grass, bottled beer, and sickly petrol-fumes. Mouths scented with candyfloss screamed against the mechanical music. Steel octopi revolved, their tentacles studded with lights.

A huckster in a cowboy hat yelled: '... skill, ladies and gents, try your skill....'

Beckett liked the fair and the crowd. Seeing the people, he felt enjoyment by proxy. Walking alone through a crowded fairground was his nearest approach to feeling a member of humanity. He turned the coins in his pockets with pleasure.

He strolled past the mosque frontage of the Ghost Train; then past the Hall of Mirrors, outside which LAUGH! LAUGH! LAUGH! flashed in coloured bulbs. Girls in bright dresses slid down the Helter Skelter. He watched them, trying to see their stocking-tops and knickers. The lifted skirts roused the state of desire, but not desire for a specific object. It was a hunger, not really for sex but for something indefinable.

The summer evening, the fair, the lifted skirts, evoked bygone summer evenings, bygone fairs, other skirts. He was melancholy, filled by half desires without names.

As it grew darker, arc lights were switched on and shone on lips and eyes and cheekbones. The first dew blackened the grass. Blue sparks screamed along the wires of the Dodgem Cars and a carriage hurtled down the Scenic Railway, followed by a dying trail of shrieks.

At the rifle range he set down his money for six shots. He selected a rifle and frowned down its barrel. Although it was only an inferior discard he felt for it an approval that almost amounted to love. When he took aim the fairground receded and there was only him, the rifle, and the cardboard target. He squinted down the sights. He did not fire until his hand was completely steady.

Five shots went into the bull; the sixth was in the inner ring.

'You're a crack shot, sir,' the attendant said, giving him the cardboard target with the hole eaten in the centre.

Beckett took his prize of cigarettes. He was still locked tightly in the world of rifle and target and triumph so that, on leaving the stall, he stumbled against a man who had been standing directly behind him. He apologized to the man without looking at him.

He walked back across the damp grass of the common towards the main road. Ahead of him a couple strolled arm in arm. He heard the bubbles of their soft, relaxed laughter. They did not reach the road, but turned aside into the darkness of the common.

Returning home on the Tube, the mechanical music was still with him, in his stomach like loneliness. He felt in his pocket for the target, but it was not there. He must have dropped it. He still had the cigarettes, though. He lit one.

He got off the Tube at Notting Hill Gate, and paused to look at a poster advertising a horror film. A scaly monster was threatening a girl in a torn dress who crouched behind a tottering skyscraper.

When he looked up he met the eyes of a man who was staring at him intently. The man wore a seedy pin-stripe suit. He was pale, and privation had planed away his face until his features had set in a numb, wolfish expression. His pale eyes, with pinpoints of light, were those of a fanatic with a hysterical grudge against himself.

When he met Beckett's gaze, he turned away and rattled the drawer of the chocolate machine, but he had not put a coin in.

Momentarily, the incident disconcerted Beckett. The man seemed vaguely familiar, but he could not remember where he had seen him before.

Beckett had a long stride and reached home quickly. He was inserting his key in the front door when he again saw the man, who was rounding the street corner. The man hurried in hurting shoes, as if he had corns. He had evidently followed Beckett and been forced to trot in order to keep pace.

Beckett was annoyed. He disliked being bothered. He asked nothing of people and expected that they should ask nothing of him. He used the lavatory in the house, then left again. The man was no longer in sight. Beckett walked to the Paradine Café snack-bar.

The proprietor said: 'You're late tonight.'

'Yes.'

'Been a hot day.'

'Hasn't it?' He waited for his food, staring without interest at the Coca-Cola advertisements, the smeared glass tops of the tables, and the radio flanked by ketchup bottles.

The proprietor was asking a man in overalls: 'Heard the cricket? Hudson still not out.'

Beckett took his food and coffee over to the corner

table, and sat down. Then he noticed that the man was standing outside the café, peering through the greyish net curtains. A folded newspaper protruded from his jacket; Racing Results hugging the heart like hatred.

Beckett thought that, as he was being followed, he might as well come to terms with his follower. Accordingly, he beckoned the man in.

'Well,' the man said. 'Knew I recognized you. How're you keeping? Enjoying your food?'

'Do you want a tea or something?'

'Well, I'll tell you, I'd rather have a bite to eat. Honest, I haven't eaten for three days and I'm bloody starving.'

'Have what you want. Put it on my bill.'

The man went up to the counter, and presently returned with egg-and-chips, slices of bread-and-marge, and a tea. 'Thanks a lot. I got the cheapest...' His voice was poisoned with pride. 'I'm not putting you to any expense.'

Beckett said: 'Please yourself.'

'Can't remember the last time I ate. Not my fault. Been ill.' He tapped himself on the chest. 'Lost my job.'

'Hard luck.'

The man shook ketchup on to his food. 'Knew I recognized you. Funny, I was just thinking "I know that bloke" when you beckoned to me.'

'That isn't surprising. You followed me from the Tube station to my house and then to this café.'

'No, I mean I know you from way back. Seen you somewhere in Soho. Where do you get? The Belgian Café? Mick's? The Constantinople?'

'I do go to those places from time to time, yes.'

'Knew I'd seen you. Never forget a face. Sometimes I can't place it at first — and then bang! Suddenly it comes back. Know that bloke from such-and-such.' The man ate voraciously and talked through mouthfuls. 'You know Silent?'

'Yes.'

'Baroness Tania?'

'Yes.'

'German Erik?'

'Yes.'

'Dutchie?'

'Yes.'

'All the old familiars. The Belgian and Mick's crowd. Knew I'd seen you around. Seen you in Mick's the other night, with a blonde girl. That right?'

'Possibly, yes.' Beckett's own memory was returning. He now remembered that this was the man who had talked of an appointment outside Cinerama, and who had tried to sell Silent a camera.

'There you are; told you I knew you. My name's Jacko, in case you didn't know. Pleased to make your acquaintance.'

Beckett said: 'Quite probably we've seen each other round Soho. But why did you follow me tonight?'

'I haven't been following you.'

'Yes, you have.'

Jacko said: 'Don't be funny.'

'If you followed me because you wanted a meal, well, that's fair enough. I mean, I'd always feed someone who was broke. I'm broke myself often. But admit it. Don't make a mystery out of it.'

'I said I didn't follow you and I didn't.'

His obstinacy angered Beckett. 'Then don't trot along behind me all the time.'

'Now, don't get narked. You been okay by me; bought me a meal and all that; but that doesn't give you the right to insult me. Does it now? I've got my pride.' Jacko finished the meal and wiped up the plate with the last slice of bread. 'Got any fag papers?'

'No, but have a cigarette.'

'Ta. I generally roll my own, see, but I'm right out of papers. Comes cheaper if you roll them. It's since I've been ill and lost my job that I haven't any money. Still, not to worry. I spend the nights in the all-night caffs round Fleet Street and Covent Garden. Get a bit of kip with my head on my arms on the table. Pal of mine's got a gaff off Tottenham Court Road, and he lets me keep my gear there till I get my own place.'

'All right. Well you've had a meal, which is your admission ticket to this café, so you can stay here in the warm for a bit. I've got to go now.'

'My company bore you?' Jacko looked with fierce pride at the worn cuffs of his jacket and his warped nicotined fingers. 'Or perhaps you don't like to be seen with me?'

'It bores me when you follow me around. Please stop doing it.' Beckett got up, paid the bill, and left the café.

Jacko followed him out, and plucked at his sleeve. 'Look, you done me a favour, so I'm going to do you one. Put a bit of good in your way. There's this bloke I know —'

'If you genuinely want to do something for me, leave me alone. That's all I want.'

'Look, how would you like to buy some stuff? I sell things second-hand, see. Pick up a bit of cash on the side that way. But I could let you have it cheap, whatever you wanted. Books, a raincoat, or there's a good electric shaver, almost new. The stuff's in this pal's gaff I was telling you about, but I can get it for you tomorrow, anything you want...'

'I don't want anything, except to be left alone.'

'Doesn't do to be unsociable. Makes you miserable.'

'Go away!' Beckett said. Then, as Jacko continued to trot after him, he turned and shoved him hard in the chest.

Jacko lost his balance and staggered backwards. His face was white and twisted with hysterical hatred for Beckett's strength and his own weakness.

Beckett walked away. He was conscious of his hand which had shoved Jacko, as if the hand had become large. The incident had upset him, and he could not regain his emotional balance. He wondered whether he had been too harsh to Jacko. He stifled his conscience by thinking angrily: I hate being bothered... I hate being bothered.

Chapter 6

WELL,' ILSA SAID, 'so this is where you live.' She slouched with her fists in her raincoat pockets. Her beret and belted raincoat made her look like a Resistance heroine.

'Yes. Sorry it's untidy.'

'Darling, you'll have to find some very domesticated woman and marry her. Otherwise you'll always be uncomfortable and not cared for. How about Katey? She does all the cleaning at the flat. And I wish you wouldn't always live on top floors. It kills my feet.'

'Yes, I always seem to have an attic, don't I? But I like the roofscape,' he said. 'Your raincoat's wet, love. Take it off and hang it behind the door.'

'Thanks, I will.' Shrugging out of the raincoat, she exclaimed: 'Damn!'

'What's the matter?'

'Broken a nail.' She inspected the scarlet claws.

He took her hand. After a moment, she withdrew it. There was an embarrassment. He said into the pause: 'Would you like some coffee?'

'Love some.'

He went down to the bathroom to fill the kettle. When he returned she was lounging in the armchair, swinging a bored foot and flicking ash on to the floor.

He put the kettle on the gas ring, then shut the window. Rain beat against the panes. A brilliant zigzag of lightning lit the sky, followed by a crash of thunder.

Ilsa said anxiously: 'I hate storms.' She combed her fingers through her wet, waif-like hair.

Beckett thought: Good, then perhaps she'll stay the night. Aloud he said: 'Yes, it's bad, isn't it? Likely to go on all night, according to the weather report.' He started to tidy the room. On the hearthrug were the remains of a meal: the saucepan he had eaten out of, the bathtowel he had spread on his knee because the saucepan was hot, the book he had read while eating, and an apple core in the ashtray. He removed these things from sight.

Ilsa watched him. After a while she said: 'I wish you had a radio.'

'Shall I get one?'

'Yes.' She said in a twangy voice: 'This is Radio Luxembourg, the Station of the Stars.' She followed this announcement with an imitation of a pop singer.

Becket said: 'Fine. But can you pitch it a bit lower?'

'Huh? Why?'

'The landlady. I'm not supposed to have visitors after ten-thirty. Especially beautiful girls.'

She accepted the compliment as a matter of course, saying merely: 'What a drag.'

'I know. It makes me feel so humiliated, having to ask my friends to be quiet on the stairs, and keep their voices down. The old cow makes me feel guilty every time I come in the front door. I want to find a place without a landlady on the premises. I detest the whole race. The constant pettiness and prying, the complaining notes pushed under the door. That's why I left the Paddington place, you know. The fool woman was always shoving notes under my door, complaining that I burnt the light too late, or that I walked up and down and disturbed the people below, etc., etc. Finally I told her I was sick to death of reading her everlasting drivel, and that she must either stop pestering me with notes or find another tenant.'

'Heavens! What did she say to that?'

'She asked me, who did I think I was?'

They laughed, then Ilsa said: 'I can't help sympathizing with the woman. You do give the impression that you think yourself superior to other people. It's a very irritating trait of yours.'

'It's only because I *am* superior.' He said it as a joke, and then realized that he meant it. He had always had a conviction of his superiority; a conviction so basic that it was hardly conscious.

She said: 'You're bloody conceited, Joe Beckett.'

'I know. Can you stand it?' He took her hand and raised her out of the chair. They stood facing each other. He said: 'You obsess me. You know that, don't you? I've got you in my blood like fever.'

He tried to kiss her, but she quickly averted her face so that his mouth only brushed her cheek. She shrugged him off. 'Stop it, Joe. You're to leave me alone.'

'But why?'

There were pinpoints of light in her grey eyes. She looked mean and nasty. 'Because you get in my way, that's why.'

'I don't see that.'

'I can't explain any better.'

'Well, try.'

'All right, I'll try. You said you felt superior. Right? If life proves unpleasant to you, you evade it by hiding in superiority feelings. A sort of sour grapes. Well, I am a very insecure person, but my cure is different from yours. I've got to have people loving me, admiring me, telling me I'm wonderful. Love and admiration build me up, so I don't feel insecure any more. But you despise me, Joe. You despise me, my friends, my amusements. All the things that are necessary to me. Instead of building me up, you undermine me. That's what I mean by saying you get in my way. And I won't stand for that.'

'I see. At least, I think I see.'

Her voice took on a more conciliatory tone. 'Besides, my darling, I'd be bad for you. I'd hurt you. I'd betray you by going off with other men. Oh, I might promise not to, and really intend not to. But I'd do it just the same. I can't stop with any one man. I've got to have new men, new conquests. I suppose I need constant confirmation that I'm attractive.' She pushed her hair back with quick, nervous fingers. 'I remember once when I was a kid, a neighbour of ours got run over and killed. Stupid thing to happen in the country, where there are only about two cars a day. Anyway, I thought: Suppose I was to die tomorrow? You know the way kids get obsessions? Well, I got this sort of obsession that I was going to die tomorrow. At first I was frightened, and then I thought: Well, if I'm going to die tomorrow I'm going to rip it up like mad today. And I did, too.'

'What did you do?'

'Oh, invited all the other kids in to slide down my dad's haystack. Dad was furious. I got slapped and sent to bed for it.'

'And what about the next day, when you didn't die?'

She laughed, dismissing it like a promise made under stress. 'Oh, I'd forgotten about it by then. I never could think of any one thing for long. But you dig what I mean, don't you? I always live as if I'm going to die tomorrow. Rip it up and run wild; get all the kicks I can out of life while it lasts. I can't stay with any one man, Joe.' Her voice had risen to a strident, ugly pitch. Then she altered again, and looked at him nervously. 'You do understand, don't you? I don't want to be a bitch to you like I am to the others.'

'I wish you would stay with me,' he said. Then he knew that it wasn't true. He only wanted her now.

Torrential rain was still falling and the sky was a battlefield of thunder and lightning. He looked out of the window. Behind him, Ilsa continued to talk in a hard, sophisticated voice, and made stagey gestures. 'But, I mean, we can still be platonic friends. When people say they don't believe in platonic friendship, well, I think they're completely crazy. Well, I mean. I've got tons of platonic friends, and you'd be the favourite of the lot, darling. And we'd keep it as a terrific secret that we really love each other.' She came and stood beside him, flashing a smile. 'Friends?'

'Don't be such a child, Ilsa. Do you think men are made of wood or something? I'm not, and I'm not going to be one of the string of men you keep hopelessly in love with you in order to gratify your vanity. That sort of situation may appeal to romantics, but not to me.'

'Oh, Joe, don't be horrid, when I've offered to be friends.' She pointed to the boiling kettle. 'I'm going to be awfully nice and make the coffee, it you'll tell me where everything is.'

Beckett frowned, preoccupied.

'Did you hear, my honey? Where are the coffee things?'

'Oh, thanks. In the cupboard under the washstand. The mugs are there, too.'

He watched her making the coffee. The light shone directly on her face, showing up the flaws. Her skin had a stale pallor, there was a sharpness about the bone structure, and her eyes were tired from late nights.

She put the filled mugs on the mantelpiece, saying brightly: 'Here you are, then. The Barnes coffee-making service. With a smile.'

He went to pick up his mug, but instead turned and seized her. He kissed her destructively, forcing her mouth open.

'Joe-Joe...'

'Ilse-Ilse. Oh, honey...' He cupped his hands over her trim little behind and pressed her against him.

'Oh, honey!' Her breath caught sharply. 'Oh, please, darling, don't.' Ilsa the trembler, the unreliable, was a cornered little animal now but behind her eyes was a wary, vicious glint. Ilsa was penitent only when caught; Ilsa with eyes honest-wide made promises that afterwards evaporated when she sold you out and left you only the nail-slashes of her smart remarks and smart-set laughter.

Beckett clasped all this to him for the sake of the small percentage of their love for each other. Keeping his mouth on hers, he started to ease the back of her skirt upwards. She was wearing some sort of nylon panties. He groaned silently with excitement. With his free hand, he switched off the light.

The springs of the bed creaked as they collapsed on to it. He raised his hand and wrenched at the buttons of her blouse, excitement making him clumsy. Then he said: 'Wait a moment.'

'What is it?' Her face in the twilight looked wan, and from under her rumpled hair she regarded him with the eyes of an ancient child. There was something pathetic about this, and about the way her raped blouse hung agape, that made him pick up her hands and kiss them. Then his previous train of thought reasserted itself.

'Wait a moment, I'm going to bolt the door.'

'Oh yes, better, I suppose.'

When he returned she held her arms wide to receive him. They lay in silence except for his breathing and her occasional whimpers. Suddenly she said: 'Wait, I'm going to take my nylons off. They're my best ones; I don't want them laddered.' Her voice sounded unnatural after the silence. Recognizing this, she gave a nervous laugh. 'I bet they've got splashed, damn it, from walking in the rain.'

Naked, she had a Cockney body, pale and thin. But it was lithe, for her habits of jiving and late nights kept her body fit and unpampered. Her tuft of pubic hair had a jaunty look.

Beckett said in a hard, hating voice: 'I adore you.'

She said: 'Darling.'

'Yes?'

'Does my face change when I make love?'

He propped his bare elbow on the pillow and looked down at her. 'Yes. Your face looks all clean and shining in the moonlight. Like a newly born angel.'

'Yours does too. You look like a god.'

A bit later she said: 'You are in love with me, aren't you?'

He lied quickly: 'Yes.'

'Then say it. I want to hear you say it.'

'I love you, Ilsa.'

'Say it again, Joe. Keep saying it. Say you love me. Keep saying it. Don't stop.'

He woke with a start and sat up in bed. The luminous dial of the clock said nearly two.

Ilsa woke too, and asked: 'What are you doing?'

'Going to get a drink of water. Do you want one?'

'No, thanks. I say, I'm streaming with sweat.'

'So am I.'

'Has the storm stopped?'

He listened. 'I think so, yes.' He got out of bed, treading on something soft: the pile of their clothes. He padded across the room and switched on the light.

Ilsa shielded her face with her arm. She murmured sleepily: 'Joe-Joe.'

'Yes?'

'Still love me?'

He returned and sat on the edge of the bed. 'Of course.'

She flung her arms round his neck. 'Promise you'll stay with me. Promise to be kind to me and love me for ever. And oh, darling, I promise and faithfully swear that I'll always stay with you.'

He kissed her lips. 'I've got a lazy and conservative nature. There's no reason, as far as I can see, why I should leave you.'

'Then keep me safe, love me and look after me, and I'll never get into any scrapes.'

He stood up, putting on his raincoat for a dressing-gown and thrusting his bare feet into his sandals. He emptied one of the mugs of cold coffee into the slop basin, and took the mug with him.

The house was in darkness. He groped his way down the stairs. The unbuckled sandals were loose and made a noise. He curled his toes, trying to keep the sandals on and make them less noisy. His warm skin contracted where the wet raincoat touched him. Thus he clopped slowly down the unlit flight.

The bathroom was on the ground floor. A strip of worn lino ended at the iron claw-feet of the bath. The bath was marked by horseshoes of rust under the taps. There was a large, old-fashioned gas geyser. On the medicine cupboard was a cup from which someone had drunk cocoa, a stub of shaving soap, and a litter of spent matches.

He ran water into the mug, wiping it clean with his fingers. Then he filled it again and drank thirstily. The coldness went straight down to his stomach. He wanted to urinate but could not be bothered to shuffle laboriously to the lavatory, so he used the bath.

The window had been made opaque by covering it with adhesive paper. The paper was varnish brown, with a pattern of fleurs-de-lis. He pushed the window up, letting the cool night air blow in on his forehead. Somebody's socks, which had dried stiffly on the string from geyser to window-frame, swayed in the breeze.

He had contained a wolf, which had become steadily more ravenous the longer he had led his monkish life. The wolf panted towards the moment of orgasm, the moment when he knew that there was nothing except this. Then the wolf disappeared, leaving only a man who felt anticlimax and disillusion, who grasped air instead of a prize, and who resented Ilsa's presence in his room.

He conscientiously went back over all the things he had said to Ilsa, and tried to discover whether he had meant them. He did not know, but suspected that he had not.

He thought: No prizes in life. Only mirages that disappear when you arrive at them. Freedom from sexual desire results from gratifying it. But there must be another sort of freedom. Not just a passive lack, an emptiness, but an active, positive freedom.

He looked out of the window. The row of solid buildings opposite were a negation of his love-making with Ilsa. His thoughts wandered to building construction; to men in overalls, to planks and scaffolding, to the bulldozers whose jaws scooped up mouthfuls of rubble.

Somewhere in the house a clock struck twice. He switched off the bathroom light, and groped his way back to his room, Ilsa lay with the spun silk of her hair on the greyish pillow, and the warm smell of sleep around her.

Chapter 7

THE SUNLIGHT made metal patches on the office window. A fly buzzed dustily against the letter T of TONS & PAC.

Beckett looked at the clock. It was only three minutes later than the last time he had looked at it, a desert of boredom ago.

On his desk was a pile of invoices to be entered in the ledger. The first stage in the task was to pick up his Biro. But he could not do it. Even the thought of doing it drained away his energy.

The cover of the ledger had a marble pattern. He stared at the ledger until it seemed alive, swelling like yeast. He did not think. Thought had been replaced by consciousness of the ledger.

The door of Presgate's glass tank was ajar. His cracked, clerical voice could be heard dictating to a typist: '... we would advise that Credit Note Number — look it up on the carbon — was despatched to your good selves on the 28th ultimo comma against our invoice....'

Beckett looked at the clock again. It seemed stationary. He realized that it was no good hoping for five-thirty. Five-thirty was in the future and did not exist. Only the present existed. He was fixed in the present like a man in a photograph. And tomorrow he would have to endure it all again. Not only tomorrow, but for all his life until he retired at sixty-five. He was resentful. He had only one life; why should he be forced to waste it in this manner? It would be different if he believed in immortality.

His thoughts started down this new track. Hard work and active patriotism declined with the decline of belief in immortality. When people knew they had only one life, they were not inclined to waste it by working or end it by dying for their country.

He daydreamed of a small private income. He did not want much and he was enough of a moralist to admire austerity. He wanted only sufficient to live modestly, to purchase food, cigarettes, and books, without having to waste time at a job. Syd asked him: 'What's the matter? Have you got the total wrong again?'

'Yes. I loathe sums. I never could do them. At school I enjoyed algebra and geometry, and loathed arithmetic.'

'Why not try brains, the new wonder head-filler?'

'Oh, drop dead.'

Beckett got up and wandered out of the office. In the corridor he felt dizzy with boredom, as if he were going to faint.

He went into the cloakroom, which, to his relief, was empty. Waves of faintness broke out like sweat. A notice on the wall forbade staff to throw cigarette-ends down the washbasins. All the hot taps were fixed with wire so that they would not turn. He leant against the wall, and pressed his forehead against the white, lavatory-smelling tiles. The coldness made him feel better. Then he sat on the edge of one of the washbasins and smoked a cigarette.

After a while he supposed he should return to the office. He yawned. A tap was dripping and he turned it off. Then he turned it on again and washed his hands, tipping liquid soap from the container. The roller towel was damp as usual.

On his way back to the office, he knocked on the managing director's door and was told to enter. Mr Glegg was fat, like a pig, with his neck seeming thicker than his head. He had a small moustache. He was sitting weightily behind the two telephones and the fan arrangement of *Packaging Worlds*.

Mr Glegg said: 'Won't keep you a minute.' He shuffled through some papers. His stertorous breathing gave the effect of stupidity. He ironed the topmost paper, picked up his fountain-pen, and signed the document.

Beckett thought with sudden surprise: How can he sign anything? His name means nothing. He isn't real. There was something absurd about the flourishing signature, the mark of a man who certainly thought himself real.

Mr Glegg set the papers aside, breathing. Then he asked: 'What can I do for you?'

'I'm resigning. I want to leave on Friday.'

'Oh.' Mr Glegg waited for an explanation. When none came, he said: 'Pastures new? You've found another job?'

'No.'

Mr Glegg clasped his hands over his stomach. 'This firm is like a boat in which we must all pull our weight. We are all cogs in a vast... all cogs. Everyone of us, from myself... I take work home with me every night, Beckett, did you realize that? And often I come in on Sundays too. I could tell you young fellows something about hard work. And/or all staff who pull their weight, and show keenness and ability, there are good channels of advancement and ... keenness has prospects. And the conditions and hours are excellent, very excellent.'

'Oh yes, I suppose it's no worse here than anywhere else.'

Mr Glegg talked on about the excellence of the firm and the crass folly of leaving it. Beckett did not listen. It was nothing to do with him. He watched Mr Glegg's lips, which writhed like pink worms under the moustache. He knew that Mr Glegg kept a bottle of anti-halitosis gargle among the gin-and-tonic bottles in the cabinet. He gargled before appointments with customers.

'... your progress here has not altogether given satisfaction —'

Beckett cut in: 'All right. We both know that I'm inefficient, habitually late, and completely uninterested in the work that poverty forces me to do. Having agreed this, let's end the matter without a long and boring discussion.'

Mr Glegg stared at him, his mouth dead-fish open. Then he banged his fist on the desk. 'Get out!'

Beckett went.

Later, walking with the rush-hour crowds towards the Tube, he saw the broken glass. It lay like a crystal fortune in the gutter. The wonder of it took him aback. He wanted to shout aloud the miracle of a broken milk-bottle.

It was a small incident, but it made him happy, as if he had been touched by grace. The happiness lasted, so that when he walked through the square where he always spent his lunch hours, he was pleased by it. The open-air café was pleasant, and there was a nostalgia about the iron tables, the pigeons, and the fallen leaves. He would miss his lunch hours spent reading in the square.

The experience of seeing the glass, and others like it, were a compensation. They were the occasional visions into super-reality given to the victims of unreality.

Chapter 8

IN THE DAYS that followed his departure from Union Cartons, Beckett did not bother to look for another job. He decided to lay off work until he ran out of money.

He spent most of his time in his room, reading. Between books, he lay on the bed and looked at his view of washstand, armchair, and wallpaper. Occasionally, he had a beer at a pub that had tables on the pavement.

Sometimes he visited Ilsa at Earls Court. It was her fortnight's holiday from her office, but she did not go away because she could not bear to leave her habitat of cafés, pubs, and clubs. Her latest craze was to get brown. The back steps of her basement flat led up to the garden. The earth was barren except for old slop buckets and a few clumps of dusty grass, but she spread a blanket and lolled around listening to pop-song programmes on her red-and-cream plastic portable radio. Her favourite programmes were the Hit Parades, and it was of vital importance to her to know which tunes were in the Top Twenty. Under the dish-rag of London sky she chatted gossip, or was bored, or painted her toe-nails silver.

Indoors, in her flat, she nibbled incessantly at her diet of biscuits and tea made with condensed milk. She never seemed to eat a proper meal unless she was taken out to a café or Katey cooked for her. Even in the daytime she always had the gas fire and electric light on; and the curtains with their Martini, Cinzano, and Dubonnet design were closed, making a permanent artificial night.

In the grey wastes of SW5 she seemed like the one bright flame. Her radiance touched the whole district, so that Beckett, on his way to visit her, thought the 31 bus-stop at Earls Court a most glorious place. Passing the row of flyblown little shops where she got her groceries and cigarettes, he endowed them also with the magic reflection of her radiance.

When he was with her he generally felt bored but he would rather be bored by her than interested by intelligent conversation. She had a passion for things which were trivial and fifth-rate and chatted about the latest scandals in her circle of friends, the plot of a film she had seen, or the clothes she wanted. Beckett listened, bored by her talk but enraptured by her presence.

The second week of her holiday she had to go home to her parents' farm in Sussex. She whined and complained at the prospect. 'The only decent thing is when they've gone to bed I stay up and swig the drinks they keep in the bottom of the larder. Luckily they never seem to notice how the level goes down.'

'Your parents seemed pleasant people to me.'

'Oh God. They're absolutely impossible. Dad never thinks of anything but the farm, and Mum never thinks of anything except making scones and bottling fruit and the socials at the Women's Institute. They're both terribly limited, really.'

'Poor love.'

'I don't know how I'll endure it. Oh, honestly.'

The night before she left for Sussex she spent with him in his room. Her smart tweed suitcase was in the middle of his floor, her best dress for tomorrow hung in his wardrobe. She had her period and could not make love. Instead they lay, with limbs entwined, talking softly into the night.

She moved as if she were uncomfortable.

He said: 'Huh?'

'Sorry, I want to scratch my thigh.'

'Where?'

'Here. Oh, thanks.'

'I can feel your bones. Sharp as a chicken's. You are *thin.*'

'Cheek. I'm slim, not thin. Sort of boyish.'

'You're thin. Skinny Liz. Oh, darling, I adore your thin body.'

'M'm. I love being scratched.'

'I'll have to get you a Chinese back scratcher.'

'What are those?'

'Oh, you know, one of those things like wooden toasting forks.'

'Marvellous.' Then she said: 'Aren't I vulgar, darling, to like being scratched?'

'I like vulgarity.'

'Oh, so do I. I'm terrifically vulgar.'

They were automatically caressing each other, occasionally giving little sighs of pleasure. He said: 'What do you do that's vulgar?'

Giggle. 'Well, for instance I pick my nose.'

'So do I.'

She giggled again. They were both suddenly wide-awake, a conspiratorial midnight-feast awakeness.

He continued: 'And also, I smell my socks to find out whether they are still wearable.'

One of her caresses made him sharply intake breath; he exclaimed: 'Oh, darling...'

'Darling. Am I good in bed?'

'Yes, of course.'

'Good. I'd hate to be no good in bed. And I have got sex appeal, haven't I?'

'You know you have. All your men friends are trying to make you.'

She wriggled with flattered delight. 'Are you glad?'

'It makes me feel proud and victorious to have my property admired. But on the other hand I'm always worried that somebody will steal you. It's like being the winner of a valuable prize that everybody wants to steal.'

'Yes?' Then she whined: 'Can I have a cigarette?'

'Does that mean I have to get out of bed and get them?'

'Oh, honey, be nice.'

'Oh, all right. Actually I want one too, but I thought that if I waited for you to ask first you'd have to get up and get them.'

'Well, that's where you went wrong.'

'Lazy little beast.'

She said smugly: 'I know.'

He lit both cigarettes and gave one to her. They lay in companionable silence, with only the sound of lips on filter-tips and the exhalations of smoke. He had one arm round her shoulders. They lazily rubbed their feet together.

Then she giggled and said: 'Well, go on, you haven't told me anything really vulgar yet.'

He grinned too, pressing closer to her. 'I can't think of anything else. Oh yes, I use the slop bucket because I can't be bothered to go down to the lavatory.'

'Lazy hound. Do you know, Katey did it in our kitchenette sink, and the sink came away from the wall. We had to call the plumber.' The traitress added: 'Of course, she's rather fat. Disgusting, really, I think, all that fat wobbly flesh, and great breasts and things. Like that Georgia you were so keen on.'

'Stop teasing me about Georgia.' Then he added: 'Poor Katey.'

'Oh, she wasn't embarrassed. Are you ever embarrassed?'

'It's one of the penalties of being civilized. We're all afraid we're going to fart in public.'

'Did you ever do that? What was the most embarrassing thing that ever happened to you?'

'Oh, I don't know,' he considered. 'I remember I was once trying to make some fabulous girl....' He squeezed

98

her shoulder. 'Before I met you, of course.'

'So I should hope. Go on.'

'Well —'

She interrupted. 'How do you mean, fabulous? What was she like?'

'Oh, blonde. A fashion designer. Very svelte.'

'What, better than me, do you mean?'

'No, of course not.'

'All right,' she said. 'Go on.'

'Well, I had everything laid on for the big seduction scene. First I took her to some very sexy French film, and then back to my room. I had prepared the room beforehand, and everything. Swept the floor, tidied up, clean sheets on the bed. Put the clock back half an hour so that she would miss her last bus. I'd even bought a bottle of drink, which I couldn't afford.'

'I didn't know men were so cold-blooded. Planning it all in advance, and putting clean sheets on and everything!'

'Sorry to disillusion you.'

'Never mind. What happened?'

'Everything went off fine at first. We both got slightly drunk, we were sprawling on the bed and I was kissing her. My hand was working lower down all the time. And she wanted it too, I could tell that. Then we decided to get undressed, and somehow everything went wrong. I stood there naked, and it was as if I had taken off my desire together with my clothes. I didn't want her any more than I wanted a lump of dead meat. I had gone completely limp, and as sober as yesterday's empty glass. All that was left of the drunkenness was a bad taste in my mouth and a cold distaste for the whole adventure.'

'How terrible,' Ilsa said.

'The damn' girl was writhing around on the bed, she kept saying: "Oh come to me, darling! Oh take me,

99

darling!" which killed the last vestiges of my desire. However, being the perfect gentleman, I climbed on top of her and gallantly did my best. But it was no use. I couldn't do a thing.'

'How terrible,' Ilsa said again. 'Was she furious?'

'She was quite nice about it, actually. Said she quite understood, and all that. But all the same I felt awful about it. And I'm sure she told the whole story as a huge joke to all her friends.'

'Poor darling, did he have his reputation ruined, then? Never mind, I'll always supply you with any references you may need to impress girls.'

'Thank you.'

She leaned across him to throw her cigarette-end at the grate. There was an expression of furtive excitement on her face, like a child behind a door. He pulled her down so that she lay half across him.

She said: 'Will you miss me when I go home for the week?'

'Of course. Hurry back soon.'

'Did you miss me when we parted for nearly a year, before?'

'Yes.'

'I missed you, too. Did your bed list grow any, during that time?'

'They were only loveless one-night stands.'

'Do you write your bed list down?'

'No, I trust to memory.'

'I write mine down,' she said. 'It's in the back of my diary.'

'Ilsa, you must be faithful to me.' His voice went loud. 'I'd rather see you dead than with another man.'

'Would you really?'

'I mean it, Ilsa.'

Alarmed, she protested with wide-eyed cross-my-heart honesty: 'Oh, honey. I will be faithful to you.' She stroked his cheek. 'Honestly. Honest and true.'

'Darling!'

After a while she said petulantly: 'You've had so many women.'

'No, I haven't.'

'Haven't you?'

'Not compared with some men. And most of mine were meaningless one-night stands. You know, drunk after a party, or in the back of a car, or a quick bash on the sofa before her husband came home. That sort of thing doesn't amount to much.'

'But it's fun, it's experience, and you're not tied to the other person.'

'You don't really mean that, Ilsa. You go in for that sort of experience because you think you ought to want to, not because you really want to. You do it because it's fashionable.'

'But I do want to.'

'You don't. No woman really does. Women are promiscuous for emotional reasons, not because of physical desire.'

'Oh, all right, expert.' She yawned. Then said: 'Who was the first woman you ever slept with?'

'Girl called Margaret. She was older than I was. She worked in a transport café I used to go to.' He smiled into the darkness, caressing Ilsa, and remembering the wood in autumn and the woman's plastic handbag lying amid the fallen leaves. 'She seduced me in a wood.'

'Was it nice?'

The irrelevance amused him. 'Oh yes.'

'How old were you then?'

'Nineteen.'

'Same age as I am now. You were a bit old to still be a virgin, weren't you?'

'I suppose so. I was pretty much of a moralist and a prig.'

'You still are, in some ways.'

'I think people should be. I mean, people should have some central notion, they shouldn't just live haphazard.'

'You live haphazard yourself, though.'

He said: 'Yes, I suppose I do. But I don't like it.'

'Are you sleepy?'

'A bit. Are you?'

'A bit,' she said. 'I bet it's terribly late.'

'Yes.'

'And I have to get up early to catch the train.'

'I'll come with you to the station.'

'Will you?' she said. 'Thanks.'

'We can have a coffee or something on the platform.'

'Nice. Oh well, I suppose we'd better go to sleep now.' Then she asked: 'What did you do before you were nineteen and met this woman?'

'Masturbate.'

'Did you? I did that when I was a child, but not when I was an adolescent.' She sighed, sleepily. 'I used to look up my parents' medical encyclopaedia, too, and read the dirty bits.'

'Sweet child.'

'Oh, I was. I used to go to Sunday School, and they made me Virgin Mary in their nativity play because' — she switched to a twangy American accent — 'I was such a pure-browed lily-white kiddo.'

'Who, you?'

'Yeah, me.' Normal voice again: 'I used to grow my nails long and pinch the other kids, and make them carry my books for me."

'I bet they loathed you.'

'No, they didn't. I was the most popular girl there. They were always inviting me to tea.'

'We really ought to go to sleep.'

'Yes.'

'Turn over then, and I'll cuddle you.'
'All right.'

In the morning she was already removed from him, insulated in her world of make-up things which she had regimented on the washstand. She peered into the mirror that she had moved from the mantelpiece and created her mask from numerous bottles, tubes, and jars.

He sat in vague irritation as the dust of face powder settled on his threadbare carpet. He watched the line of her arm as she pencilled her eyebrows into the correct arch of aloof disdain.

At Victoria he carried her case down the platform. She walked slightly ahead. Her hair was swept up into a Grecian knot at the back; her dress was new to him: slim-fitting white with a gold belt.

He felt like a porter trudging after the model in a travel advertisement.

On the step of her compartment she coolly inclined her mask face, proffering an alabaster cheek to be kissed.

When Ilsa had gone Beckett reverted to his monastic life, as if there was a battle to be fought out with the four walls of his room. He got the daily papers in order to follow the case of the little girl who had been raped and murdered. An arrest had been made. He wondered a lot about the killer's state of mind. He formed an idea of a man bored and frustrated within the cage of his own personality, who had determined to break out into a more intense life even at the cost of his own ruin.

When he saw the newspaper photographs of the murderer, the stupid face above the open-neck shirt belied his theories. The man was twenty-eight; he had been in a low grade at school and even now could hardly read or write.

Every day Beckett walked down Portobello Road and bought cheap meat and vegetables at the market.

Once he met Michael, who said: 'Oh God, dear, isn't life boring? I wish I'd been in the SS; how marvellous to wear one of those dramatic black uniforms.'

When Beckett mentioned that he was out of work Michael insisted on buying him a spaghetti meal at an espresso bar. Beckett felt touched and grateful at this gesture. Over the meal, Michael talked politics. He had a good, though fascist, political sense, and an admiration for the dictator figure. Michael the narcissist played to his reflection in the mirror opposite while talking.

They had been in the espresso bar for some time when Dyce came in. He saw Beckett and started towards him. Then he noticed Michael, and a look of annoyance crossed his face. Instead of joining Beckett, as had been his original intention, he merely nodded curtly before selecting a table as far away as possible. He seemed to have an intense dislike of queers.

Dyce had a coffee, and a croissant, and flipped through a copy of *Oggi* from the pile of magazines. On his way out he sat down at Beckett's table for a brief conversation. Ignoring Michael, he asked Beckett: 'How's life treating you these days?'

'All right, thanks. And you?'

'I want to talk to you one day soon. I have a proposition to make which may interest you.'

Surprised, Beckett said: 'Yes, certainly. Call round any time; I'm in practically all day. I'll give you my address.'

'Don't bother. I already have it.' Dyce stood up, and remarked to Michael: 'About time you got a job, isn't it?'

'Is it?'

'Wake up to it: you're a man, you should be self-supporting by now. Lot of lads your age are helping to support their parents as well. Pity you weren't born into the working class. Mining village or something. That would have killed you or cured you.'

'Well, actually, if you want to know, I get on very well with the working class. I think Cockney boys are fab.'

Dyce tightened his lips. Then, turning to Beckett, he said: 'See you again, Joe. Keep fit.'

When Dyce had gone, Michal said: 'Oh God, dear, isn't he *norm*? Isn't it depressing when people are all moral and norm?'

One day Beckett bought a second-hand radio. He ran it from the light and put the set beside his bed. It worked all right, even the light behind the control panel. He was pleased about the control-panel light working. He turned the knob and got music from various stations. If he moved, he would take the radio with him.

The radio enabled him to listen to a gramophone record performance of Vivaldi's *Four Seasons*. He lay on the bed, with his feet raised at the pillow end. The music possessed him. He was immobile and relaxed, like the drowsiness after drinking wine. On the window ledge above his head was a jam jar containing a branch of chestnut leaves. The leaves lifted against the window. The music and the leaves seemed so miraculously beautiful that he wondered how, if God had not made the world, it was so wonderful. He wanted the music to go on for ever. When it ended he felt cleansed and blessed and slightly dazed. He turned the radio off, and wrote in his notebook: *The function of music and painting is to give praise.* Then he lay on the bed again, trying to make the peace last. It was one round to him in his battle with the four walls.

The purchase of the radio made a hole in his dwindling supply of money. He had, however, no inclination to find another job. He had no inclination to do anything except hang around, bored, in his room. At Union Cartons he had not been free because he had been confined in the office. Now he was no longer obliged to sit at a desk between nine and five-thirty, but he still was not free. He concluded that freedom was not lack of obligations, and that boredom and depression excluded freedom. Having thought this far, he came to a standstill. He had discovered what freedom was not, but not what it was.

One evening he walked through the slum district of Notting Hill. The air smelled of gas from the Kensal Green gasometer. He passed a fence sloganed BAN THE BOMB, and a block of Peabody Buildings with tiled entrances like public conveniences. In Goldthorne Road the people leaning out of the windows looked like laundry. More people sat on the front steps of the houses. All the radios seemed to be turned on; a programme could be heard continuously by walking down the street.

The sounds of loudspeakers replaced that of the radios. An open-air meeting was being held at the end of the street. People drifted towards the meeting, a fat woman in bedroom slippers, a wiry little man with tattooed arms, and a group of young men who swaggered and shoved one another.

On the portable platform the speaker was advocating that the Negroes should be cleared out of Notting Hill. "... they take our houses. ..." The overcrowded population cheered.

Technicians, sitting on the roof of the loudspeaker van, looked bored and swapped cigarettes.

Beckett looked round the crowd, and soon discerned

his acquaintance Reg Wainwright. Wainwright, with his grey, crew-cut hair, powerful build, and tartan shirt, would have stood out in any crowd. Beckett elbowed his way towards him, and asked: 'Are your communist friends going to break up this meeting?'

'No. The best policy with these colour-bar meetings is to ignore them, not to give them the publicity they want.' Wainwright knocked out his pipe on the sole of his shoe. 'They won't get far with this audience, anyway. This is a working-class area, and the workers aren't anti-coloured. The white workers and the coloured workers will unite against the capitalists; they won't fight each other.'

"... importing cheap coloured labour threatens white workers ..." Cheers and whistles.

Beckett said: 'So much for your workers. They're not angels, you know, not a special race. They're just human beings like everybody else. These meetings don't succeed on rational points alone. Overcrowding and the under-cutting of wages are rational points, but the main force is the hatred waiting to be unleashed in all of us. Hatred can be summoned up with appalling ease, and directed against West Indians or Jews or Catholics or any other minority group you care to name. Hatred gets more following than the housing problem.'

'Then education must change matters,' Wainwright said. He added, with the incomprehending agony of a lover of humanity: 'I cannot understand it.'

At that moment, the crowd parted to let three West Indians through. The three men were brave to walk through the ranks of barely muzzled hostility. They did not cringe or look afraid. They had the easy, insolent West Indian hip swagger, and one of them ate fish and chips from a newspaper packet which he held under his chin. Their dark, deer eyes ranged over the heads of their hunters.

A ripple, like a snarl, broke out in the ranks of the whites. It only needed someone to make the first move and the three men would have been mobbed. But the English are frightened of making the first move. It was only when the Spades had got clear of the crowd that somebody shouted after them: 'Bloody niggers!' There was a murmur of general assent.

Then the crowd returned its attention to the platform.

Wainwright repeated: 'I cannot understand it.'

Beckett realized that he himself, like the others, had tensed like a dog ready to spring. Like the others, he had shared in the mob hatred at the cool effrontery of the West Indians. He said: 'I can. I can understand it. I regret it, and theoretically I'm opposed to prejudice and race hatred. But in practice I understand it.'

'You amaze me. You, a civilized, intelligent man....'

Beckett interrupted: 'There's a man over there who seems to be waving to you, Reg.'

'Where? Oh yes, I know him. He's a party member, a good type. He probably wants me to go across to the pub with him. Do you feel like going over for a quick one?'

'No, I don't think so.'

'Oh, come on. A very quick one.'

'Some other time.' Beckett did not want to listen to the two communists talking their code.

'Well, let's make that some other time definite. It's a long time since I've seen you. Come round one evening, why don't you? You know my address in Camden Town.'

'All right.'

'Well, do that.'

'All right.'

He watched Wainwright shoulder his way towards the pub and the communist friend trotting to keep pace. Wainwright was a good man, whose physical strength and mental ardour had seemed to increase with his years. Wainwright, despite his lack of literary talent, slogged away to produce, every ten months or so, another novel portraying folk at the factory bench or works floor. He had also written a historical novel which had achieved some success as the dust jacket portrayed a girl in low-necked historical costume.

Beckett returned his attention to the meeting. He thought: Yes, it's the irrational the speaker appeals to. Not the rational. Not to the desire for better houses or higher wages, but to the dormant wild beast in men. The beast which can be so easily awoken.

Recently, he had read an account of a Nazi concentration camp. The article had factually stated the number of Jews who had been gassed. Incidents had been mentioned, including the endeavours of mothers to push their children out of the gas chamber at the last moment before the doors shut. On one occasion, a new detachment of prisoners had arrived at an ill-timed moment, and had been greeted by the sight of corpses being shovelled on to the pyre. The new prisoners had panicked, women among them had screamed, and as a result the Nazi guard had immediately shot down the whole detachment.

Beckett's immediate reaction had been a burst of sadistic joy. He knew that if, at that precise moment, he had seen a woman prisoner with her arms yearning for a lost child, he would have kicked her in the face. The shooting of the new detachment had pleased his sense of order. They were damn' nuisances, screaming and panicking like that. Shooting them was the only orderly thing to do. He loathed the prisoners for their ugliness, their suffering, and their lack of pride. The photographs of these degraded sufferers, squatting behind their barbed wire, had revolted him so much that he had thought it a pity that the whole lot hadn't been gassed. He had preferred the photographs of the Nazi guards, who had at least looked clean and self-respecting. The prisoners, with their insistent, shameless misery, were as nauseating as Christ's bleeding heart in the picture.

The next moment he had been overcome by shame at his thoughts. He was not at all anti-Semitic. Many of his acquaintances were Jews and it had never occurred to him to differentiate. He was in fact opposed to anti-Semitism and to all racial prejudice. The article, however, had fired the violence in him, and when people were taken at the peak of violence they were capable of atrocities.

It was as if he harboured a wild beast, and surely, he thought, he was not peculiar in this. The guards at concentration camps were ordinary men from all walks of life, not a separate race of monsters. However much humanity protested its horror and nausea at these atrocities, there was no escaping the fact that sadism lay dormant in ordinary men. The wild beast thus harboured was a gorilla.

Others contained a different beast, a lean and lonely wolf. Once, walking in the woods near his parents' home, he had seen a respectable, middle-aged man spying through the bushes at a courting couple. The man had been tense with excitement, and had panted. On another occasion, on a Tube platform, Beckett had noticed that one of the posters bore a pencilled scrawl: 'I want to play with your fanny.' The few passengers on the platform had been neat and stiffly dressed, and it had occurred to him that they were all a pretence, and that the only reach for truth was in those crude, semi-literate words scrawled on the poster.

Then there were the vast sales of the Sunday papers dealing in sex and violence, which were read for vicarious thrills.

Surely most of the public, which included the man in the wood, the writer on the Tube poster, and the readers of the Sunday papers, had normal sexual outlets. They were not deprived of normal sex; but they wanted something different.

He thought, that's the trouble with a man like Wainwright. He blames human institutions, instead of human nature.

He considered the animal in himself. In congested streets, he daydreamed of mowing down the slow-moving crowds with a machine gun. If he saw a fat woman waddling across a zebra, or an old man tottering off the kerb, he longed to be a maniac killer driver. When he passed the children's playground in Kensington Gardens he tried to see the knickers of the little girls who stood on the swings. If others could read his thoughts like tickertape across his forehead he would be a social outcast. Yet in actuality his behaviour was decent enough. He was not a sadist or a satyr.

The crowds broke into fresh cheering. Next to Beckett, a housewife, with neck flushed and eyes bright with excitement, screamed: 'That's right, we don't want half-caste kids....'

A photographer's bulb flashed. The group of Teds in front of him started to horse about. "There you are, Len, front-page photo of you and me...' The Teds had spent the previous part of the meeting discussing a TV programme.

When the meeting was over, and the crowd dispersed, Beckett noticed a solitary West Indian standing on the pavement. He approached the man, offered him a cigarette, and remarked: 'It's hard on you, this sort of thing.'

The man shrugged. 'Oh well.'

'D'you work round here?'

'Yes, on the Underground. I'm a ticket-collector.'

Becket was shy, and uncertain what to say next. He felt a bit of a fool, but all the same wanted to show his friendship. He exchanged a few more remarks with the man, then said: 'Oh well, I must be off. Glad to have met you.'

The site of the meeting was now a wasteland, littered with propaganda leaflets and cigarette packets. A troupe of children, white and coloured, ran across it playing catch.

Chapter 9

I N CAMDEN TOWN the heat swarmed like a plague of flies over the dirty buildings. The fumes of the traffic made the High Street smell like a garage.

Beckett decided to stroll through the park before calling on Wainwright. After a while he lay down on the grass, pillowing his head on his clasped hands. He watched the pink flamingo clouds.

Somebody called his name. He looked up, and saw Georgia standing a few yards away. She was smiling, with one hand raised to shield her eyes from the sun.

He was not pleased to see her. He had kissed her at the party because he had been drunk and she had been the nearest female. Now he felt awkward, because he had treated her badly.

However, he stood up and tried to look enthusiastic. 'Well, hello, Georgia.'

'Hello... Joe.' She said his name in a special way, as if they shared a secret. Her eyes, smiling into his, were provocative.

He said: 'Do you live near here?'

'Yes, quite near. Do you?'

'No.'

She said: 'Isn't it a lovely day?'

'A bit hot.'

'Yes.' She smiled at him again, fiddling with her bead necklace.

He said: 'Were you going anywhere particular?'

'Just for a stroll."

'Oh. Would you like a cold drink or something at the open-air café?'

'What a nice idea.'

They walked together under the shadow of the trees. She was wearing a floral cotton dress, with white shoes and handbag. Her auburn hair caught the glint of the sun.

Outside the café they drank lemonade with a cool, cheap-scent taste from waxed cups. Georgia smiled lazily round at the people and the umbrella-shaded tables. 'I'm so glad I saw you. I live in Camden Town, you know, and I often come to the park and doze in a deck chair.'

She was holding a book. Beckett asked: 'What are you reading?'

'Oh, a novel from the book club I belong to. They send you a book a month.' She handed him the detective story. 'I never read newspapers; they're too depressing. Rebellions and H-bombs and crimes and things. Do you know what happened in my street recently? I bet they'll put that in the papers. This poor old shopkeeper, who was very nice — I used to get my groceries there — was killed and the till was robbed. And do you know how much the killers got out of the till?'

'No?'

'Four-and-threepence-halfpenny. Or was it three-and-fourpence-halfpenny? Anyway, it was practically nothing. Isn't it terrible that the poor old man was killed just for that?'

'Who did it? Did they find out?'

'Oh, some Teds, of course,' Georgia said.

'This is an age of non-belief. General scepticism always produces the sort of blasé youth who sneers at all institutions and beliefs, and who is contemptuous of morality to the extent of having no values. For someone without beliefs or values, for someone who is a spiritual bankrupt, crime is merely an experience. He'll cosh a shopkeeper more for the experience than for the trivial contents of the till. And if you ask him why he did it, he'll say something like: "Why not? Just because I felt like doing it. Wanted some money for a cinema ticket."'

'What do you mean by the age of non-belief? What doesn't the age believe in?'

'Religion, which is the only thing that can give meaning to life. The collapse of an absolute value leads to the collapse of relative values. When God collapses, so does honour, honesty, patriotism, and the like. I'm not saying that it's altogether bad that such things should go. Rabid patriotism for instance does a lot of harm, and causes muddled thinking. But on the other hand, such things do give an inner logic to a man's life. They give him some sort of central touchstone. Without them, he can just drift in a signless world where no action is good or bad. Life without meaning is life without morality. Hence the great increase in the sort of crime which stems from a momentary whim, as opposed to the old-fashioned crime where a man stole because he was starving.'

Georgia gazed at him admiringly: 'You are clever, Joe.'

Beckett could not help feeling flattered by her admiration. He was excited by his clarity of mind, his thoughts. He sat tensely on the edge of his chair, like an eager student expounding his ideas. 'To a man without beliefs, any action may be preferable to his present state of inertia.'

Her interest had sagged. She gazed vaguely round again.

He said impatiently: 'What are you looking for?'

'The Ladies. Will you excuse me?'

'Surely.' He watched her walk away, swinging her white handbag. When she had been gone a few minutes he got up, with the intention of waiting for her by the café exit. It was then that he saw Jacko, sitting at a table behind theirs.

Beckett made an angry movement towards him, and Jacko cringed back in his chair. Jacko's eyes were mocking, a parody of servility.

Beckett checked his movement, and merely asked: 'What are you doing here?'

'That's better. Wouldn't do for you to assault me again, would it? Not with all these witnesses. Besides, I've come up in the world a bit...' Jacko indicated the pile of cakes on his plate. 'I can afford to pay for my own food now. Cream cakes. I like them.'

'Never mind that. What are you doing here?'

'It's a free country, isn't it? Or so I was always told; pardon me if I'm wrong. I've got as much right to sit here as you have.'

Beckett hesitated, and realized that he was being unfair and unpleasant. He said: 'Yes, you're quite right. Look, I'm sorry about that incident the other day. But I get moods of being unsociable, when I don't want to talk to anybody. I expect you get those sort of moods yourself from time to time, don't you? Anyway, I'm sorry.'

'Still feel unsociable today?'

'No, no, it isn't that. But we're just going, anyway.'

'Going, eh? Why? Afraid your lady friend wouldn't like the look of me?' Jacko flicked a speck of dust from his lapel with fierce, shabby pride.

'It's impossible to say anything to you if you take offence so easily.'

'I understand you very well. You'd rather keep me hidden away like a shameful secret, like a secret vice, wouldn't you?'

'You're being ridiculous.'

'No, I'm not. I may be a bad habit, but all the same you need me, see? Why don't you take me with you, then I wouldn't have to follow you. I only follow you because you won't take me with you openly.'

Beckett realized he was dealing with a near-lunatic. He didn't know what to say. Embarrassment made him laugh.

Jacko's face went white with hatred. 'All right,' he said. 'All right. You think I'm funny, do you? Well, if you want to know, I wouldn't come with you even if you begged me on bended knees. I hope you rot, Mister Joe Beckett. I hope you bleeding well rot.'

'Oh, I'm bound to, eventually.' He saw Georgia emerging from the privet-lined path, and went to meet her.

She preceded him out of the café enclosure. 'Who was that you were talking to, Joe?'

'Nobody. An acquaintance.' He felt shaken. Losing his temper always had a bad effect on him. It left him feeling jarred and off-balance. The encounter with Jacko had disturbed him. The memory of the twisted, insinuating face cut with the coldness of a premonition between himself and the sunshine.

She asked: 'Were you going to do anything particular this evening?'

'Well, I'd arranged to visit a friend of mine.'

'Oh, I see.' She sounded disappointed. 'What a pity. I was going to invite you to have a meal at my flat. I live quite close, really.'

'That's very kind of you.'

'It wouldn't be any trouble. There's ham in the fridge.'

It would have been churlish to refuse. He said: 'Thanks, Georgia, I'd like to.' Leaving the park, he explained: 'This friend of mine, and his wife, have a house in Gulliver Road. They let rooms cheaply to students, including coloured students who find it difficult to get lodgings on account of race prejudice. The house is run on community lines. He's a left-wing writer. Reg Wainwright. You might have heard of him.'

'No, I'm afraid not. I'm not very well educated.'

117

Reaching Gulliver Road, Beckett pointed to a spiral of smoke which rose from a front garden. 'That's him, burning the place down.'

'Not really, I hope,' Georgia said.

Wainwright was standing beside his bonfire, holding a can of paraffin. He wore old corduroy trousers and was naked from the waist up. His face and neck were sunburnt ruddy; his powerful shoulders looked white and gleaming by contrast. He watched his bonfire with an expression of pride and absorption. Above him danced the dizzy heat of the flames. He wiped his brow with the back of his hand.

Beckett and Georgia also watched in silence.

Wainwright picked up a long straggling weed and threw it on top of the others. It struck sparks when it hit the fire. Then he saw them. 'Joe! Good to see you! How long have you been standing there like a deaf mute?'

Beckett opened the gate and they went in. 'You should be a countryman, with a smallholding.'

'Yes, it's a private ambition of mine. I enjoy making something out of the earth.'

Beckett introduced Georgia.

Wainwright smiled into her eyes in his firm, honest way. 'I'm glad to meet you, Georgia. Excuse me for not shaking hands but I'm covered in paraffin.' Then he turned to Beckett. 'Yes, I'd like to have a plot of land. Or maybe retire into the country to write books.' He led the way up the path, rubbing his paraffin-smeared hands on his chest to clean them. 'But it won't be yet awhile. I belong here, among people. I won't be one of those ivory-tower writers who see nothing but their own four walls. Besides, I've got too many commitments here in London. Apart from this house, I've just taken on the editorship of *The Humanist Quarterly;* did I tell you?'

'No, you didn't. Congratulations.'

'Oh, it's a thankless task. But I'm pleased about it.'

There was a romp of children and dogs round the house. Beckett could not tell how many of each. Wainwright conducted them into the living-room, and shouted in a booming voice: 'Marion! ...'

The answering call came: 'Busy...'

'My wife,' Wainwright explained. 'She won't be long. Would you people like some beer?'

Georgia said: 'Not for me, thank you.'

'Joe will. I know him of old. Excuse me while I find some glasses in the kitchen.'

When Wainwright had gone, Georgia sat down on the edge of a chair. She folded her hands on her handbag on her lap, and giggled at Beckett.

He grinned back, then looked round the room. The furniture was pushed back against the walls, giving the effect of a Youth Hostel common-room. There was a large table, covered by a blanket, on which was Wainwright's typewriter, a bottle of glue, a bottle of milk, back numbers of *The Humanist Quarterly,* and a screwdriver. The noticeboard on the wall displayed newspaper-cuttings, a notice for a lecture on Ethical Thought, another for a meeting for Colonial Freedom, and a typed washing-up rota.

Georgia, who had been following his gaze, giggled again. 'They're very organized here, aren't they?'

'Yes.'

'I like Reg Wainwright. He's nice, isn't he?'

'Yes.'

'Are all those children his?'

'I think only two are. The others probably belong to the neighbours. Marion seems to provide half the kids in the district with buns and home-made lemonade.'

Wainwright returned with a quart bottle of light ale and the glasses. He had put on a shirt. He asked

119

Beckett: 'Well, what did you think of the meeting the other day?'

'Nothing much happened after you left. The crowd cheered in obedience to the cheer leaders.'

'Idiots.'

Beckett asked: 'Are you writing anything at the moment?'

'Ah yes, a historical novel set in the Middle Ages.' Wainwright poured the beer and handed a glass to Beckett. 'Cheers! Yes, I find a lot to occupy my mind in that period of history.' He began to expound on the corruption of the Church, touching on its preoccupation with wealth and power, politics, the breeding of hatred, superstition, and heresy hunts, and the Church deliberately keeping the people in ignorance. He explained that religion was nothing but a ruling-class institution to keep the underdogs under.

Beckett did not disagree with Wainwright's remarks, but he thought them shallow. He said: 'Of course the Church was corrupt and immoral. But any organization, religious or political, must be corrupt and immoral if it wants to impose its concept of order on humanity. It's an evil inherent in order.' He realized that he was more or less repeating Father Dominic's words. He had an ambiguous love-hate feeling for the Church. When talking to a Catholic, he attacked the Church, but when talking to a materialist he defended it 'And, anyway, force and threats of hell-fire couldn't enforce religion by themselves. Religion couldn't persist if it didn't have very real roots in human nature, and if it wasn't psychologically satisfying.'

'It isn't a question of psychologically satisfying. It's a question of true or false.'

'Oh, nonsense. Nothing is true. People make their own truths; they invent something that works for them. You do it yourself. You campaign against petty politicians, but you must know that men have less freedom than they think, and that the petty politicians are formed by their contexts.' Looking at the bottle against the light, Beckett saw that there was quite a lot left, which made him feel happy. 'Don't you ever have sensations of unreality when you attack people?'

'No. I can't say I do.'

'I suppose the leader, or dictator figure, has more freedom than most. He is thrown up by the waves of his time, but he precipitates and directs the flood. And the masses flock round him because he has the qualities they admire secretly but lack themselves. He's got a powerful personality and the courage to stand alone. He's an idealist, and mows down ordinary morality because it would obstruct his path. He takes the responsibility for the means that secure the end, and thus becomes the conscience of his nation. However, he fails eventually, because immoral means infect the end. Also because he inhabits a world of petty men who lack free will and who are moved by circumstances, and their rot eventually poisons his cause. I should say the leader does more harm than good in the world. His virtue is that he is dynamic; the dynamic force by which history bounds forward into change.'

Marion Wainwright came in. She was about thirty-five, with a faded prettiness. She was pregnant, and wore a maternity smock over her skirt. She wore sandals and a pair of her husband's grey socks.

Georgia, who had been gazing at the two men in turn with an expression of admiring vacuity, now inspected Marion to make sure that she was not more attractive than herself. Seeing that Marion's pregnancy removed her from the competitive field, Georgia beamed at her in a friendly manner.

Wainwright provided his wife with a chair and a glass of beer, then resumed his discussion with

Beckett. 'Do you admire such a man?'

'I can admire the driving willpower of a Hitler or a Napoleon while deploring the lives lost in their wars.'

'No. You cannot separate them from the evil they caused.'

'Yes, I can. Men are always drawn to the heroic. They admire the heroic even while condemning the harm their heroes have done. Heroes seem to have the inner logic they lack themselves, and a man with inner logic can aspire. Isn't it aspiration that distinguishes man from the animals?'

Wainwright said: 'You're a terrible fascist, Joe.'

'I don't think so. I deplore the fact that there is something in the nature of man which makes it almost impossible for his heroes to take the form of saints instead of bloodstained tyrants.'

Marion picked up her knitting. At the same time she followed the argument with an intent frown.

From outside, a child's voice shouted: 'Goal! ...'

Beckett said: 'I'm only pointing out facts. I'm saying that men can, and do, simultaneously deplore wars and admire the man who caused the war.' He leaned forward, gesturing with his beer glass. 'Oh, for Christ sake! Look at the cinema queues for a film about any ruthless and determined man, — from Napoleon to Al Capone. People uphold the laws against gangsters in real life but nevertheless they flock to admire, and identify themselves with, Al Capone on the screen. I know it's a contradiction, but it's a contradiction in human nature, not a flaw in my argument.'

Georgia asked Marion: 'What are you knitting?'

'A pullover for Stephen, our eldest.'

'Oh, how nice. Can I see the pattern?'

Marion handed it over.

'Oh, how nice.'

Marion said: 'I'm probably the most undomesticated

wife in the world. It takes me ages to finish knitting anything, so I have to make it several sizes too big.'

'Well, he'll soon grow into it. How old is he?'

'And out of it. Children's clothes are hell. My two are always outgrowing their things.'

'Oh yes,' Georgia agreed eagerly. 'My little girl's just the same. I'm always buying her frocks, and then in next to no time she's complaining they're too small. I think it's just an excuse to get a new one; she loves going to a big store and trying things on.'

'Yes.'

'She won't wear anything that's too short for her. She's very clothes-conscious, really, for her age. A real little girl.'

'Mine just scruff around in T-shirts and jeans.'

'Oh, I do like a little girl to be dressed up to look pretty.'

'I prefer rough clothes, so it doesn't matter if they climb trees or roll on the ground.'

'Yes, don't children get grubby quickly?' Georgia said complacently. 'My little girl has to have a clean frock every day.'

'Eleven.' Marion answered an earlier question. 'Stephen's eleven.'

'Teresa's six. The awkward age.'

Marion said humorously: 'Aren't they *always* at awkward ages?'

'Oh, goodness, yes.'

Wainwright told Beckett: 'The trouble with you, Joe, is that you have no beliefs and no commitments. You flatter yourself on your objectivity, but the result of your fence-sitting is that you're cut off from humanity. Your objectivity may mean that you don't hate, but a man without hate is also a man without love.'

'Oh yes, I agree.'

'I can't make you angry, can I?'

Beckett said with surprise: 'Were you trying to?'

'For your own sake I'd like to get some sort of reaction, other than your usual indifference.'

'All right.' Beckett picked up the bottle and poured out the rest of the beer into the three glasses. 'Let's finish this. All right, I'll take you up on one point. You say I'm not committed; but I'm sufficiently committed to prefer the truth, even if it's a vision of futility, to swallowing lies in order to give meaning to my life.'

Wainwright asked Georgia: 'And what do you think?'

'Oh, I don't know, really.' She glanced at the clock.

Beckett, seeing her glance, said: 'Well, we'd better be going, Reg. I think Georgia is worried about the meal she has waiting.' He drained his beer.

'Oh no,' Georgia said. 'It's been very nice meeting you. I'd like to read some of your books.'

Outside, she slipped her hand through Beckett's arm. 'Oh, wasn't he nice? I thought he had a very warm personality.'

'Yes, he's very decent. He puts his humanist principles into practice in his own life.'

'Of course, I couldn't really follow everything you both said, but I thought you were both very clever. But I did think his ideas were a bit kinder than yours. I mean, when he was talking about wars and things, you could tell from his face that he hated the thought of people suffering in wars. You could tell he loved people.'

'Oh yes.'

'I suppose Marion is a brainy type, too?'

'I don't know, really.'

'What does she do, then?'

'Runs the house and writes short stories.'

'Oh well, she must be brainy, then.' Then she added: 'Well, I'm glad we didn't meet any of the black fellows you said live there. I mean, I know we're all equal, and they're as good as us, and all that, but they give me the creeps. I wouldn't fancy kissing one of them.'

Her room was large and pleasant, and looked more like a drawing-room than a bedsitter. The carpet and curtains were pale green, and the armchairs oatmeal. The divan, with cushions on it, looked like a sofa. There was a bowl of flowers on the table.

'Here we are,' Georgia said. 'I have this room, with bathroom, and kitchenette attached, so it's just big enough to be called a flat.'

'It's a good place.'

'I try to make it homelike. Well, I'll pour you a drink and then I'll go and prepare the food.'

'Can I do anything to help?'

'No, you just sit down and make yourself at home. Would you like gin-and-orange, or whisky-and-soda?'

'Whisky, please. Neat.'

She poured him a large drink and then went out to the kitchen. Alone, he looked round the room. A prod at the divan told him that it was interior sprung. He inspected the tiles in the bookcase: *Death Strikes at the Rectory; The Questing Heart; Lady in Waiting, an Historical Romance.*

From somewhere in the house he could hear a vacuum cleaner. Georgia called from the kitchen: 'It's the couple upstairs. They're both out at work all day, so they do their cleaning in the evening.'

He called in answer: 'Oh yes.'

The books in their bright dust-jackets looked new. They were all her Woman's Book Club editions. There was nothing he wanted to borrow.

He returned to the armchair and picked up his whisky, feeling grateful to Georgia for providing it. The hum of the vacuum cleaner was pleasantly lulling.

After a while she called: 'It won't be long now. Help yourself to another drink while you're waiting.'

'Thanks...' He poured himself another whisky and took it out to the kitchen. 'Sure there's nothing I can do?'

'No, nothing, thanks. It's almost ready.'

The clean, modern kitchen made him feel scruffy and ill-nourished, as if he had eaten from tins and gas rings for too long. Georgia had tied an apron round her waist, and he wanted to hug her.

'Here,' she said, 'you take this plate of salad in, and I'll follow with the tray.'

The meal consisted of ham, eggs, salad, French dressing, and buttered rolls. She put the things down on the low table between the armchairs.

He said: 'You are wonderful.'

She said in an Irish accent: 'Sure, 'tis nothing.'

The food was good, and she replenished his glass when necessary. The drink relaxed him.

There were two framed photographs on the mantelpiece, one of a man, the other of a child. He asked: 'Who are the photos?'

'My husband and my little girl.'

'Oh. Where are they now?'

'My husband and I separated years ago. He sends me some money through the bank, which is how I can afford this place. My little girl lives with my mother. I go and see her as often as possible, and sometimes she comes here for weekends.'

'I see.' He found it difficult to imagine her married. It was strange to look at her and realize that she had a past life in a different setting from her present one.

'Teresa, that's my daughter, doesn't look like that now. That photo was taken three years ago, and now she's left the toddler stage and reached the child stage. She's lost one of her front teeth and there's a funny little gap when she smiles.'

'Oh yes.'

'And she's getting on very well at school. The teacher said she's one of the best in the class at reading.'

'Oh, good.'

When they had finished eating, Georgia said: 'Well, I'll just move this out of your way...' and removed the tray and table. Then she turned on the electric fire. It was made to look like a basket of logs. The order and ease of her living bemused him. It was pleasant to have someone thoughtful enough to clear away, so that he could stretch his legs and did not have to look at dirty plates. He compared it with the messy way in which he lived. He had an unsatisfactory method of piling dirty crockery into the china bowl, carrying the bowl down to the bathroom to wash up, and afterwards poking the scraps down the plug hole with his fingers.

He leant back in the armchair, letting comfort and whisky spread over him. He imagined having a servant, a housekeeper. It would be pleasant to have someone to look after his comfort. On the other hand, there would be the disadvantage of a woman talking when he wanted to read.

'Now,' Georgia said, 'tell me what you've been doing with yourself lately.'

'Oh, nothing much.' He offered her a cigarette, leaning close to her when he lit it.

'Thanks.' She smoked as if it was a deeply satisfying sensual experience, her eyelids sexily lowered.

He said: 'All this is very pleasant. The room and the meal and everything.'

'I'm very glad you came. I would have spent a lonely evening otherwise.'

'Me, too.'

'Then what about Ilsa Barnes? I heard that you two were together again.'

'Where did you hear that?'

'Ah-ha, the grapevine! Actually I'm delighted, I think Ilsa's a sweet girl.'

'Do you?'

Georgia regarded the tip of her cigarette. 'Well, she's certainly very bright and amusing, anyway. I saw her about a week ago at a party. She was sitting on the edge of the table, and showing rather a lot of leg, and another girl made a bitchy comment about this. And Ilsa said, quick as a flash: "Well, you could hardly do it with *your* legs, could you, *dear*?"'

He felt a quick stab of jealousy that Ilsa should exist and say things and swing her slim legs when he was not there. She had no right to exist out of his life. He said: 'Anyway, she's staying with her parents at present.'

'For long?'

'No, only a week.'

'Well, anyway,' Georgia said, 'you're happy with her, and that's the main thing.'

'Happy? No, she doesn't make me happy. Another person can make you unhappy, but can't make you happy. Happiness has nothing to do with other people. Sometimes, for instance, I know I'm a god and that everything is good. It's a feeling of certainty and affirmation. But this feeling comes when I'm alone.'

'Do you often feel like that?'

'No, on the contrary, generally I feel only a paralysing despair. It settles on everything like grey dust.'

'Can't you decide which of the two is right?'

'It's not a question of one being right. They are just states which occur.'

Georgia did not answer. Instead, she put her hand on his arm. He automatically covered her hand with his own.

He said: 'It annoys me when people talk of happiness, as if it was an object that could be kept. Something you get when you marry, together with vases and tea services. My definition of happiness is spiritual intensity, and it certainly can't be kept. Most people have to grub along as best they can without happiness; it's senseless to try and chase it and pretend that happiness is a necessity.'

She considered this for a while, then asked: 'But how do you feel about Ilsa?'

'Oh hell, Georgia, I don't know. My feelings for people are so contradictory. I say things I don't mean; I even feel things I don't mean. There are always elements of unreality and absurdity in my relationships. Sometimes I think that I don't really feel anything for people at all, and only pretend to because it's the expected convention.'

'Don't you think you fight yourself too much? That may be the reason you can't genuinely feel. I may be wrong, Joe, but my intuition tells me that you should stop fighting yourself and learn to accept yourself.'

The whisky and her kind, womanly voice hummed in his head. He was not really listening to her.

She said: 'After all, proper living means accepting yourself, being adjusted to yourself.'

He woke with a start, and energetically thumped the chair arm. 'You're wrong, Georgia, you're wrong, wrong, wrong! There are thousands of people who contentedly accept their stupid, limited, mediocre selves. They're even proud of themselves, for God's sake! They call themselves the little man, or an ordinary man, or the man in the street, as if mediocrity was something to be proud of! Not one of them interests me in the least. The men who interest me are the ones who are dissatisfied.'

'I'm sorry, I didn't mean to annoy you.' Her blue eyes, staring into his, had the unfocussed look of a drunk woman's.

'You didn't annoy me. How could you annoy me? I think you're sweet.'

'Do you?'

He pulled her out of her chair to sit on his knee. Kissing her was an oblivion. It was any mouth, any arms.

After a while, she said: 'Excuse me a minute...'

'Where are you going?'

'I won't be a minute.'

He released her, and watched her leave the room. Alone, he said to himself: 'You're a bit drunk, boy.' He went over and threw himself on to the divan. The embroidery on the cushions made him laugh; he picked at the flower design. Lying and laughing and picking at the embroidery silk, he felt irresponsible.

He heard music outside and got up to look out of the window. The music came from the pub on the corner.

He could see a man in a raincoat and brown felt hat walking very straight along the centre of the pavement, as lonely men do. Farther up the street a youth came out of a house, wheeling a bicycle. Beckett said aloud in North Country: 'Eee lad, it's a right rum do all right.'

He heard Georgia's footsteps returning, and lay down again on the divan.

When she came in, she said: 'I see you've made yourself comfortable.'

'Very comfortable. Come and join me.'

She had taken her nylons off, and he guessed that she had also removed her roll-on. When she snuggled against him, he noticed that she smelled of fresh soap.

'Talk to me,' Georgia said.

'What about?'

'Oh, anything. There's something friendly and reassuring about a human voice.'

He smiled, strumming his fingers on her bare shoulder. He could hear singing from the pub across the road: 'Saturday Night at the Crown'. It occurred to him that they had been singing that same song all the time he and Georgia had been making love. Then he thought: no, they must have begun and ended with that song, and sung others in between. But he could not remember any of the other songs. Only 'Saturday Night at the Crown' to a honky-tonk piano.

The pub music was broken by an angry voice, drunk and Irish. 'Don't you shove me!' the voice yelled. 'Don't you shove me!' Other voices joined in, but the Irish one rose above them, solitary as the cry of an animal. 'Don't you shove me, that's all! Don't you shove me!'

'They always make a row in that pub,' Georgia said. 'Do you think there'll be a fight?'

'I don't know.' He sat up, preparing to get out of bed and go to the window.

'Ah no, don't go.' She pulled him back. The odour of sex stirred between her thighs when she moved.

He looked down at her, seeing her placid face, and the mark where her brassiere strap had cut into the soft flesh of her shoulder. The thought came coldly: I could strangle her now... He imagined his hands seizing her throat, his thumbs gouging in. And then the completed act, with the woman sprawled on the bed and the embroidered cushions fallen on the floor.

When he examined the urge it disappeared. He knew he would not do it. His analytical mind prevented any spontaneous actions.

'I'm glad you're here,' she said.

That completed the disappearance of the urge. She had re-established herself as a person; as Georgia who had talked about her daughter, who had been kind enough to give him a meal and drinks, and who as a final kindness had gone to bed with him.

He felt depressed. He wanted to be out of the warm bed and pleasant room. Already in his mind he was out

131

walking the streets, where at every corner there might be something which would make him feel pleased inside. It might be a building with a street light shining on it, or a man eating chips from a newspaper in a doorway, or a match briefly illuminating a face. Whatever it was, he wanted to be out, seeing it. He wanted to smell the adventure in the night air.

He got out of bed and pulled on his trousers.

She said: 'What's the matter? You're not going, are you?'

'Georgia love, I can't stay. I must get back home.'

'Why bother? It's comfy here, and the landlord doesn't live on the premises, so there's nobody to complain if you stay all night.'

'All the same, I must get home. I've got things to do in the morning.' He heard the flat tone and lack of conviction in his voice, and thought: I am a rotten bastard.

She knew he was lying, but bowed her head in humble submission; 'All right.' She got out of bed and went to the fireplace, extending her hands towards the artificial coal.

The firelight shone ruddy on her face, her breasts, her rounded belly. He noticed a varicose vein on her thigh and quickly averted his gaze before he could be sure.

Georgia slipped on her dressing-gown, tied the sash, and wriggled her feet into fur-trimmed slippers. 'I'll make some tea, shall I? Sex always makes me feel thirsty; are you the same?'

'Yes, thirsty as hell. It's the whisky, too.'

'Yes.'

He quickly finished dressing, then followed her out into the kitchenette.

She asked in a too-casual voice: 'I suppose you haven't seen anything of Dickie lately, have you? Dickie Dyce?'

'I did see him once, briefly. In an espresso-bar.'

'Oh.' She plugged in the electric kettle. 'Did he mention me?'

'No.' Then he added: 'I only spoke to him for a few seconds.'

'Oh.'

'Can I do anything to help? Get the cups out or anything?'

'No. No, thank you.' Pause. Then she said: 'Dickie stayed here with me for a week.'

'Did he?'

'Yes.' She busied herself with the tea-making, bustling to conceal her hurt. 'I thought he was very nice when I met him at the party. He seemed very polite and considerate and romantic. Opened doors, and helped me on with my coat, and all that sort of thing. But as soon as he moved in here he changed completely. He got very nasty. For instance, he made a fuss when his meals weren't ready exactly when he wanted them, yet I never knew when he was coming home. And he jumped on every little thing I said, and told me I was a damn' fool. I felt I couldn't do or say anything right, however hard I tried. He seemed to think I was his slave.'

'Why didn't you tell him to clear out if he was such a boor?'

'I don't know, really. I suppose he dominated me. He has a very masterful personality. But somehow or other, when he was here, I felt I was being forced to love someone whom I didn't even like, really. He took away my will and replaced it with his own, if you know what I mean. And also, I never really trusted him. I didn't like him being in the flat when I was out. It wasn't exactly that I was afraid he'd steal anything ... I don't know what it was. I just didn't trust him.'

Beckett said: 'Well, anyway, you're well out of it now.'

'Yes. By the way, you don't know where he's living now, do you?'

'No, Georgia, I don't.'

'He hit me once, and gave me a black eye. That's the sort of brute he was.'

Watching her bend over the teapot he felt a sort of impatience at her humbled shoulders in the dressing-gown, her disordered hair. He could understand Dyce ill-treating her. She had a masochistic element which incited violence.

She continued: 'And, also, he seemed to be a pathological liar. I mean, he was always telling tall stories and boasting about his adventures, and somehow I never knew whether it was truth or lies. In a way I don't think he really knew either.'

'Pathological liars are impossible to live with.'

'Yes. What causes it, do you know?'

'Not really. I suppose it's the desire to make life more exciting for themselves. A liar creates exciting circumstances, rather like a backcloth for an actor. And a good liar, like a good actor, believes in his own act.'

'Yes, I suppose so.' She poured tea into marigold-patterned cups. 'I hope I haven't been boring you with my troubles.'

'Not at all, of course not.'

'I don't really want to live like this, you know, sleeping with any man who turns up.'

'No.'

'I really want somebody steady, somebody I can love and take care of. But whenever I meet somebody I think will fit the bill, it turns out he doesn't really want love and care. He only wants one thing. And when he's had that, he leaves, and despises me into the bargain.'

Beckett felt embarrassed.

She said: 'So you're with Ilsa Barnes?'

'Yes.'

Her face was veiled by her chestnut hair. She looked down at the fur trimming of her slippers. 'My trouble is that I'm too old.'

'You're not old, honey.'

'Old enough to husband-want, to want a father for my little girl.'

'There's no reason why you shouldn't get one.'

'There is. It's a fault in myself. I'm too eager, and that puts men off. But don't worry about me, Joe. I'm like a cork, you know, that keeps bobbing up. Life just can't keep me down.'

Chapter 10

I T WAS A TIMELESS Sunday. The thousands who lived
alone in bedsitters had nothing to do. Some read
the papers, others strolled round the block, more
sat in pubs or coffee-bars. Beckett went for a walk. He
heard a gramophone from an attic window; a woman
blues singer. The woman had an adult, disillusioned
voice. He imagined her, a Negress, sitting on a bar-
stool facing a desert of empty glasses, singing the blues
to the disillusioned dawn. She sang straight and honestly, without gimmicks.

The music hung like the summer sky over
Tewkesbury Road.

The combination of the sunshine, a tree against a
house, and the music, touched Beckett, making him
feel happy. It was as if the music formed a centre, and
everything fell into place around it. He was suddenly
rested and at peace, giving his consent.

He became aware that a red sports car was kerb-
crawling beside him. He recognized Dick Dyce at the
wheel.

Dyce asked: 'Where are you headed for?'

'Home. I've just been to get the Sunday papers.'

'Feel like a drink? I think we can just beat the closing
time.'

'Okay.' Beckett got in the car and they drove off.

Dyce said: 'Well, what do you think of her?'

'The car? Smashing. Is it new?'

'Almost. It's this year's model. How much do you
think I gave for her?'

'No?'

'Three hundred quid.'

'You're joking. You must have paid more than that.'

'Not a penny more.' Dyce's manic laugh was hoisted like a triumphal banner. 'It's a stolen car. Man I met in a club gets these stolen cars, alters the numbers on the engines, chassis, etc., gives them new number-plates, paints them up, and provides faked log books. He sold me this one for three hundred, but I could have had a cheaper car for only one hundred.' There was a bursting exuberance in Dyce's voice, as if he delighted in challenging fate by not only buying stolen cars, but by boasting about it.

Beckett said: 'Well, it's all right if you can get away with it.'

Dyce laughed again.

'There's a pub round this next corner.'

The pub windows were frosted glass with a pattern of cherubs in plain glass. They went inside. Green plastic-covered benches lined the walls and a tray advertising Guinness screened the fireplace. The place was full of Irishmen, out from Mass in the nearby church, with royal-blue best suits, Brylcreemed hair, and fresh, ruddy complexions. The two young women with them were stately swans in babyish dresses and angora cardigans, holding gin-and-oranges between gloved genteel fingers. Cigarette smoke and fumes of slopped beer swirled round the full-moon globes which lit the saloon. There was a thud of darts from the partitioned public, and the banshee voice of an Irishman howled the *Rose of Tralee* into a microphone.

'I saw Georgia the other day.'

'She's a very silly girl,' Dyce said. 'What are you having?'

'No, I'll get them.'

'Nonsense, old boy, I invited you.'

'Well, thanks then. I'll have a brown ale.'

'Have a short.'

'No, I'm all right with beer.'

'One brown, one whisky-and-soda,' Dyce ordered, batting his newspaper on the counter.

Sitting at the corner table, Dyce continued: 'A very silly girl. Man-crazy. Wants stability, of course — cheers — but can't get it. Anyway, she provided me with somewhere to stay temporarily, which is all I was concerned with. I've got a flat now, bloody good place, costs me a packet.' He took a card from his pocket. 'Come round and see the place sometime.'

'Thanks, I will.' Beckett read the address: Flat 34, Grosvenor Court Gardens, SW1. He put it between the pages of his notebook.

'Georgia made a terrible fuss when I told her I was leaving. "Dickie, don't go ..." all that sort of thing. The trouble is, she's such a spaniel that, after much of her company, one gets an overwhelming urge to hit her. Know what I mean?'

'Yes. She's pleasant enough, but masochistic.'

'What's your attitude to women?' Dyce asked.

'I suppose my ideal would be to press a button and find a beautiful blonde in my room. And then afterwards press another button to make her disappear.'

'Ah, that would be ideal indeed.'

'When I'm sex-starved I can't think of anything else but sex. I get excited by looking at a pin-up girl like the one on the Clayton's Ginger Ale ad over there. Or by seeing girls' thighs when they slide down a fairground chute. But this desire is often an inner state not caused by a particular girl in the same way that hunger is an inner state, not necessarily caused by seeing a café window.'

'Although the café window certainly helps.'

'Oh yes. But what I mean is, my desire is for sex, not for a specific woman. And the push-button idea appeals to me immensely. It's certainly better than having some girl hanging round expecting breakfast when I want to get rid of her.'

'I know that feeling,' Dyce said. Then he stretched, flexing his muscles, and yawned. 'I must tell you a story. Something that really happened. Want to hear it?'

'Okay.'

'I was about fifteen at the time. During the summer I went hitch-hiking with my cousin Clive, who was several years older than me. We hitched up North and at one in the morning we were stuck on the road above some industrial town or other. They had a blast furnace there, and the sky was lit up by its glow. I rather fancied myself as a socialist at that time, and I was mentally composing a speech about the poor buggers sweating away day and night shifts for the cruel capitalists, plus some calculations as to wages in relation to supporting a family, beers, instalments on the telly, shoes for the kids, fish-and-chips, etc. I'd got all this lined up in my mind and was just about to start spouting and impress Clive, when he suddenly pointed to the sky and exclaimed: "Look at all that money lighting up the sky!"

'This completely took me aback. I refrained from saying my piece while I took in this new angle. I'd automatically identified myself with the workers, you see. It wasn't until Clive's remark that it occurred to me to identify myself with the bosses. It was the turning-point in my thinking. Until then, my interest had been with the underdogs. Afterwards, my interest was in ensuring that I would be a topdog.' Dyce grinned. 'Well, that's it. You thought I was going to tell you some sexy story, didn't you?'

'What happened to your cousin? Did he become an industrialist?'

'No. Like thousands of others, he lost his purity of

ambition, and resigned himself to a humdrum life. But I didn't lose my purity of ambition.' Dyce's slit eyes scanned a horizon. 'That ambition was born in me that night, a penniless boy stranded on an open road. It was never to be stamped down into the ranks of the underdogs. At the moment I'm an adventurer. I climb and fall just for the hell of it. But one day I shall play, no longer for experiment, but for keeps. And from that last game I intend to emerge as a topdog.'

Beckett glanced at the clock. It was almost closing time. The public bar was singing 'When Irish Eyes Are Smiling'. He drained the rest of his beer and asked: 'Have another?'

'No, I've got an appointment. Let's go and I'll run you home.'

Dyce preceded Beckett through the swing door. 'Damn' ugly barmaid in that place. Wonder why they employ such old hags. I suppose the poor fool of a publican is married to her.'

Dyce's verbal cruelty made Beckett feel slightly uncomfortable. 'Don't run me home if you've got an appointment, I can easily walk.'

'Nonsense, old boy. The appointment can wait.'

In the street they noticed that a small crowd had collected some fifty yards away, and they walked over to investigate. As they approached, Beckett pointed out a stationary car, which was wrenched round at an unnatural angle on the wrong side of the road. There were skid marks behind it and the driver's door hung open. He said: 'Accident.'

'Looks like it.'

They pushed through the spectators. A man was sitting on the pavement, propped against the wall, with his legs thrust out stiffly. A piece of wire was twisted into his flesh from forehead to jaw.

Dyce said: 'Christ!'

Beckett realized that it was not wire, but blood. More blood, bright like Technicolor-film blood, was splashed on the road. Something in the quality of the victim's skin made him know without doubt that the man was dead.

The police arrived and started to disperse the crowd, detaining those who had witnessed the accident. Beckett and Dyce moved off with the others. They said nothing because there was nothing to say.

They got into the car, but Dyce did not start it. Instead he asked: 'You haven't got much of a moral code, have you?'

Beckett was still thinking of the accident, and had to adjust his thoughts. 'What do you mean?'

'Just what I say. You have no morals.'

'If you want a serious answer; most Westerners are conditioned to the Christian habit of classifying actions into good and bad, right and wrong. It is possible to throw off this conditioning and to conclude that a life without meaning is a life without morality. One then becomes an amoralist. However, to practise amorality (as apart from holding it in theory) one needs a naturally hedonistic personality, which I myself lack.

'In fact I find that far from wanting pleasure, I generally have to use my will to force myself to indulge in it. Does that answer satisfy you?'

Dyce started the car. 'Shall we drive round for a bit? I'd like to put her through her paces for you.'

'By all means.'

'Can't get up much speed in London, I'm afraid. This car was made for the M1. However, I'll do my best.'

'Right.'

'The reason why I questioned your morality was that I was talking to your friend Wainwright yesterday,' Dyce said. 'Surprised that I know him? I know many ill-assorted people. He told me that you

141

admired the politically expedient rather than the politically moral.'

'Yes, I take it for granted that politicians have necessarily to be crooks. It rather shocked Wainwright.'

'It would.' Dyce had his foot jammed down on the accelerator. The car was now doing an alarming speed. The hood roof was down, and their ensuing conversation was conducted in shouts against the wind. Dyce shouted: 'There was also your conversation with Georgia. When you told her that this is the age of disbelief, which breeds motiveless crimes, you also said that for a man without belief, any action would be preferable to his present condition.'

Beckett shouted: 'How do you know about my conversation with Georgia? You haven't seen her since.'

'I may have got your exact words wrong, but that was the gist of your remark.'

'How did you know about that conversation?'

'She's a beaut, this car. Makes me think of all the other things I'd like to have if —'

'That conversation?'

'— if my rich aunt kicks the bucket and leaves her favourite blue-eyed nephew some money.' Dyce gave a blast on the horn, and a pedestrian, who had started to cross a Zebra, leapt back to the kerb and angrily shook his fist. Dyce had avoided hitting him by inches.

Beckett shouted furiously: '*Will* you answer me?!'

'Sure ... nearly got that pedestrian ... what are you asking?'

'I'm asking you how you knew about my private conversation with Georgia.'

'Oh, that. Jacko told me.'

'Jacko?'

'Yes, I got him to follow you,' Dyce said with a delighted grin. He pressed his foot harder on the accelerator, and the car shot through a cross-roads.

Beckett turned on him. 'Stop laughing. I want an explanation.'

'Don't threaten me, you idiot, with the car going at this speed. Do you want to crash and kill us both?'

'Then slow down.'

Dyce decreased the car's speed gradually.

Beckett said with irritation: 'If you weren't such a damn' fool, you'd know better than to risk getting pinched for speeding in a stolen car.'

They drew up in Tewkesbury Road. Dyce switched off the engine. There was sweat on his forehead. He folded limp arms on the steering-wheel. 'It's you who's the fool. You nearly crashed us. I didn't realize you had such a bad temper.'

'On the contrary, I have an easy-going disposition. If people insult me, nothing happens except that some time later I realize I should have been angry. The only thing that enrages me is interference; people trespassing on my privacy. And you have trespassed, by setting that whining little down-and-out to follow me around.'

'Oh, Jacko. He's lonely. He just wants to serve anyone who will give him a chance. Like a stray dog, licking your hand if you pat him.'

'I don't want my hand licked.'

'Who does? But I wanted to find out what sort of man you are. And what I found out, I approve. How would you like to work with me?'

'Doing what?'

Dyce took a cigarette from his case, and flicked the lighter. 'Taking a risk. To make some money.'

'Money?'

'People think of money as materialism. It isn't. It's a religion. You said life has no meaning. Well, sure, I agree. But we need a meaning, don't we? So we make one for ourselves. You know, dedicate ourselves to a career, or the arts, or a political party. Or to making money. Money's nothing without making it.'

Beckett said: 'You mean, just as a football trophy is nothing in itself, but only meaningful because it's gained by winning matches?'

'That's it. The money addict sees life in terms of finance. You like analogies, don't you? Well, it's like a Christian seeing life in terms of a battle between God and Satan; and the Communist lot seeing it in terms of the class struggle. Get me? I look at life through money-coloured spectacles. I see the money like the ether, permeating everything. Collecting in pockets here, banks there, financing industry, changing into power like matter changing into energy. And obtained by wits, work, or violence. There are plenty of mugs who work fixed hours for a wage. They're ignorant of the financial game. They haven't felt its excitement in their veins. Funny thing is, my aunt felt it coursing through her veins. She was born into a poor family... you know that, don't you? We're working-class, the Dyce family... but she was ambitious and unscrupulous. She knew what she wanted and she made sure she got it. Married for money, and when she'd hooked the man, she pushed him by fair means or foul to the top. She was the driving power behind his career. Then when she'd got her money, she hung on to it. Used all sorts of pious maxims as reasons for not sharing the pickings with the rest of the family. Only one she's got a soft spot for is me, because she realizes that I'm another addict who is as unscrupulous as she is.

'She's a pathetic figure now, poor old bag. One of these widows who put all their money in investments and live meanly on the interest. She's too stingy to repair her house or live decently. She eats scraps, and she's a kleptomaniac. Always pinching worthless trinkets from the local stores.'

Beckett said: 'I understand your obsession, both with making money and money itself. But to me, money only represents freedom from work. I don't need much money. My tastes are simple and I only want enough to live modestly without having a job.'

'You're not a money addict, then?'

'No.'

'You should be. Everyone should centre their lives on some interest or another. It's a form of self-discipline. Good for you.'

Beckett's curiosity was aroused, so he invited Dyee up to his room. On the stairs Dyce suddenly gripped his wrist, saying: 'Try and get away from this!' Beckett tried to jerk free, whereat Dyce retaliated by trying to twist his arm.

Finally Beckett broke free of the steel grip. He was rather irritated by Dyce's he-man act and compulsion to engage in duels of strength or willpower.

In his room a shaft of sunlight fell across bed, worn carpet, to the blue-and-orange flowers of the wallpaper.

Dyce sprawled in the armchair, his head resting on the damp bath-towel which hung over the chair-back like an antimacassar. 'I happen to have discovered that my aunt has left her money to me. The trouble is, that she refuses to die. Now her house, occupied only by herself and a deaf female companion, must be quite a good proposition for a burglar. Suppose a burglar did break in and accidentally made a noise which woke my aunt. She might start to scream, and the burglar might, in a panic, kill her.'

Beckett stared at him.

Dyce said: 'It's a dangerous occupation, being a rich woman.'

'Is that your proposition? Are you suggesting that I should be that burglar?'

'The burglar would take a few things of value from the house. But this would only be for form's sake. He would really collect when the will was read, when I, as heir, would share the proceeds with him.'

'But it's murder,' Beckett said.

Dyce said lightly: 'Everyone has to die sooner or later.'

Looking at Dyce's face, for a moment he saw it as Ilsa's. The two laughing faces, greedy for excitement and with a childishly undeveloped sense of moral responsibility. He said: 'You must be crazy.'

Behind the laughter, Dyce's eyes were narrowed, calculating the risk. 'Sure. And you are, too.' Then he asked: 'You haven't got any whisky on the premises have you?'

Beckett was silent for a while. Then he returned his attention to Dyce and said: 'No. There's some beer.' He opened the wardrobe and took out a full bottle from among the empties.

'No, thanks, old boy. I don't share your plebeian tastes.'

Beckett stood with the bottle in one hand, a cup in the other. It occurred to him, factually and without emotion, that life would never be the same again.

Dyce said: 'Well, are you interested in my proposition?'

'Are you seriously arranging the murder of your aunt? Or are you joking?'

'I'm completely serious.' Dyce guyed: 'Cross my heart and hope to die.' Then he asked: 'So what are you going to do about it? Rush round to the police station?'

'No.'

'But don't you condemn me as an utter scoundrel?'

'No, that's meaningless. I never condemn people.'

Leaning forward, Dyce said: 'Then will you help me? Listen, if she is killed, I, as the heir, may well be

146

suspected. But I will be away at the time, with a genuine alibi. And who will suspect you? Suspicion may fall on known criminals or teenage hoodlums, but not on a quiet young man who spends most of his time shut in his room, bothering nobody. There will be nothing to connect the crime with you.'

'Apart from the question of risk, I couldn't do it.'

'There are twenty thousand pounds at stake. Ten thousand each. I always split fifty-fifty, otherwise an exciting adventure degenerates into a sordid squabble, don't you think?'

'Twenty thousand,' Beckett said. 'Is that a lot of money?'

'It's a fair amount, old boy.'

'I can't conceive an amount larger than a hundred pounds. Up to a hundred I can more or less translate it into goods. But over a hundred is meaningless to me. I don't even know the difference between twenty thousand and two thousand; both sums are too large for me to visualize in terms of buying-power.'

'You'll soon get the hang of it once you've got the money.'

'Is it enough to free me from working?'

'Plenty. You could live on it for the rest of your life. Stay in London with your books, or pack up and wander round the world, living on a comfortable weekly sum.'

'It's the life I've always dreamed of.'

'Sure. And why shouldn't you have it? You see through conventional morals. You've said you're an amoralist and an unbeliever. Listen, I don't pretend to be one of these brainy types. As long as I've got enough wits to deal with life, I'm satisfied. But even I can see that unbelief is a blank cheque for action. Whereas you've been living as if it produced paralysis instead of action.'

'It does. If there is no absolute, there is no meaning. Everything is pointless. And if things are pointless, you don't do them.'

'All right, you know best. But you aren't going to lie down and give up, are you? Show a bit of fight! Remember that drunken session at the party? You told me that murder would be a violent dynamite to blast the bars of the prison. Well, then, blast the bars! Don't just find excuses for inaction; cure it!'

'That's just in the field of talk.'

'Then what do you want to do with your ideas, for Christ's sake? Spout them, so that everyone can admire the mastermind? Look, ideas are useless unless you act on them. But you refuse to act on them. You stick them on a pedestal, and then cover them with a glass case to protect them from the realities of life.'

'And what do you want to do with them? Twist them to your own advantage, by getting me to murder your aunt so that you can collect her money.'

'My dear chap, you're quite right. Naturally I'm concerned with my own advantage. If I'm not, who else would be? But in this case, my advantage coincides with your passion for liberation. Besides, you must admit that a share in the money would be useful to you.'

'Very. It would free me from wasting my time at some boring job.'

'I'm a scoundrel,' Dyce said. 'But I have my own sense of honour. I want to work with a man who is above the rabble of common criminals, a man who sees farther than his own grubby hands snatching the pickings. There are any number of miserable little scavengers like Jacko, whining and grovelling for the price of a tea, or five minutes of one's time, or the loan of two bob. Stub out your cigarette and they'll rush for the fag-end to put in their tins. Well, I've lived at that level of poverty before now, but by Christ I did it like a man. I lived as a bum but I didn't become one. And I knew that at any minute I could stop living like a bum if I wanted to, whereas these scavengers have no control, they're bums and they'll always be bums. I can live rich and live skint and it doesn't touch me. But they are just weaklings; they drifted into petty crime and then couldn't get out. I'm an experimenter, I'll choose crime and then when I've learnt all that's necessary from it, I'll experiment with something else, and choose some other way of life. And you would choose as well, you would deliberately choose crime. Not for the same motives as mine, but the point is that we would both be choosers, not drifters.'

'You understand my ideas very well, don't you? That makes me suspect them.'

'No, I'm a fraud, old boy. But I've equipped myself to deal with brainy types, because at one time I was always beaten in arguments. Just as I've equipped myself to deal with drunken navvies, because at one time I was always beaten in fights.'

Beckett lit a cigarette, then remembered and offered the packet to Dyce, saying: 'Sorry. Have one.'

'Thanks. Of course you realize that, even if you do not actually kill the old hag, you'll still be a murderer. You've promised not to inform; and that makes you legally and morally responsible.'

'I understand that if she is killed I am guilty.'

'That's it. And she will be killed. If you won't do it I will. You're condoning her death, so whether or not you actually kill her doesn't matter a snap of the fingers. I'm telling you this because there's something I want to make clear. If you refuse to kill her it will be because you're a coward. Not because you're moral.'

'Stop arguing with words. This is too important.'

'Important, yes!' Dyce bounded to his feet in one

easy, animal movement. 'And we won't get caught, either. I don't intend to hang. There are too many things I want to do. Believe me, Joe, this job is going to be foolproof.'

'Have you worked it all out, then?'

'Yes. Your part and mine. If you're with me, that is. Are you?'

The bar of sunlight had crept across the room to illuminate the tin tray under the gas ring, the packet of lard and the litter of spent matches.

Beckett said seriously: 'I shall have to think it over. I need a week or two to do so.'

Dyce started to say something, but Beckett cut in: 'There's nothing more to discuss. I've told you I'll make a decision within a couple of weeks, and the matter ends there.'

Dyce hesitated, then said: 'All right!' He grinned suddenly, and punched Beckett's arm. 'All right!' he laughed. 'All right! All right!'

Beckett said nothing.

'By the way, before I go, I'll return this....' Dyce handed him the cardboard target with the bull in the centre eaten by shot. 'Your rifle-range target. Dropped on the fairground. Another service of the invaluable Jacko.'

When Dyce had gone Beckett spent some time striding round the room. Occasionally he beat his fists on his forehead.

Murder would be a deliberate choice, an act of will in a world without free will. It would result in mental and spiritual torture to him; but torture was preferable to non-feeling. Better to be wrecked in the rapids of life than condemned to be the eternal spectator sitting on the bank.

His interest had always been in the criminal, never in the victim. Following, in the newspapers, the current trial of the man accused of child-murder, Beckett's interest had been exclusively in the man. The fact that there was one less child in the world did not interest him. Similarly, when Dyce had told him of his intended murder, he had automatically identified himself with Dyce, not with the aunt. Dyce was more interesting than the woman. The victim did not interest him, and therefore he had immediately promised not to inform.

As Dyce had said, to condone was to be guilty. If Beckett did not actually commit the murder, it would be through a sense of disbelief in the situation.

Thinking of various murder cases, it occurred to him that the criminal had been caught because he had subconsciously wished to be caught. The urge towards extreme experience stretched past the crime to the consequence which was the completion of the experience. The desire for punishment to follow crime was the result of society's long conditioning in Christian morality. He must guard against it.

If only he could decide what to do; whether to go forward into crime, or to shut his eyes and pretend he had never met Dyce.

Chapter 11

IT WAS ONE OF the better times. He lay in bed beside Ilsa and felt very clear and alone, knowing that his own existence was the only truth.

He raised himself on his elbow and looked down at her. She was exhausted and immobile; her eyes were closed. He watched her hard, pale face with the dew of perspiration on her forehead and darkening the roots of her hair. She had a spent, half-dead look like a medium after a séance or a mother after giving birth.

He kissed her without losing the certainty that was hard as a diamond inside his head.

She opened her eyes. 'Hello, you.'

'Give me your hand, and I'll lead you out of the window and over the stars.'

She said fondly: 'Crazy boy, we'd fall.'

'No, I wouldn't fall, and I'd support you so you wouldn't fall either. Ilsa, I'm convinced I'm going to be a great man; that I have limitless potentialities.'

'Oh, sure,' she said cynically, sleepily. 'And as a start you're going to flip from star to star round the universe.'

'It isn't conceit, you know. It's just sudden awareness of my own strength.' He climbed out of bed and went to the window. 'Come and look out.'

Reluctantly, she obeyed. 'What I suffer for you! Being dragged out of bed into the cold....'

'Look at the roofs. And the sky. And under the sky, all the lands stretching from here to Africa.'

Seeing that some comment was expected of her, she said: 'Do you want to travel?'

'Yes. Don't you?'

'I'd like to go State Side. That's where all the high times are. This old country's dead.'

'It isn't dead. I'm English.'

They stood together looking out; a naked man and a naked girl looking through a dingy lodging window. He put his arm round her shoulders. He was fascinated by the paradox which had fitted an ordinary, limited girl with such a perfect body. He felt that his strength and destiny were such that he could take her with him; carry her without even noticing her weight.

After a while, boredom made her shift from foot to foot. He said from his superior hardiness: 'Get back into bed, love.'

'I'll be glad to.'

He pulled on his raincoat for a dressing-gown and continued to gaze out of the window like a god surveying his territory.

From the bed, Ilsa said: 'Christ, cigarette...' She stretched out an arm to reach her handbag. She grasped the bag clumsily; it opened and the contents fell on the floor. 'Damn,' she said. 'Be a honey, Joe.'

He retrieved her scattered belongings.

'Joe...?'

'You're beautiful, love. You really are.'

'Joe...?'

'Yes?'

'I think I'm in love with somebody else.'

He continued to retrieve her things, putting them in her handbag. 'I see.'

'Oh, darling, I didn't want to do this. It kills me, doing this to both of us. But I couldn't help it. I honestly couldn't help it.'

'You tell me this now.'

'I've been trying to tell you all evening, but I couldn't. I kept thinking: I'll count to five and then tell him. But whenever I got to five, either you said something, or something happened, or I just didn't have the courage. But I wanted to tell you before we — you know — went to bed.'

Then why didn't you?'

'I've *explained* why I didn't. And once we'd started kissing I couldn't break off.'

'I didn't notice you trying to break off.'

'Of *course* not. I've *said* I *couldn't* stop once we'd started. But I did mean to tell you before bed. I have got a moral code, you know.'

'Have you? I thought you were a complete little tart.'

'Oh, shut up, Joe. That's not fair. You don't mean it.'

'I'm afraid I don't feel like being fair.' Then he asked: 'And this man. Is he in love with you? Yes, of course, he must be. You get everyone you want, don't you?'

'He said he couldn't live without me.'

'Then he must be either a fool or a liar.'

'Oh, stop it, Joe. Don't talk about it like that. You mustn't hate Larry; I want you to meet him and be friends. You can't let me down about this. You're the only person I can rely on.'

'Please let's get this straight; it's you who are letting me down.'

'Oh yes, I know, darling, and I do feel terribly bad about it.'

'If he says he can't live without you he's obviously a very possessive type. You know you can't stand possessiveness. You'll be sick of him within a week.'

A note of self-satisfaction crept into her voice. 'Well, actually, I like possessiveness. I mean it's very flattering. It's only that I react against it.' He kept an angry silence.

She exclaimed: 'Oh, I know, you're right, I know. I know I'll get sick of him, and I'm telling you because you're the only person I'm honest with. But I can't help it, Joe. I wish I could help it but I can't. It's like being called by the Pipes of Pan or something, and the tune they play is life and excitement, and I can't resist them. I've got to go dancing after them.' Then she added: 'And I did warn you, didn't I, Joe? I did warn you I wouldn't stay.'

He didn't answer.

'Joe? I did warn you.'

He still didn't answer.

'Didn't I warn you?'

'Yes. You warned me.'

'Well, then.'

'Oh, for Christ's sake, shut up.'

For a while neither spoke, then a sudden thought struck him. 'Have you slept with him?'

'Don't shout at me like that.'

'Have you?'

'I said, don't shout at me. I'm being very decent, trying to break this gently to you, and you've no right to shout questions that aren't any business of yours anyway.'

He yelled furiously: 'Have you or haven't you?' He raised his hand as if to strike her.

Made hysterical by fear, she yelled back: 'Yes, yes, yes! I have, I have, I have!' Then, as the threat of a blow receded, she became calmer. With fear still flickering behind her eyes like a faulty connection, she hurriedly made excuses. 'It was only once, honestly it was only once. I had to go home for a week; you've no idea how utterly boring my home is.' As she gained confidence, her voice became a complaining whine. 'Just this stupid old farm, where nothing ever happens from one year to another. Dad out all day looking after the stupid old animals. Mum never thinking of anything but housework and cooking and all that boring stuff. They wouldn't even let me go to the village pub, bloody hell, although there's never anyone in the pub except a lot of local yokels with faces like mangel-wurzels or whatever those things are they plant the bloody fields with. And I couldn't even play my records because they don't like rock or jazz, and anyway their gram came out of the Ark and only plays seventy-eights. Well, anyway, I escaped for a day and went up to London. I was coming straight here to see you, honestly I was, but I thought I'd just pop into the Cellar Club on the way. And then I met this Larry. I didn't like him much at first but we went out for a drink together and, Christ, did I get drunk!...'

He said: 'You sicken me.'

'Don't, Joe. I can't bear it when you're angry. Nobody must be angry with me. Everybody must love me.'

He stared at her, taking in this new shock.

'Everybody must love me,' she said again.

'What do you want to be? Everybody's little darling? You've got to grow up, Ilsa. You can't be a spoilt child all your life, grabbing what you want and evading responsibility for what you do.'

She spread her fingers, sulkily examining the nails. 'I haven't done anything so very awful.'

'Haven't you?'

'No.' She turned her hand, and examined her nails from another angle. 'Not enough for you to stop loving me.'

'You don't understand. I loved your body. No, more than that, I worshipped and adored it. Every inch. Every time you did so much as move your little finger it was a miracle. I'd rather watch you perform the most humdrum task than look at the most beautiful scenery imaginable. And now that I've found out what you've been doing, I feel disgust and nausea in exact proportion to the adoration I felt before. I never want to touch or even look at you again.'

She stared at him in silence, nervously pushing her

hair back from her forehead. Then she burst into a furious tirade. 'You loved my body! Yes, that's all you ever cared about! You never cared the least little bit for me as a person. You weren't even aware of my existence as a person. Other people are only objects to you. You've got no real contact with them at all. Well, I'm just about sick of being regarded as an object.' She lit a cigarette, and stabbed the air with the cigarette as she talked. The smoke made blue wraiths over her head. 'You don't care about me; you only think of yourself. Oh, you're always kind and generous, but in such a patronizing way, like patting a pet animal on the head. Your kindness and generosity is only a way of asserting your superiority. You don't consider me an equal. I can't really affect you, so you can afford to be kind.'

Beckett felt suddenly tired. He was conscious of the absurdity of his appearance; sitting on the edge of the bed with bare hairy legs protruding from the raincoat. He said: 'Yes, you're quite right. I'm sorry, Ilsa. I can't help the way I am. I'd like to be able to make contact, but I can't. I didn't realize that you'd guessed it, though.'

'I'm not a complete ninny, you know. Although you consider me one.'

'No.'

'And what's more, you've no right to be angry because I've been unfaithful, I bet you're not faithful yourself, are you?'

'That's different.'

'It isn't different. I don't see that it's different at all.'

'I'm a man.'

'That's a bloody unfair argument.'

'I don't care if it's unfair or not. It just happens to be the way I feel. I need a faithful partner. Whether or not I'm justified and fair in that need, doesn't matter. The thing is, I need one.'

157

Ilsa said: 'You don't realize that I exist in my own right, too. You don't recognize me, or anyone else for that matter, as a person. I love people and I want them to love me. But you don't care; you're just indifferent to people. Do you know, when we're together I feel that you're not really there at all. Nothing I say really touches you. You live behind a glass wall. You don't love, you only lust. And, anyway, you won't have to bother with me any more because I'm getting the hell out.' She got out of bed and switched the radio on to full volume. Latin-American music beat against the furniture. She started to drag her clothes on, lighting a second cigarette from the stub of the first and parking it on the mantelpiece while she dressed.

He shouted against the music: 'How will you —?'

'What?'

He turned down the volume of the radio. 'Do you mind not waking the entire house?'

'Yes, I do mind.' She turned the volume up again.

He turned it down.

She turned it up.

He shouted: 'Stop it, for Christ's sake, I'll murder you.' He turned the volume down again and they stood glaring at each other in silence. He took a deep breath and enquired : 'How will you get home, now that you've missed the last Tube?'

'Walk.'

'You can't do that. I'll give you some money for a taxi.'

'Thanks, but I'd rather walk.' She tapped her foot to the diminished music, shut off from him as she made up her icy face in the mirror.

'It's a long way.'

'I'm not complaining.'

He paced up and down.

She said: 'Must you act the caged tiger?'

'Oh, shut up.'

After a while, she said irrelevantly: 'I'm going to take a job in a club.'

'Are you?'

'Yes. The owner's a friend of Larry's. He says I've got the looks and the right sort of personality.'

'I hope you're successful."

'Don't worry; I shall be." She slashed lipstick on her mouth.

There was a pause. Then he exclaimed angrily: 'It's just the sort of rotten job you would take. Flirting with a lot of tired old businessmen.'

'So what? It's none of your business.'

'I detest you.'

'Fair enough, I detest you too.' She dragged the comb through her hair, then clipped on her ear-studs and patted them. After a final peer into the mirror, she said: 'Well, goodbye. I'm going now.'

'Got all your things?'

'Yes.'

'Goodbye, then.'

She stood, tense, in her gay flimsy dress, in the doorway. 'You'd better give me some taxi-money after all. It's too far to walk.'

'Cold, too.'

'Yes, isn't it? I'll make myself some tea when I get in.'

"Do you want some here? I mean, have a cup if you like.'

'No, thanks all the same, I'd better get home.'

He gave her a pound note. He only had thirty-seven and threepence left. 'Here you are.'

'I don't know how much it will cost.'

'Keep the change.'

'I'm only borrowing it. I'll pay you back.'

'Don't bother.'

'I will.'

'All right,' he said, 'you will.'

'You don't believe I will?'

'What does it matter? I don't care whether I get the pound back or not.'

'But I will pay you back! I will, I will! I don't want to owe you anything.'

'All right,' he said. 'You've made your point.'

She looked at him, pushing the hair back from her forehead. Then she said: 'Goodbye.'

'Goodbye.'

She stilll hesitated. Then she made a sudden dash for the radio and turned the volume on full. The next second she was out of the room with the door slamming behind her and the sound of her high heels clattering down the stairs.

The music blared. Something about Señore and Amore. He turned it off. The illuminated panel no longer pleased him; he had a general sensation of tastelessness. He noticed that her cigarette had burnt out on the mantelpiece, blistering the paint. Her lipstick, with the cap off, was beside the mirror.

He noticed a pocket diary on the floor. He must have missed seeing it when he retrieved her belongings. The entries, in her neat office-girl backhand, stated that she 'Went to jazz club. Wore new check shirt and tight jeans', or 'Bought sweater from Marks & Sparks, as was payday', or 'Had coffee in Troubadour with Katey'. She had listed the records she had bought and the films she had seen with comments 'not bad' or 'v. good'. Drawings of a bottle beside the written entries denoted the days on which she had got drunk.

Looking for references to himself, he found 'Went to cinema,' and 'Went to bed'.

Over the days of her holiday in Sussex she had scrawled 'FOUL TIME!'

The last entry read: 'Met a boy called Larry. He is dark, he has a black sweater over a red shirt. He is keen on B. Bugloss (like me!). We went to bed.'

Beckett found the remains of a wrapped sliced loaf in the cupboard, and made a sandwich with cheese and a hunk of raw onion. He sat in the armchair, eating, and dropping crumbs down his bare chest. His thoughts were not of Ilsa, but of Dyce, whose proposition was always present at the back of his mind. It was a constant factor, like a headache.

The next evening he had still not arrived at a decision. Sometimes he knew he would do it. At these times he imagined his future supplied with a private income. It would be a pleasant modest life, devoted to study and research into the nature of existence, and made extraordinary by the secret of the crime he had committed. It was an attractive prospect, but it was immediately destroyed by the knowledge that he would not do it. At the times when he knew he would not do it, he felt relieved, as if he had thrown off a burden. Yet soon the idea of the crime became attractive again, and he started rebuilding his ideal life. These two states, knowing he would do it and knowing he would not, succeeded each other endlessly.

He decided to visit Gash. He was admitted by the landlady, who again thanked him for paying for the window. Beckett hardly heard what she said. His replies were so strange and incoherent that she asked him whether he was ill.

'Oh no,' he said. Then added: 'It's the heat, you know. It's been terribly hot these last weeks.' He wiped his brow.

'It gets you down. I thought the thunderstorm would clear the air a bit, but it's got just as bad again.'

Beckett gabbled some sort of reply, then knocked on Gash's door.

Gash greeted him with: 'I'm pleased to see you.' Behind his old man's, womanish face, with its aureole of hair, the new window-pane shone clean like steel. He held up his hand in blessing.

Beckett was reminded of Father Dominic's hand holding the chess piece. 'I met an acquaintance of yours recently. He's a priest now, but you knew him when he was at school. His name's Dominic.'

'Yes, I remember the Dominic boy. He was very clever for his age. It was a great occasion when he was elected president of his school debating society. He worked all night in the bedroom, writing his speech. Poor Mrs Dominic couldn't get him to go to bed. And the motion he was proposing was astonishing — "that falsehood is preferable to truth".' Gash was quite excited. 'I remember it all clearly. The charming parents, the pale, serious boy. His bedroom, which he used as a study, was a holy of holies to him. His parents were not admitted except by special invitation. He invited me up once, for the purpose of an argument whereby he tried to convert me to Catholicism.'

'Did he? Well, he's still at it. He tried to convert me, too.'

'With any success?'

'No, I can't be reconverted. But he made me feel more interested and friendly towards the Church. Also he surprised me by agreeing that actions are determined and therefore there is little freedom.'

'Little free will,' Gash corrected him. 'There is still freedom."

'Aren't they the same?'

'Not at all. It was thought that there was an immaterial tenant of the material brain. The tenant was called the mind, the personality, the I, or what you will.

Then determinism announced that there was no such tenant, and that the brain was a sort of automatic signal-box without an 'I' at the controls. But however much the tenant is planed down, it cannot be entirely abolished. It still remains in the form of consciousness. Consciousness is the seat of freedom.'

Beckett scratched his head, trying to follow.

Gash went on: 'Man is the intersection point between the God dimension and the human dimension; between timelessness and time. That point of intersection is consciousness. It is there that we receive the God-force with its qualities of freedom and timelessness. That is why I believe we have freedom, in spite of our limited free will.'

The room smelt of thug cat and Dettol and the stale smell of insanity. Here Gash half starved and slept on the floor, and talked of the God force.

Gash continued: 'It wouldn't occur to young Dominic — to Father Dominic — that we have this freedom, for unless he is much changed since I knew him, he is no mystic. With him, everything is an intellectual problem. However, I'm surprised that he overlooked the most vital doctrine of his Church: that man is the temple of the Holy Spirit.'

'Mr Gash, do you mind if I ask you an impertinent question?'

'Not at all. I don't think I should find it impertinent.'

'Well, I heard you were once in a mental home, and I wondered if it was true.'

'Perfectly true. I was sent there because it was thought that I was incapable of taking care of myself. My sole preoccupation was to concentrate the force inside me. The force that can be called the God force or the life force or the Holy Spirit or what you please. I practised the concentration of this force until I could live in a state of ecstasy which would be unbearable to the normal man. Consequently, I grew careless about the routine business of life: crossing roads, carrying on conversations, eating food, and such things. Finally it was decided that I was in need of control and protection, with the result that I spent the next year in a mental hospital.'

'How terrible for you.'

'The hospital was excellent; very well run. I had no complaints, except that leisure was discouraged and we were supposed to fill our time with all manner of trivialities known as occupational therapy. Unfortunately, the whole treatment was designed for the sick; whereas I suffered, not from sickness, but from excess of health.'

'I see.' Beckett looked at the new glass. A million pinpricks of light dazzled him. He picked up one of Gash's books and glanced at the title on the spine. Then he faced Gash, and said: 'I asked, not because I think I'm going mad, but because I'd like to go mad and can't.'

'An interesting affliction.'

'Look. Last time I was here, you talked about the moments of assent, of affirmation of life. I've had that experience, but I also suffer from its opposite condition.'

'Go on.'

'Well, I remember once, when I was a child, my mother gave me a book of noble lives to read when I was convalescing from flu. One was Pasteur, I remember. Another was Father Damien, who founded a leper colony. In this chapter it mentioned the fact that a leper can't feel hot water. I mean if a leper immersed his hand in hot water, he wouldn't know it was hot.' Beckett looked at his own hand.

Gash nodded, to indicate that he was following.

'You can imagine a leper immersing his hand in hot water. They tell him that it's hot, and that he should have certain reactions to heat. He accepts what they say as correct, but it's meaningless to him. The word "hot" draws a blank with him. He has no reaction; he feels nothing.'

'Yes.'

'I am a spiritual leper. I am told that there is a point in life, but "point in life" is as meaningless to me as "hot" is to a leper. I lack the correct feelings and reactions, the correct convictions. If a leper has an impaired physical sense of touch, I have an impaired spiritual and emotional sense of touch. My sense of touch is dead.'

Gash asked: 'What are you going to do about this problem?'

'There is something I could do. An action violent enough to shock myself back into life. But it's drastic, criminal. I can't tell you about it.'

'You're not a criminal. I don't think you would belong in their world.'

'No. That's the point. I'd choose crime, I wouldn't drift into it. Suppose a man has grown up with certain beliefs and values. Then he loses them. He will become intellectually a nihilist, and emotionally numb like the leper. But eventually it will occur to him that if there is no meaning in life, he is able to impose his own. If he wants to live for pleasure, he can do. If he wants to go anywhere on the face of the earth, he can do. If he wants to substitute a goal of his own for the overturned goals of religion and social morality, he can for instance set out to make as much money as possible.'

'Well, yes.'

'And if he refrains from these things, it is either because he is blind or because his sight is so clear that it destroys everything he sees. The blind man has bandaged his eyes before the glare of his awful freedom. He won't live for pleasure because he has self-imposed duties to society and his family. He won't roam the world because he has limited himself to the area of

165

his job, his place of residence, his timetable. He won't make money because he is somewhat afraid of it, and considers it immoral. In short, he prefers to construct a safe pattern of living as a barricade against his freedom.

'That was the blind man. Now the clear-sighted. He looks around at his possibilities: pleasure, travel, money, etc. But his wretched eyes act like a pulverizing gun. One blast from his eyes, and the thing looked at crumbles into dust. He sees in advance the futility of all goals, and so never attempts to reach them. Instead, he stagnates, seeing nothing worthy of his beliefs, nothing to make him move in one direction rather than another. The man thus paralysed is not free. But there is one course possible to him: if he can't feel the normal human blood in his veins, he can inject himself with poison, with fever.' When he had finished, Beckett could still hear his last words, in his flat assertive voice, hanging in the air. He thought with depression: People dislike me, as a clever prig student is disliked.

Gash said: 'When I was a young man of about your age I had everything I could desire. A good career, a wife whom I loved, and more money than I knew how to use. I was successful in business, society, and love, and I enjoyed myself enormously. Then I started to lose my taste for my manner of life. It was like losing one's taste for food when one has a cold. Everything I looked at seemed tinged with futility and greyness, and I felt a permanent vague dissatisfaction which had, so far as I could see, no tangible cause. This condition worsened and I began to suffer from headaches. I tried a holiday abroad, which only brought temporary relief. I next toyed with various ideas, including, under the influence of the Dominic family, that of joining the Catholic Church. None of these mental fads lasted for long. Finally I took a drastic step. I resigned my position with my firm, parted from my wife, friends, and family, and went to join a small religious community who had a house in Scotland. These men practised disciplines for the attainment of spiritual ecstasy, which I still practise daily.'

'I find your life story very interesting. But I could not do the same myself. So I hope you're not advising me to become a monk.'

'I was advising nothing,' Gash said. 'The point I wished to make was that freedom follows an act of rejection. I must add that, in my opinion, all men who are capable of greatness have to go through a preliminary trough of spiritual deadness. This deadness is the necessary preliminary to rebirth. I believe that the great are drawn from the ranks of the twice-born, from those who have undergone death and rebirth.'

'What is rebirth?'

'I could answer your question, and many other questions. I could chart your future spiritual development. But it would be of no use to you.' As Beckett looked startled, Gash continued: 'Don't be alarmed, I'm not a charlatan, claiming to read your future! I meant that, from my own experience along the same path, I could chart the progress of the path for you. It would be useless because experiences cannot be given. You must undergo them yourself. When you have done so, you will make your own definition of rebirth and won't have to ask me for mine.' Gash put his hand on Beckett's shoulder. 'I have only one piece of advice. Don't rush precipitately into some rash action which you may later regret, but wait for the experience of rebirth which will assuredly come to you sooner or later.'

The old man's face was near his own; the smell of decay hung from the womanish soft mouth. Beckett felt sudden revulsion. He thought, rebelliously, that it was all very well for Gash to talk. Gash was even more divorced from the everyday world than he was. All the same, Gash's voice had the ring of authenticity, like the voice of a workman who thoroughly knows his job.

Gash removed his hand. 'Well, go now. But come and see me again, any time you please.'

In the doorway, Beckett said: 'By the way, I asked you about the mental hospital because popular gossip says you were confined for a sex crime. I don't know what you feel about this. Personally, I should be rather flattered at being considered the local sex maniac!'

Gash said: 'How amazing! I'm sorry to disappoint the gossips. But tell them that in my youth, although never actually qualifying for the status of sex maniac, I was very passionate and never ran short of beautiful, charming, and cultivated women.'

'I'll tell them!' Beckett said.

Chapter 12

BECKETT'S MONEY diminished rapidly. He lived cheaply, buying meat sold as pets' pieces, and scavenging vegetables from the gutter in Portobello Market. He made his excursions in the evenings, when the stalls were closing and many vegetables were dropped. If he was too late the road-sweeper beat him to it, and swept up the vegetables into the Royal Borough of Kensington cart.

He received a letter from Ilsa enclosing a fifteen-shilling postal order. Her writing style was flat and undistinguished, punctuated with exclamation marks. She related that Katey had caught a summer cold, that they had got a cute chianti-bottle lamp for their living-room, that yesterday she had been to the cinema and the film was v. good; that she liked her new job but some of the customers were bloody mean about tips. There then followed complicated explanations why she was sending fifteen shillings instead of a pound. This made him laugh. It was somehow typical of Ilsa to fall just short of the mark.

That evening he had an alteration of vision. It was as if the mechanism of his sight had been sharply jolted into a clearer and truer focus, so that he saw clearly instead of partially. He happened to be looking at the washstand at the time and suddenly all the objects on it looked different. Trying to define this difference, he could only express it as more intense being. The rose-patterned china bowl, the empty milk-bottles, his tooth things and the ball of socks to be washed, all existed more intensely. They no longer looked like their names, but like clusters of living electrons that formed perpetual-motion matter. Life was the sinews of these objects, these wrestling shapes and shadows that were twisted into the substance of the marble slab.

He thought that there must be shutters on the human senses and capacity for experience. Generally the shutters were half closed, admitting only imperfect, lazy sense-impressions. On the few occasions when the shutters were raised, the world appeared, not fully, but at any rate more clearly than usual.

Why then could not men always live and experience fully? Why were they shuttered, as if reality was so blazing that it could be seen only through a protective screen? Why did the state of boredom and depression, the polar opposite to vision, occur so frequently?

His thoughts were interrupted by a rap on his door. The landlady called: 'Mr Beckett... visitor...'

He ran down the three flights. In the front hall stood his mother. She was wearing a fawn hat with a decoration like curled antennae on the front, a beige jacket, and her churchgoer best dress that she had bought three years ago from the High Street drapers. Her prayer-clasped hands were in net gloves, and from her right wrist dangled a navy holdall containing her handbag and her plastic mac.

He said: 'Hello, Mum.'

'Darling boy...' She held him tightly. 'My darling boy.'

He smiled at her.

She smiled back.

The landlady watched them stolidly with her grudging, dissatisfied eyes, and her arms folded on her chest like a garden-fence gossip.

Beckett said awkwardly to his mother: 'I live on the top floor. Come on up.'

Passing the landlady on the stairs, his mother said: 'Excuse me...' fluttering a nervous smile.

Beckett whispered: 'Don't smile at that old cow.'

'What, dear?'

'Oh, nothing.'

'Why shouldn't I smile at her?'

'She's a lower form of life and should be ignored.'

'Really, dear!'

In the room, he said: 'Well, this is a surprise. I didn't expect to see you.'

There was a hint of reproach in her voice. 'Didn't you, Joe?'

'No!' he said jovially. 'Well! Sit down.'

'I had to come up to town to see Aunty Anne, dear, so I thought I'd look in and see you first.' She sat, and looked round cosily. 'My darling! So this is your room, where you live. I've often pictured it in my imagination, trying to imagine the place you live in.'

'Bit of a mess at the moment, I'm afraid.'

She prodded the bed, evaluating like a woman at a sale. 'I believe I've got just the thing for a cover for this bed. Those old curtains that used to be in your bedroom at home. You remember, the flowered ones. I'll take the curtain rings out, and wash and iron them for you.'

'The bed's all right without a cover.'

'Yes, that's what I'll do. The colours should come up nicely if I put some salt in the water.'

'I don't *need* them, Mum.'

'Oh, let Mother do this for you! It would be no trouble, really, dear.'

He said ungraciously: 'All right.' He filled the kettle and put it on the gas ring. 'Anyway, how are you, Mum?'

'Better, dear, though I haven't been at all well lately.'

'Haven't you? I'm sorry to hear that.'

'I told you, in my last letter, that I was ill. Didn't you read my letter?'

'Yes, three times.' It was true: he had read her letter thrice. But the words had slipped over the surface of

171

his mind without making an impression, and he had not registered that she was ill. Now he felt guilty, and resentful at her for causing his guilt.

'I *did* hope you'd answer my letter. Especially as I told you I wasn't well.'

'Yes. I meant to write back, but somehow I never —'

'I don't expect long letters. Just a postcard from time to time would be a comfort.'

'Yes.'

'Otherwise Mother worries.'

'Yes.'

'Well, never mind, dear. We're together now, and that's the main thing.' She smiled, her tired, anxious eyes loving him. 'My boy! Tell me all your news.'

'There isn't much, actually, Mum.'

'Well, there must be something.'

'Not really.'

'Have you made any nice friends?'

'I know some people, yes.' He knew what she was getting at, but perversely feigned stupidity, determined not to help her.

'Anyone special, dear?'

'What do you mean, "special"?'

'Well, special.'

'What do you mean?'

She was forced to say it. 'Any nice girl?'

'No.'

'Oh, I am disappointed. But perhaps you'll meet someone you like soon.'

'Yes.'

'Darling!' Then she asked: 'What about that girl you mentioned last summer?'

'What girl?'

'What was her name?'

He said reluctantly: 'Ilsa Barnes?'

'That was it. What happened to her?'

'Oh, well. Nothing, really.'

'Don't you see her any more?'

'Not really, no.'

'But you seemed so fond of her, Joe.'

He grunted noncommittally.

'Perhaps you *will* see her again?'

To buy her off, he agreed: 'Perhaps.'

'Of course, dear.' She said brightly: 'Ilsa! That's a German name, isn't it? Is she German?'

'No, English. From Sussex.'

'Sussex! What part of Sussex?'

'A place called Lowhurst. Near Rye, somewhere.'

'Oh, I know Rye. It's a lovely place. I went there once for a holiday when I was a girl. I expect it's a lot changed now, though. Fancy that! I don't know Lowhurst itself, though. Well,' she said, 'so Ilsa is a country girl. That's nice. I expect you show her round London, don't you?'

'Oh no. She's been in London three years now, and probably knows it better than I do.'

'Still, I expect there's a lot she hasn't seen. St Paul's for instance, or the Crown Jewels in the Tower. Has she seen those?'

'I don't expect so; no.'

'Well, then!' she said triumphantly. 'You'll be able to take her, won't you?'

'Yes.'

'Aunty Anne and I went to the Tower last time I was in London. There was such a feeling of history there, of people in times gone by...' She had an expression of timid enthusiasm, like a child wanting her hesitant hope confirmed. Then, unselfishly, she stopped discussing herself to discuss him. 'After all, dear, your Ilsa comes from the country and London must seem very strange to her. She'll be glad to have a nice boy like you to take care of her and show her around. And Joe...'

'Uh-huh?'

'Make sure you *are* a nice boy, won't you? Don't lead her astray. Remember she's a country girl, a long way from home, and I'm sure her mother worries about her, as I do about you, dear.'

Embarrassed, he said nothing.

'I'd so like to have a daughter-in-law. I want to be a granny *soon!*'

'Mum, need we discuss this?'

'But you'll want to get married one day, won't you?'

'Not particularly.'

'But why not, dear?'

'I just don't.'

'Now don't be silly, Joe.' She said in the irritating voice of a woman in the right: 'All these ideas about not marrying and wonderful free-love are all very old-fashioned and very very boring. People discovered long ago that free-love wasn't half as wonderful as they had supposed; there is nothing free about behaving like an alley-cat. And there is nothing of love in it either, because a man must trust and respect a girl in order to love her. If a girl lets you paw her about, how can you trust her not to let other men paw her about behind your back? Believe me, if you really love a girl, you'll have a regard for her honour and self-respect. You won't want to drag her through the gutter to satisfy your animal lust.'

Surreptitiously, he looked at his watch. It was ten past seven.

'Joe...'

'Yes?'

She said with annoyance: 'Haven't you been listening to me?'

'Yes.'

'Then why don't you *answer,* dear? It's so annoying when you don't answer.'

'There's nothing I want to say.'

'Well, there's plenty I want to say. These ideas about not marrying; I suppose they're ideas you've picked up from these fine friends of yours, who do nothing all day but drink coffee, and set the world in order, and think they're such geniuses with their second-hand mistresses and second-hand ideas. I'm sure all these friends of yours would think I'm very boring, a silly suburban woman, because I stand up for the morality they laugh at. I suppose they never ask themselves where they'd be if it wasn't for people like me. It never occurs to them that if nobody got married then they would never have been born. It's only because decent people, whom they despise as being conventional, got married and sacrificed themselves to bring up children, that they're able to sit there discussing their fine ideas.'

He said coldly: 'If you *must* attribute to me a lot of mythical friends...'

'Well, you know very well your friends are like that. The few I've met all looked as if they could do with a good wash, physically, mentally, and morally. They all looked as if they needed a long walk over the moors, so that the wind could blow some of the silly ideas out of their heads. But it isn't them I'm interested in. It's you.' Her voice softened, was yearning. 'I know Mother is a cross, nagging old woman. Yes she is, dear. But it's only because she loves you, and doesn't want to see you go down the drain. This idea about not marrying may seem very fine and free to you now, but what's going to happen when you're old?' Her voice sharpened again. 'What will you be like then? One of these lonely, dirty old men who go round pinching young girls' bottoms because there's nothing else left for them?'

Beckett frowned.

She said: 'There you are, I can speak up, I can talk as frankly as any of your wonderful friends.'

'Yes. All right. You can. Now please let's drop the subject.'

'All right, dear, if you want to. Oh, Joe darling, I did so want to have a nice evening with you, and now I've broken all my resolutions by nagging you. Will you forgive your nasty cross old Mum?'

'There's nothing to forgive.'

'Yes, there is, dear. I shouldn't nag you. It's only because I love you so much.'

The kettle was boiling. 'Coffee?' he offered.

'That would be lovely.' She asked in a bright, different voice: 'And how's your job?'

'Oh, that. Well, actually, I've left.'

'Left your job?'

'Yes.' He made two cups of Nescafé, stirring them hard to vent his irritation.

'But *why,* Joe?' She took the blue-and-white striped mug. Sip. 'What a pretty mug! Is it yours or the landlady's?'

'Mine.'

'Oh, yours. She doesn't provide crockery, then?'

'No.'

'Oh, what a pity. If I'd known you could have had some crockery from home. It would have saved you buying it.' Another sip. 'Ah, this is nice. I was dying for a nice cup of something hot to pull me together after the journey. Journeys are really exhausting.'

'Yes.'

'I did look in at the station buffet, but it was so crowded I decided not to stay.'

'No.'

She said: 'But why did you leave your job?'

'I don't know really. Because I was fed up.'

'But you must know, dear.'

'Nobody really knows why they do things.'

'Now, that *is* a silly thing to say. Of course people

176

know why they do things. I certainly know why I do things; I should think it very peculiar if I didn't.'

Beckett lit a cigarette.

She said: 'I do so worry about you, the way you keep drifting from job to job in that shiftless way.'

He thought she had finished, but she continued in a timid, yearning voice: 'You were so lovely when you were a baby. People in the street used to stop and look into your pram. And now when the neighbours and people enquire about you I just don't know what to say. I can't tell them you just drift from job to job.'

'Why not? I don't care if you do.'

'But *I* care, Joe. I met Mrs Delapole the other day. You remember, her son used to be at school with you. Anyway, Mrs Delapole said that he had a very good job now; something to do with an engineering company. His firm sends him abroad for them, it's all very exciting. And he has an expense account, and a secretary, and two telephones on his desk. And then Mrs Delapole asked about you, and I just didn't know what to say.'

'What the hell does it matter what you say? Tell her to mind her own damn' business, if you like.'

'Now, Joe. Mrs Delapole is a very nice woman, and she's always taken a friendly interest in you.'

'Well I didn't ask her to.'

'I have to tell her the truth, and it's so humiliating. It's so humiliating to be pitied for having a son like you.'

'I'm sorry, but I don't intend to order my life with the sole aim of impressing your neighbours.'

'But it isn't as if you were stupid and only fit for menial jobs. You have a good brain; you were always top of your form at school — far ahead of the Delapole boy, who was rather mediocre I always thought.'

'Mum, I am not at school now. If you want to talk to your inaccurate memory of a schoolboy, all right. But don't expect me to acknowledge your concept as myself.' He struggled for words, making chopping gestures with his right hand. 'It's as if somebody insisted on calling me Smith or Jones instead of my right name, and then wondered why I didn't respond.'

'Yes, I know, dear; of course I know you're not a child any more. But, you see, I want to feel as proud of you now as I did then. Other mothers can feel proud of their sons. I don't know why I'm the only one to have a problem child. I suppose it must be my fault. I must have slipped up somehow. Although the good God knows I've tried to be a good mother. I've worked for you and prayed for you. But I suppose I didn't work and pray hard enough.'

He said uncomfortably: 'Oh no, you've done everything right.'

'I can't have done everything right, or you wouldn't be in the mess you're in now. Oh, Joe, darling...' She held out her arms to him and cradled him back and forth. 'My only son.'

He was in a cramped position, the brim of her hat jabbing his cheek. He said, in what he tried to make an emotional tone: 'Darling Mum.'

'My own boy.'

'Mind the coffee, Mum, you're spilling it.'

'Oh yes...' She released him, and dabbed her eyes with her gloved knuckles.

For something to say, he remarked: 'Yes, I would have tidied the room if I'd known you were coming.'

She was saying: 'I should have thought you'd *want* a more interesting job. It would be so *exciting* to go abroad for the firm. I can quite understand that you'd get bored with a dull job, but surely one that involved travelling would be just the thing for you. The Delapole boy went to Germany, and he had free time to go around and see all the sights and everything. Mrs

Delapole showed me some snaps he'd taken of the Rhine Valley, and it looked absolutely beautiful, dear.'

Her thin face had a wan beauty as she spoke. A tremulous hope shone at the back of her eyes and flitted round her mouth. In spite of her physical frailty, she had indomitable willpower, love, and humility. She only needed a man's touch to bring out the joy which was in her. Being denied this touch, she had bowed her shoulders patiently and got on with the housework; But the timid joy was still there, waiting for the touch which could bring it to flower. When she spoke of things like the history in the Tower and the scenery of the Rhine Valley, there was a pathetic radiance in her face which could have transformed her if it had met an answering beam of love.

Beckett felt depressed. The feeling of certainty which he had experienced earlier when he was looking at the washstand, and the excitement of thinking about the problems of vitality versus boredom, had gone. His mother had destroyed it.

He did not disagree with what she said. On the contrary, he knew that he was wasting his life. But it was irritating when she told him something that he knew only too well already. It was more irritating when she judged him by standards, such as good jobs and sexual morality, which he himself considered irrelevant. He was indeed wasting his life, but not in the way she supposed. Her advice, therefore, was as meaningless as suggesting remedies for a cold in the head to a man who suffered from a broken arm.

She was fumbling in her handbag, producing a box of pills.

He said:'What's that?'

'I have to take them, three times a day, Dr Murchison said.'

'D'you want some water?'

'Yes, please, dear.'

He was irritated, feeling the pills to be a reproach directed at him. He handed her a cup of water with averted face, not watching her as she swallowed it.

She started to recount her illness, starting from her first symptoms of feeling a bit off-colour, and then continuing with the various visits of the doctor and what had been said on each visit, telling him how the family had managed to cook and housekeep and look after her.

Beckett, who found accounts of feminine ills boring and somewhat nauseating, hardly listened. He stared out of the window, commenting 'Yes' or 'No' or 'I see' whenever her voice paused.

'... and Aunty Anne was *so* kind,' she was saying. 'She came to see me three times and brought me grapes. I did so appreciate it. And Uncle Xavier and Aunt Margaret were very good, too.'

He nodded morosely, simultaneously bored by the doings of his family, and depressed by the implication of his callousness compared to the kind relations.

'Are you listening, Joe?'

'Yes, of course. It must have been terrible for you, Mum.'

'Sometimes I feel I can't reach you at all. It's a terrible thing to feel about my own child. But when I talk, you don't really listen, and when I ask you questions about your own life, you just grunt as if you can hardly bear to answer.'

'Do I? Sorry.'

'I *am* your mother, and it's only natural that I should be interested in your life, your job, your girl friends. But I can never get any information out of you at all. It's like talking to a wall trying to talk to you. And yet I'm sure you talk half the night to your friends.' She sighed. 'I suppose you think I'm just a boring middle-aged woman.'

'No. No, of course not.'

'Yes, you do.' Then she tried another tactic, saying in a renouncing, martyr voice: 'All right. I've done all I can for you, I've talked till I'm hoarse. From now on I just give up. You can ruin your life, you can go down the drain, for all I care. I give up. I'll just forget that I've got a son, I'll cut you out of my heart.' She smiled briskly at the space beside him, to demonstrate that she had already started the operation. 'Yes, I'll probably find it very easy once I've got used to the idea. It will be nice to only have myself to consider after all these years. It's about time I was able to be selfish for a change.'

Beckett was unimpressed. He knew she was acting. He pitied her clumsy attempts to act, and pitied her because her acting could not affect him.

She said: 'It will do you good to realize you can go too far with people, that the greatest love can be destroyed if you treat it too badly.'

'Yes, I'm sure it will.' Then he said: 'Well, I expect you're hungry, aren't you? Come on out and we'll have a meal.'

She demurred at first, because she did not want to be an expense to him. Then, when he insisted, she gave in.

He made an excuse to leave the room, and borrowed ten shillings from the Irishman. That, together with Ilsa's fifteen shillings, would be sufficient.

When he returned, his mother said: 'I didn't really mean that, darling.'

He smiled encouragingly at her. 'Didn't you?'

The next thing she said was: 'Are you going to put a tie on, dear?'

'No.'

'Oh.'

There was a pause. Then she said: 'I just thought you'd look nicer with a tie.'

'I'm all right without, aren't I?'

She touched the front of his shirt, pleading: 'Look nice for Mother, dear.'

In silence he buttoned the neck of his shirt, took a tie from the wardrobe and put it on. He turned towards her. 'Shall we go?'

He did not take her to the Paradine, the workmen's café he frequented, but to a smarter restaurant in Westbourne Grove. He had a warm feeling of protection towards her as he shortened his stride to match hers. Her hand was through his arm, and her bright eyes smiled up at him from below the brim of the antennae hat.

She warned him against habitually eating in cafés. She said that they heated the food up, which destroyed the vitamins. Continual café meals were bad for him, and would make him an easy prey for germs.

In the restaurant, she sat opposite him across the red-check tablecloth. Her hands, work worn, with the wedding ring dimmed by the years, touched the cutlery on either side of her plate. She turned her head. The line of her profile and neck was graceful and the hat brim cast a soft shadow. Then she looked at him with her timidly loving eyes.

They were thus smiling into each other's eyes when the French waitress served the food.

His mother's eyes achieved a final orgasm of love, then she said: 'I should brush your hair back from your forehead, dear. You look much nicer when you're tidy.'

Annoyed, he pushed the lock of hair back in such a way that it immediately fell forward again.

'Let Mother do it....' She stretched out her hand to touch his hair.

'Do leave me alone.'

'All right, dear. But you can look so nice when you take the trouble. It isn't a sign of genius to go round looking like a tramp, you know. It's quite possible to be intelligent *and* tidy.'

After the meal he escorted her to the Tube station. She was going to Acton, to Aunt Anne's. She suggested that he should come, too, but he invented an excuse.

Walking back alone, he felt depressed. It was always like that with his mother. Their remarks to each other, innocent on the surface, were really calculated to irritate in a subtle way. However much they tried, they could not resist the urge to irritate each other.

She judged him by standards which he did not acknowledge. Such things as jobs, important in her view, were merely incidentals in his. At best, a job he was doing seemed absurd; at worst, an immoral waste of time. Work was merely an annoying action to be got through with as little attention and energy wasted on it as possible in order to obtain sufficient money for cigarettes, rent and, food. He could never take a job seriously, it was merely so much time detracted from the important business of living.

Their different sets of values made communication between his mother and himself as impossible as if they spoke different languages. She had been a good mother, devoting her life to love and sacrifice for him. It was probably this which made him selfish in his dealings with her.

His thoughts wandered to his parents' bedroom at home. It was really his mother's room, reflecting her taste. His father had no taste and never noticed his surroundings. On the mantelpiece was a crucifix with her rosary twined round it, a picture of the Virgin Mary, a bottle of Lourdes water, and a blue-glass swan. These same things had always been there for as long as he could remember. They had been part of his childhood. He remembered once, at the age of two or three, rising early and creeping into his mother's bed. The curtains had been closed and the light which filtered through had been coloured pink by the cloth. This pretty, rose-tinted light had been his first association with his mother. The tinted light had established for him her femininity. Just as his father had first been established as a god-like being who had two eggs for his breakfast, while his mother and Granny Dolan had only one.

His mother had wanted him to be a priest. She had often said that she was living for the day on which she would first receive Communion from his hands. It had been a lasting blow to her when he had rejected, not only the priesthood, but the faith which was her whole life.

Beckett thought: Sorry, Mum, sorry.

In his room, he noticed one of her gloves lying on the bed. He stared at it unwillingly. It was a nuisance. He did not know whether to post it to her, which would mean the trouble of writing a letter and buying a large envelope, or whether to assume that she would buy a new pair, in which case he could throw it away. That presented a new problem. Did one callously throw away one's mother's glove?

For the moment he put it in the wardrobe. Then he stood with depression weighing heavily on him, wondering what on earth to do with the remainder of the evening.

Without money Beckett could no longer buy pets' pieces, and there were no more shillings for the gas meter. The dairy discontinued his milk because he had not paid the bill. For three days he lived on Camp Coffee Essence without sugar or milk, made with hot water from the bathroom geyser.

On the third day he lay on the bed and stared at the

pattern of blue-and-orange flowers on the wallpaper. He thought, as usual, of Dyce, for like a man with stomach-ache he could think of nothing else. Now that he was penniless, he felt the attraction of the money reward which Dyce had offered.

It seemed to him that most people had two choices. They either worked and earned money, or did not work and were penniless. It was, in fact, a choice between two evils, of starvation on one hand and a life wasted in performing boring tasks on the other. He thought angrily: Why the hell should I do either? Life is short. Why should it be spent unpleasantly?

He had no money, no food, no hope. He did not want to work. He did not want to do anything. He forced himself to go out for a walk. In the streets, his dead senses revived a little. The trees along the pavements and the neon ODEON sign gave one of those moments of sharp pleasure in being alive.

When he returned the room was twilit. Out of the corner of his eye he saw a baby's skull on the bed. He felt a shock of horror. When he turned to look he saw that it was not a baby's skull, but the fold of a shirt which he had tossed on the bed.

An acquaintance, casually met in Ledbury Road, gave him a tube of Thyrodine pills. Soon Beckett wrote in his notebook:

The official use of Thyrodine is for slimming. It acts by burning up the body's stored energy, thus reducing the need for food. However, the amount of energy released by T. is greater than the amount ordinarily released. This surplus energy goes to the brain, increasing mental activity and producing insomnia. Therefore, T. is often used by such people as students before an exam, and down-and-outs who can afford neither food nor a place to sleep.

He somehow got hold of small sums of money with which to buy cigarettes and occasional food, and took Thyrodine daily. At first the pills made him feel fine. His brain was active, turning out ideas like a works' conveyor belt on overtime. When he read, his mind was too active for the mere assimilation of words. It raced off at a tangent of criticism and ideas suggested by the text. He abandoned reading and, instead, filled his notebook with writings on various subjects from medieval history to the psychology of crime. He worked out chess problems on the portable set which he always carried in the pocket of his suedette zipper jacket.

The only adverse effect of the pills was that all sense-impressions seemed slightly offbeat, as if a gravitational pull had been lessened, thereby altering the relationship of objects to him and to each other.

After a week on Thyrodine the headaches began. A knife-pain shot through his brain. At nights he could not sleep, his mind was a dynamo which would not cease despite his physical exhaustion. His exhausted body seemed to be falling away from his relentlessly churning mind. He lay awake, unable to stop thinking, until the thin, acid light of morning brought the rattle of milk crates and the chorus of bird-song.

He compared the ideas represented by the various people he knew. Wainwright was the social man, with his leaflets, and his meetings like undergraduate rags. He loved and had faith in ordinary people. His energies were extroverted and concerned with material things.

Father Dominic was the political man. He despised the ordinary people, whom he considered fit only to be pressed into a semblance of order according to the blueprint devised by the few superior intelligences.

Gash was the religious man, shutting his senses to

the material world in order to concentrate on the God within him.

Beckett closed his eyes and saw the three as a triangle imposed on the surface of his brain. The three points of the triangle were variously served by the faithful masses who believed speeches and sermons; by men like Father Hogan with his peasant faith; by his own mother who cheerfully sacrificed her life for her erroneous belief in an after-life. They were rejected by the faithless, by Dyce and Ilsa who knew life to be meaningless and who retaliated by getting as many kicks out of it as possible while it lasted.

All three wanted Beckett's allegiance, but although he sympathized with all, he had faith in none. Yet he would have been happy to give allegiance. His was a serious nature which needed a meaning in life.

The thought of Dyce always returned, hitting him like a sick thud in the stomach. When he managed to get a few hours' sleep he dreamed of guns which either did not go off or which fired, instead of bullets, puff balls of smoke that exploded in slow motion.

Chapter 13

H E WOKE SUDDENLY to the feeling of terror. He did not know which way round the room was. He could see shapes, but could not recognize them because they were out of context.

Gradually, he became orientated. The objects fitted together into the recognizable pattern of the room. That shape was the edge of the curtain, the other was the wardrobe with his suitcase and a fringed lampshade on top.

He got out of bed and switched on the light. The sudden brightness was like waking to illness. There was some water in the kettle, and he poured it into the toothglass. His mouth was swollen and at first he could not feel the rim of the glass against his lips. Then there was the toothpaste taste of the water, and coldness going down into his stomach.

He realized that he was going to be sick. He grabbed his raincoat and groped down the unlit stairs.

In the lavatory, high tide beat in his giddy head. The sick scorched up into his mouth and nostrils. He vomited into the lavatory-pan round which his lover's arms were clasped.

Waves of heat broke out in sweat. His stomach went on heaving when there was nothing left to bring up: In between the heaves, he whimpered: 'Oh God, Oh God...'

Afterwards he sprawled on the floor, his forehead pressed against the base of the lavatory pedestal. The air had a rushing sound, like a radio tuned to a closed station. The room was a magnified heart, expanding and contracting. Its pulsations throbbed in the white pedestal, the walls, the sports page on the floor.

In the morning the Irishman stood in Beckett's room. He was muscular as a labourer. He had a glass of Guinness in one hand and a shaving brush in the other. He did not believe in work either. 'Consider the lilies of the field,' he roared in quotation from his battered New Testament. Then he advised that if Beckett was ill he should see a doctor.

Beckett, with ill body tough as whipcord, leaped out of bed and declared that he had no intention of seeing a doctor, and that occasional attacks of sickness did not bother him.

In fact Beckett was one of the people who feel very fit when they are ill. He always felt well when he was hangover-ill, as he was in the ensuing days of Thyrodine and little food. His body was planed away to its essential core of toughness. His senses were sharpened and his nerves exposed. There was a sort of relaxation and peace that resulted from exhaustion.

He went for long walks. In the streets, he was more aware of people than before, because he wanted something from them: food and money. The faces were all an adventure, as ships are an adventure to a pirate.

Often he walked in Kensington Gardens, liking the feathery sunlight on the grass. In his mouth and nostrils was a flavour like soda-water that belonged to sickness. Sometimes he went to Speakers' Corner where he engaged in arguments with strangers. Sometimes he went to Brompton Oratory because he liked the Victorian cherubs that ornamented the candelabra. Sometimes he went to Park Lane because it was an expensive area.

Once he looked through an office window and saw a man at a desk engaged in filing some papers. The sight of the man's nine-to-five servitude made Beckett exhilarate in his own freedom. He was ill and penniless, but he was free. He tramped by night as well as by day.

One evening he saw Ilsa in the street. She was wearing her teenager rig of jeans and a check shirt. Her hair was in a skimpy pony-tail, as she had done it at art school. It looked attractive with her ill, adult face. It accentuated her sharp cheekbones and the greyish shadows under her eyes. She was laughing outside an espresso-bar with a gang of arty teenagers. He saw her give one of the boys a sharp punch in the arm, then skip out of range. Her laughter was strident and taunting.

Beckett crossed the road to avoid her. He did not want to talk to her, or to her new man, or to her rowdy friends.

Sometimes he spent the night in Covent Garden, which smelled like an orchard. There was an all-night café for the market workers, with yellow-topped tables with bottles of O.K. Sauce on them, and thick crockery. He sat in a corner, grim and unspeaking like a secret agent. Once a drunk lurched in, with a Christ message of love for all humanity. The message was frustrated by the drunk's inability to express it coherently.

Beckett the tramp wandered down dustbin night streets, stole milk and a loaf from a crate outside a café, and saw the dawn break over London. He walked with solitude round his shoulders like a cloak.

When he returned to his room, he laid his hard body between the sheets stained with loneliness, and lay sleepless through the sunny morning as though his eyes had no lids.

He received a letter from his father, written on Civil Service notepaper in office ink. His father, like him, seldom wrote letters.

The letter said that his mother had leukemia although she did not know it, and had only a few months to live.

Beckett read the letter again. He waited for it to produce an effect on him, waited to feel. But he felt nothing. It was like watching to see which way a cat jumped and then finding that it did not jump at all.

He thought that his mother should be told that she was dying. He deplored the conspiracy of well-meant lies that insulted the strength, dignity, and intelligence of the dying. The faith of a Catholic should be respected; she should be told in order that she could prepare herself for death within the Church. Often, doctors opposed calling the priest to give Extreme Unction because the sacrament amounted to telling the patient that he or she was dying. Beckett disliked this practice of shielding the patient instead of honouring religious beliefs.

Then he realized that, as usual, he was riding an intellectual issue, abstracting an argument from a human situation.

A wasp zigzagged round the room with spiteful drone. It buzzed against the window, its wings visible only as speed. Beckett spent some time stalking it, and finally swatted it dead with a Penguin book.

He hoped his mother never suspected that for humans, as for insects, death was the end, the eternal cessation of consciousness. He hoped she never doubted, never lost her comforting faith in God and immortality.

Was death instantaneous? Or was there time for a moment of truth between existence and non-existence; a moment in which she would realize that God and immortality were delusions?

He regretted his many past arguments with his mother about religion. In these arguments, his prig voice had used reason against her faith. She had not been convinced. Out-argued, she had said: 'I can't argue. I just *know* there's a God. I just *know* Catholicism is the true faith.' Her subjective conviction could not be shaken by arguments.

Now, Beckett hoped that her conviction was as unshaken as it had seemed. He hoped that he had not made cracks that would widen under the strain of her slow dying. He did not want her to die in the wasteland of doubt.

He snapped his fingers as an idea occurred to him. He could ensure her faith by pretending to be recon- verted himself.

Then he had his master idea. He could take her to Lourdes. That would show that he believed, and also the visit to the shrine might cure her. He had heard that leukemia was psychosomatic, like asthma, eczema, ulcers, and other illnesses. If so, it might be cured psychosomatically. If, in fact, his mother believed that the shrine could cure her, this belief might enable her to cure herself.

Auto-suggestion, Beckett thought. It's cured other pilgrims at Lourdes...

He paced up and down, snapping his fingers and fre- quently exclaiming aloud: 'That's it! That's it!'

Recently, he had heard a modern-jazz record named *I'm Hooked*. Now the record seemed to be playing inside his head. He moved in the dope-taker's way he had acquired, as if jerked by the spastic compulsive rhythm, snapping his fingers to the beat.

He realized that he did not really believe that Lourdes would cure her. He did not believe that auto- suggestion would work. His true motive was that, by paying for the pilgrimage, he would be buying off his guilt-feelings towards his mother. He could not be accused, by others or by himself, of unfilial behaviour when he had taken the trouble and expense of the journey. However, whatever his ulterior motive, he would go through with it.

He said aloud: 'Expense!' He flopped on the bed, and

then in the same movement, like an acrobat, leaped to his feet again. He stood slackly, but still with the muscular coordination of an acrobat, with his hand pressed against his brow.

Then the jazz inside his mind, the pulse-beat hiss of the brushes on the drum skin, quickened again. He jerked in time to it. He could not turn off the mental gramophone; he was compelled to listen to the music. He took out a cigarette-paper and his dog-end tin, and rolled up a couple of the stubs that poverty had reduced him to. His compulsively jerking hand spilled some of the tobacco.

I'm Hooked. He was hooked all right, and could not get down from the music any more than a coat can get down from a coat-hook.

The thin cigarette rolled and lit, he inhaled, and said aloud: 'Don't despair. I'll get some money.'

Money, Must get some money. Money.

He heard footsteps mounting the stairs. By the tread, and the heavy, righteous breathing, he knew it was his landlady. He supposed she was coming to demand the overdue rent, did not move, in case a floorboard creaked. Only his head continued to jerk to the beat. His eyes were clenched, and his face set in the rigid expression of jazz-prayer.

The landlady knocked at the door.

Beckett heard all her movements, and at the same time kept touch with the rhythm which was fainter now, a tenuous thread.

She knocked again, louder, and demanded: 'Mr Beckett!'

He opened dead-staring gangster eyes, watching the door. Just let her come in, the old cow, the old bitch! he thought. Just let her come in, and I'll slaughter her. Smoke from his cigarette tendrilled up his drooping hand.

Outside the door, she breathed heavily. Boards creaked. She was obviously doing something. Finally a piece of paper appeared under the door. Beckett waited until her footsteps had receded, then he picked up the note.

Dear Mr Beckett, If you do not pay me the rent you owe me before Tomorrow Tuesday, I will call in the Police.

Yours faithfully,
Mrs Ackley.

Beckett refolded the paper tightly. Then, thinking, he tapped it against his palm. He decided that he was pleased on the whole. The woman had forced the issue; he would have to leave this place. He was glad, because now his fight for money would start from zero, which seemed to present more challenges and possibilities.

In the evening he dismantled the room, separating his belongings from the litter. His clothes, clean and dirty together, were bundled in the wardrobe drawer in an octopus tangle of sleeves and socks. He removed the drawer and tipped the contents bodily into his suitcase.

A canvas grip contained all his papers, notebooks, journals, and a pair of old plimsolls.

The larder was empty except for a sticky cough-linctus bottle, a restaurant's salt and pepper, an empty Batchelors peas tin, and a comic birthday-card somebody had sent him last year.

His books ranged from heavyweights to slim paperbacks. They were arranged along the window-ledge, with the surplus ones stacked on the floor beneath the window. Some of his books had been borrowed by friends and never returned. On the other hand, he had acquired books in this manner himself. Some bore the labels of public libraries or LCC evening classes; one was rubber-stamped 'Mission to Seamen".

'So many damn *books!*' He filled a pillow-case with them, stuffed others in his raincoat pockets, and piled the remainder into the china bowl with its pattern of roses.

The work of dismantling and packing took him two hours. He chucked the litter on to the tin tray under the gas ring. Then stood with shoulders hunched, fingers snapping, feet apart like a Chicago gunman's, surveying the ring of gunned-down objects around him.

'So much bloody *gear*! How on earth did I collect so much bloody *gear*?'

It had seemed to him that he lived simply with few possessions, but when it came to moving, he found he was loaded with cumbersome objects.

He got on with the work. During the packing he made the following remarks, at intervals:

'*Christ* Jesus... .'
(Singing)   'I can't live without ya,
                Nights, I dream about ya —'
'Now where did I put...'

At midnight he crept down the stairs carrying the suit-case and grip.

He knew so well the compound odours of minestrone soup, bedsitter loneliness, public lavatories, and dusty polish that impregnated the orange blooms of the wall-paper. He knew the beige linoleum route to the front door; and the sameness of the light through the fan-light, always afternoon light even when it was morning. The same unclaimed mail was on the hall table; the Vernons Pools envelope, the detergent coupons, the religious tract headed AWAKE!, the Bournemouth postcard addressed to a tenant long left.

All these things were the chemicals of evocation. It seemed strange that he was leaving them for good.

He carried his cases to Gash's house, and rapped on the window.

When the old man admitted him, Beckett said: 'Can I leave my gear at your place? I've got to do a moonlight flit because I can't pay the rent.'

'Yes, certainly you can. But I'm sorry to hear —'

Beckett interrupted like gunfire: 'There's some more stuff, which I'll have to make another journey for. Rather a lot in all, I'm afraid. Do you mind?'

'I don't mind how much there is. I'll be delighted to look after it for you. But I'm sorry to hear you're in financial troubles. You've helped me by giving me money and food in the past, and I feel most upset that I can't repay you. Believe me, I'd pay your rent for you if I could.'

Beckett snapped with impatience and honesty: 'No, no, it doesn't matter to me about leaving the room. It's of no importance whether I've got somewhere to live or not.'

'Have you anywhere to stay?'

'No, no, but it doesn't matter.'

'You would be welcome to stay with me. We could halve the blankets.'

'No, really.' Then Beckett, under the old man's calm gaze, became aware of his own tension. His nerves and tiredness were making him irritable, so that Gash's kindly questions seemed as irritant as mosquitoes.

Gash said: 'It's difficult to live in England without a home, an address. For one thing there is the climate. For another, our society lacks the tradition of charity to mendicants and recognition of the value of contemplatives.'

'I'm not a contemplative,' Beckett snapped. He added: 'I'll bring the rest of my things. It's very kind of you to let me keep them here.'

He made a second journey. He had knotted the ankles of his denim jeans to form a kitbag, and had stuffed things into it. A frying-pan handle and a tail of damp towel protruded from the top. His other arm hugged the china bowl of books. A paperback on witchcraft, with a cover depicting witches dancing against the full moon, threatened to slide off the pile.

On his third journey he brought the radio and a large saucepan containing shoe-brush and polish, a roll of insulating tape, Vick Inhaler, constipation pills, a threaded needle stuck in the torn-off flap of a Weights packet, one grey nylon sock, a screwdriver, and the alarm clock ticking on its back.

The fourth journey was his last. He had left all his gear with Gash, keeping only his suèdette jacket with his sponge-bag in the pocket. He felt enormously relieved that he had managed his exodus without waking the landlady.

He walked the streets. He felt, simultaneously, exhaustion and vitality. It was as if his brain and body had been sliced in two down the centre and each half was inhabited by a different being. The right half was vital, the left half was exhausted. The sensation of physical division was strange.

He had the cotton-wool awareness and exposed nerves of a hangover. He could either collapse into the parting waves of sleep or riproar to manic action. The combination of physical exhaustion and nervous tension made him stumble with weariness, and yet contain the potentiality of meeting any challenge, to dance or to walk frenetically at a second's notice.

He slumped along, then suddenly uttered an inward scream and started to leap, flailing his arms. Alone and manic he exhilarated in the empty streets and in the knife cold that sliced him.

Without luggage or property, he had the freedom of the night. He contained the stars, but they were still in the sky. The stars were in him, but also above him and around him.

He passed a house that had a rose garden. He stepped over the wall and stole a red rose. The smell of the flower was pleasant, making him feel happy, as if some friend had given him a garden.

As Beckett leapt and gloried along the streets, he felt wonder at the rows of sleeping people inside their boxes. He seized a stone to hurl at a window. His arm was back, ready to fling the stone which would awaken a sleeper to co-experience his joy. Then his stance slackened and his mouth opened in silent laughter. Soon he was laughing aloud, sharing his enormous complicity with the heavens. The stone dropped from his hand.

He went on down the street. He said: 'God, I'm so tired!'

At the railway station it was still artificial day. Officials, snack-machines, and timetables operated.

Travellers, weighted with luggage and anxiety, hurried to their reserved sleepers. Their footsteps in the half-empty station rang metallic like footsteps in a prison.

Lovers parted with kisses and magazines. There were groups of Servicemen. Along the benches rows of shabby men and women sat like refugees.

A gang of teenagers, with shaggy heads, sloppy pullovers, and tight jeans, were off on a rave by milk train to the seaside. Two of the boys carried guitars, and a girl was drinking beer from a bottle. Beckett half-expected to see Ilsa among them but she was not there.

He went into the waiting-room, which was often used as a doss-house by the homeless. He sank down on to the green leatherette bench. In the seaside poster, a girl in a white swim suit laughed: 'Have the holiday of your life!' into a caption balloon.

The poster made him realize the degree of his dissociation from normal life. He could hardly believe in the millions of respectable people who worked in factories, offices, or shops for fifty weeks of the year, and then dutifully entrained for the seaside for the remaining two.

He felt as dissociated as a Martian. He looked round the waiting-room to see if there were any other Martians.

The three soldiers were healthy lads in uniform and were genuine travellers.

The two men opposite were engaged in an intimate argument. The elder wore a navy duffel coat and a Paisley cravat. He had a hollowed, intelligent face, like a woman novelist. He had womanish skin and womanish, close-set eyes. He was saying: 'But surely... one ought to take into account, don't you think... a man of Adrian's temperament...'

His companion, a curly-haired lad with the physique of a wrestler, merely grunted.

'I...I mean, *if* one is a reasonable, adult human being...'

'Well, I'm dead choked about it. So lay off me, will you!'

The older man gestured humorous resignation with his cigarette-holder.

In the corner sat a small man of unkempt appearance. His fat, unshaven jaws were like a tramp's. One of his eyes had only a white, and was half closed. His good eye stared malevolently round, and he muttered: 'Bloody lot of no-goods. Look at you, layabouts. When did you last have your shoes repaired? And you, you over there? And you? No self respect, or you wouldn't be here. And do you know why you're all a lot of stinking

199

layabouts? Because you're shy of work, I'll tell you. Wouldn't do an honest day's work to save your lives.'

An Italianate youth lay full length on the bench, with his narrow, blue-black head supported on his clasped hands. He was sharply dressed in a vee-neck pullover, tight jeans, and shoes with pointed toes. He had the tough, cynical expression of one who intends to get rich quick, and doesn't mind doing a bit of laying about and hanging around in the meantime.

One man was asleep, clasping a brown-paper parcel. Beckett knew him by sight from Mick's Café. He was middle-aged, dressed like a bank manager with a homburg hat. Only his mad, sad eyes, and the, tautness of the skin over his cheekbones, showed that he was a gentle tramp.

Beckett was unable to relax. He drummed his feet on the floor. His eyes were sore and tiredness was a permanent frown between his brows. He furiously twiddled the stem of the rose. Then he gave an exasperated sigh, laid the rose on the bench beside him, and strummed on his knees instead.

The seaside poster irritated him. He would have liked to smash its glass. Everybody and everything irritated him. The one-eyed man was still muttering. 'When did you last have your shoes repaired? I've asked many people that, and I'm asking you. No, you can't answer, because you're shy of work. Haven't got any self respect.'

The three soldiers were trying to shove each other off the bench, guffawing and uttering inarticulate half-sentences. One exclaimed: 'Let's give 'em the regimental song of the Fird Foot 'n' Marf....'

A hand gripped Beckett's shoulder. 'Joe!'

He looked up to see Dyce standing over him.

'Come on,' Dyce said, 'let's get out of here.'

Beckett jumped up and followed Dyce out.

Dyce inserted coins into the Auto-Snack, jabbing the red button. 'I'm getting a ham sandwich. And for you?'

The thought of food nauseated Beckett, tightening his stomach. 'I'm not hungry.'

'I'll get two packets, anyway. I've been to an awful dance. It's like playing tennis, dancing with some of those hefty hearty deb girls. Still, they provide some decent food and drink, and you get to know people.' Dyce gave him the cellophane-wrapped sandwiches. 'Hang on to these, will you?' He slapped his pockets. 'I came here for cigarettes. Run clean out. Now where the hell is the —'

'Machine over there.'

'Fine.' Dyce strode forward, saying: 'Yes, I passed the waiting-room and happened to see you in there. What on earth were you doing? Not travelling anywhere, are you?'

The cigarettes bought, they started for Dyce's car, which was parked outside.

'I lost my room. I'm broke. I had to stay somewhere.'

Dyce stopped, and gave him a hard, long look, like a recruiting officer assessing men for physical fitness and psychological stability. Finally he said: 'You look a wreck, man. Your nerves are all gone to pieces. I've never seen anyone degenerate as quickly as you have.'

'That's not so. I'm stronger than you think. There's a core of hardness inside me, a hard core inside me,' Under the influence of the pills, Beckett's words were like an express train. 'Some things do not touch me, they are nothing to do with me. For instance, if I have a job, it is nothing to do with me. If I owe rent, it is nothing to do with me. If I stole five pounds, it would be nothing to do with me. For me, the only sins, the only things I feel moral about, are the things which soften my centre. For instance, laziness, boredom, wasting my time in trivialities, I regard as sins.'

Dyce opened the car doors. They got in and sat talking in the parked car. 'How did you get in such a state, anyway?'

Beckett's express-train mind was now racing in another direction. 'My mother is very ill. She is going to die, they think. I want to take her to Lourdes. You know, the shrine there.' He started off about auto-suggestion, a fusillade of words dealt with miracles and faith healers. He had once known a hypnotist who had cured a woman of asthma, but it had been useless because the woman had later developed cancer. The hypnotist had refused to practise any more, because he said he could only change the physical symptoms, not root out the psychological cause.

'Then why fool around at a useless shrine? You know that sort of twaddle helps nobody except the local hoteliers and relic-sellers.'

Beckett put his rose in the glove-rack on top of the AA books. 'Only ex-Catholics can attack the Church. From people like you it is merely ridiculous, because you have no conception of the greatness of the structure you are attacking. I mean —'

Dyce cut him short. 'Not another spate of words, please.'

'Well, give me a cigarette.'

Dyce did not answer. Then, very deliberately, he peeled the cellophane from the new packet, transferred the cigarettes to his case, and held the case in front of Beckett without looking at him.

Beckett fumbled out a cigarette. When it was lit, he inhaled greedily, relaxing in the comfortable seat.

Dyce was wearing a dark, well-tailored suit. His body, hard and commando-fit, emanated vitality that was almost tangible, like heat from a radiator. Beckett felt shabby and sick by contrast. The contrast was symbolized in the two packets of ham sandwiches, which

Dyce had casually bought and neglected to eat. Beckett, to whom every penny was important, could not comprehend this casual treatment of food and money.

Dyce said: 'It's idiotic, this sleeping in waiting-rooms. To start with, the police do a nightly check there. If you aren't a bona-fide traveller with a ticket they want your name and address and your reason for being there. And, secondly, if you are really set on this crazy scheme of —'

'Of what?'

'Perhaps it isn't such a crazy scheme after all, taking your mother on holiday. No, on second thoughts, I think it's a good idea, old boy.'

'Do you? I don't.'

'Now look here. I know the way it works out, all this sleeping rough and the rest of it. Seen it too many times. And it's bad. While you're sleeping rough and looking like a tramp, you can't get a job. And if you don't have a job, you can't pay for a room and so have to sleep rough. It's a vicious circle.'

'Yes, I know.' Beckett leant across and pressed the hooter, which uttered a two-note war-cry.

Dyce frowned. 'If I were an employer, I certainly wouldn't hire you. Not only on your appearance, but on your past record. I'd want a man who was smart, keen, a hard worker. And when I received your references...' Dyce held imaginary papers between finger and thumb, 'I'd find that your previous employers had described you as unreliable, uninterested, habitually late, and forever taking days off under the pretence of illness.' He made the gesture of dropping the references into a waste-paper basket. 'No, I certainly wouldn't employ you. And nor would anyone else. You're going to find it very difficult to get another job.'

'I don't want another job.'

'The rest of the community have to work.'

'Yes, but many of them enjoy it. At Union Cartons there was a girl who typed invoices; a boring enough job I should have thought. She didn't *need* this job, as her husband was earning easily enough for both of them. She said she worked because she liked it. She enjoyed the companionship of the office, and would have felt at a loose end if she'd stayed at home all day.'

Dyce said: 'Look, you're ill. You need to rest up somewhere.'

'No I don't.'

'You need food, and sleep, and to smarten up your appearance to get back some self respect. If you don't get these things, you're going to collapse in the street and wake up in Paddington General Hospital.'

'I'm all right.'

'I know what I'm talking about. I've seen it happen before. I've kicked around a bit and I've seen it happen to plenty of people. One was a girl, nice kid, but a tramp, I wouldn't touch her.' Dyce turned on him. 'Is that what you want? Do you want a girl? Some fat mother type, like Georgia, who'll take you in, and stroke your suffering brow, and feed you up, and murmur: "Poor boy, what you must have been through"?'

Beckett said impatiently: 'I don't know what you're talking about. You irritate me.'

'I'm just trying to tell you how a woman would behave. She'd look after you and sympathize with you. And it would be just about the worst thing she could do.'

Beckett pressed the hooter again. He experienced, rather than merely heard, its sound. When he tried to express this experience, the only words he could summon were: It's triumphant!' This was inadequate, so he tried again, expressing the intensity of his inner knowledge by saying the words passionately. *'It's triumphant!'*

'Maybe,' Dyce said curtly. 'Now get this, Joe. I could give you money now, this instant. I could provide you with food and a place to stay. And if I was a false friend, if I was weak enough to act emotionally instead of having the strength to act for your good, I would give you money. But I'm not going to give you money. You're on your own, and it's a service to you to make you realize it. If you want money from me, you've got to earn it, not lie back on my charity.'

'Yes, yes, I understand.'

'Good. Someone like Georgia would help you, but in return you would have to become soft and sloppy, so that her mother-love could feed on your weakness. Well, I say, keep your guts. Have the guts to either starve alone, or earn money the hard way.'

Beckett got out of the car.

Dyce said through the open window: 'Well, you know my address if you decide to take up my offer. Needless to say, I'll give you a cash sum down if you do.'

Watching the scarlet car speed away, Beckett remembered that he had left the rose on the glove-rack. Momentarily, he felt regret. Then he returned to the waiting-room.

The next day, lying on the gentle lawn in Holland Park, he knew that Dyce was right. He must either get money or starve.

Suddenly, he had an image of his mother's face. She turned her head and smiled. The image was very clear; he could see everything, from the way she had her hair to the flowered overall over her cardigan. For some reason, he had the impression that she was standing by the kitchen table cutting sandwiches for a picnic. There was no reason why the idea of a picnic should occur to him, and he concluded that the image was a childhood memory. He must have seen her smile in

that way, wearing that overall, and cutting sandwiches. They had often had family picnics.

He thought: She shouldn't die, she shouldn't die! She
had so much love: for God, for her family, for simple
things like flowers that could make her face light up.
Why should she die when she belonged to love and
therefore to life?

Agonized, he thought: Why should she die? She's so
good.

The emotion made him feel physically sick. He
groaned, and banged his head on the ground like a man
in pain.

Chapter 14

GROSVENOR COURT GARDENS was a block of service flats. A taxi drew up and a couple alighted. The man was corpulent, with greedy eyes and fat lips. The girl was about twenty-five, with a hard, made-up little face and pearl-coloured hair. Her black suit had a lace jabot, and a diamond brooch on the lapel.

Beckett followed them up the drive to the flats. He did not envy their wealth. He had a benevolent attitude to the wealthy, almost as if he owned them. He could, however, understand Dyce's envy. To Dyce, the wealthy had got more counters in the game than he had, and as such were a challenge and an insult.

The revolving doors led into an entrance hall with fern-patterned panelling. Beckett joined the couple to wait for the lift.

The couple spoke only once. The man said: 'The Van Houtens are coming at seven.'

'I thought it was half past.'

'No, seven.'

They got into the lift and glided silently upwards. The lift was filled with the girl's Chanel Number Five perfume. Beckett accidentally met her eyes in the mirror; kitten-blue, outlined in black pencil.

The lift stopped at the second floor. The man waited for the girl to alight first, but she said: 'I'm going up to Peggy's. She borrowed my white stole.'

'Well, don't stay nattering to her. I want you to hand round the drinks.'

The man got out, leaving Beckett and the girl in the lift. Without looking at her, he reached his hands towards her.

Her hand came to meet his, and they gripped. The next moment she was in his arms, with her pearl-coloured hair resting against his shoulder. They held each other close, as if to comfort and protect. Then she raised her small, expensive face to be kissed.

When the lift stopped and the automatic doors opened, she said: 'This is my floor,' and got out.

Beckett took the lift down again to the third floor. Flat 34 was at the end of the corridor. He rang the bell, and heard the double chime sound within.

Dyce opened the door almost immediately. 'Well, here you are, old boy. Come in.'

The living-room had smart modern furniture. The effect was impersonal, like a hotel room. The suite was bi-coloured in lime-green and grey. Radiogram, cocktail cabinet, television, and a pile of American magazines completed the décor. There was central heating, and wall lights with fan-shaped shades.

'Make yourself at home,' Dyce said. He moved like a combatant, easy and relaxed, but with preparedness always there like a hand resting lightly on a holster. Beckett had noticed this before. Dyce, entering a place, would scan it swiftly, in the manner of one long practised in coolly assessing vantage, danger, and cover, before issuing the command. Now Dyce was moving around the room, mixing drinks, and lowering the volume of the television. On the screen a troupe of girls in spangles and top hats were doing a dance routine. Then he took Beckett into the bedroom to show him the ultraviolet-ray lamp. 'My latest gadget. Ultraviolet rays and exercise. That's the way to keep fit. A man gets soft and sloppy in easy living conditions like these, if he doesn't discipline himself to keep in tip-top form. Look at the other men in these flats. Fat and flabby. All the exercise they get is lifting phones and getting into taxis.

Ugh. They can't even love their mistresses without taking vitalizing pills.'

They returned to the living-room. Dyce began to boast of his recent sexual conquests. Then he went on to talk of the flats, 'The front flats are the classiest, but the back are most popular because they have fire escapes.' He explained, in case Beckett had missed the point: 'I never met so many crooks as I have since I moved in here. They all run rackets. One type owns four houses which he lets to call-girls. Exorbitant rents, of course. No wonder he likes to have a fire-escape handy.' The tone of his boasting turned back to sex again. 'I've got this deb, the Hon. Pamela Watson-Stott. Daddy and Mummy have a town flat, and a house in Hampshire. They don't know about me yet, but Pam is taking me down to meet them one weekend. Have to go carefully with these deb types, though. One moment they worship you; the next they go all high horse and treat you like a serf.' He added: 'Not me, though. She tried treating me like a serf once and I slapped her haughty, vacant face.'

Beckett exclaimed wildly: 'Will you come to the point? I'm here because we're planning a murder, aren't I?'

Dyce leaned forward in his armchair, his hands on his knees, the flicker flames of excitement like careful madness in his eyes. Neither man spoke.

Then Dyce got up, switched on the anglepoise reading light on the desk, and arranged some papers round it. 'Take a look at these.'

When Beckett stood up he realized that the drinks had affected him faster than usual, because of the Thyrodine and lack of food.

'This is a map of Sealing, the country town where my aunt lives. Here is Upper Lane, on the outskirts of the town. Her house, Woodstock, is on the exact spot here...' Dyce marked an X.

Because of the central heating, the atmosphere had a hard, dry heat. Cigarette-smoke curled in the light of the anglepoise. Beckett felt as if he were suspended in space. He tried to understand the map, but could see only the shape of the paper, which made a wall against understanding. He shut his eyes for a moment, and wrenched his mind into working order.

Dyce was now displaying a sketch plan of the house, and explaining that this back door had a glass pane missing, and that this was the room where the deaf companion slept. His voice was tense with excitement. His hand, holding the cigarette, stabbed repeatedly at the plan. 'You will be absolutely safe. There will be nothing to connect you with the crime. And as for me, I shall be weekending in Hampshire, with Pamela's family, with people to vouch for my presence there all the time.' He winked. 'Even in bed. Pamela said she'd get me the room next to hers.'

Dyce then proceeded to explain the whole plan in detail. He said that he had often stayed up the entire night, pacing round the flat, sweating with fever and concentration as he had worked out the minutest details of his project. He now made Beckett repeat those details until both of them had everything firmly fixed in their minds. Beckett was accurate and quick on the uptake; his mind raced in pace with Dyce's.

They bent over the sketch again. Dyce went on talking, lighting fresh cigarettes and rapping them on the cigarette-case before lighting them. He had removed his jacket and wore rolled shirt-sleeves and loosened tie. Behind the blue haze of smoke he looked like the dealer in a poker game.

Beckett understood and anticipated everything that Dyce said. Simultaneously, he had a brilliant image of Dyce as he was at that moment, with his features decisive like a Red Indian's. The hard glare of the light showed the place where his hair was thinning and the dark circles of sweat on the underarms of his nylon shirt.

Still talking, Dyce crossed to the drink cabinet. 'It doesn't matter that we have been seen together. Because a man's aunt dies, there is no reason to suspect his every acquaintance.'

'What about Jacko? He is a link between us and might talk.'

'Not he. Every man has his price, and Jacko's is low. He can be bought with money and with the sort of tolerance a man gives to a dog who follows him up the street,' Dyce said, grinning into the mirror over the cabinet. Then he spun round. He was pointing a service revolver at Beckett's stomach. 'Don't move.'

Beckett did not move.

'Have you ever seen a man die with a bullet in his guts?'

'No.'

'Would you like to have one in yours?'

The essential was to keep calm. Beckett said easily: 'Naturally not.'

Dyce released the safety-catch. 'Why don't you take it from me? I won't stop you. Just walk towards me and take it.'

Beckett still did not move.

'It isn't loaded.'

'Isn't it?'

'That is what you don't know,' Dyce said. 'I tell you it isn't, but I might be lying. Why don't you walk towards me and take it?'

'All right.' Beckett started to walk. He thought: So this is what fear is. When he reached Dyce, he touched his hand lightly and Dyce gave him the revolver without demur.

Then Dyce exploded into his exuberant, manic laughter.

The revolver was loaded all right. Beckett raised it, aimed at the window, and would have fired had not Dyce interposed, seizing his wrist. They struggled briefly and the revolver fell on the cushion of a chair. They did not pick it up, but stood glaring at each other without speaking.

Then Dyce said: 'Stop it! What do you want to do? Bring everybody running to find out what the noise was? Is that what you want?'

'I want some fresh air.'

'Are you drunk?' Dyce peered at him. 'No, you are ill. You look terribly ill.'

'I am neither drunk nor ill.'

'Tell you what, we'll go out on the balcony for a bit. Wait while I stow the papers away.'

Beckett forced himself to keep control. After a few seconds it was all right. He picked up the revolver, and replaced the catch. Then he put it in his pocket and kept his fist tightly round it.

The balcony was reached through the kitchen. Sitting on one of the canvas chairs, Beckett had to admit that Dyce was justifiably proud of his balcony. The cool air was like a balm, an invisible hand on his forehead. Summer blessing, driven from the streets, lived in the leafy trees behind Grosvenor Court Gardens. He thought that if he owned this flat, he would sit out here in the evenings and look at the trees and at the distant road with its necklace of lights.

Dyce said: 'That business of mine, when I was fooling around. I could say that I was doing it to test your nerve, but it wouldn't be true. I'm a bit of a bloody sadist....' He sounded as if he was going to continue, but instead fell silent.

Beckett said inconsequentially: 'This is a very pleasant place.'

'The Army ruined me for civilian life, you know. Oh,

I know thousands of others were in the same position, having to settle down to a boring routine. And it didn't seem to affect them, they settled down all right. I happened to be one of the unlucky ones. I can't settle. Sometimes I wish there would be another war. I'd enlist like a shot.'

'The next war will be a nuclear war.'

'Yes, I know. No soldiers, just some official or other pushing a button. That is why I support nuclear disarmament. Not because I'm a pale-faced pacifist, but because I don't want a war that has no place for me in it.'

Beckett suddenly liked Dyce, forgetting his irritation at Dyce's old-boy mannerisms. He understood Dyce's recklessness and thirst for life. Ilsa also had this thirst for life, which was also a desire for annihilation. Ilsa danced and drank and shouted and told lies in order that she should not think and face her own vacuum. Ilsa lived with Katey because she could not stand being alone for five minutes. He said: 'You remind me a bit of Ilsa.'

'You don't understand. No bloody female's psychology is anything like mine.'

'All right, it was only a thought.'

Dyce said: 'I still remember the first man I killed. I was surprised. I fired and he fell down. I hadn't expected him to fall down, and I was surprised.'

The garage block was below their balcony. Beckett watched a car being driven out. It was a deluxe American model, with shark fins and green windows like an aquarium. 'I can't imagine having enough money to own a car like that.' He got up and went into the kitchen, where he poured out a glass of water.

Dyce followed him in. 'We will have enough money, though, if all goes well, as it must do. I think of money a lot. All those notes, in wage packets, over counters, wagered on tracks, starting businesses, buying shares, making million-pound deals, influencing everything from sex to religion and politics. Small amounts made from selling goods or services, large amounts made pure, I mean money made from money. I was brought up in a slum. I didn't have this public-school accent all my life. As a kid I spoke Cockney. But I didn't hate the rich. On the contrary I was glad they existed. My ambitions and interest weren't aroused by the Welfare State, and "fair shares for the workers" kind of crap. It was the rich who aroused my ambition, and that's why I was glad they existed. Your pal Wainwright enrages me. Middle-class bloody novelist. What right has he to be a socialist? He thinks that all workers want to abolish capitalism. Well, I was working class, and I didn't want to abolish capitalism, I wanted to be one of the capitalists.'

Something in Beckett reached fever pitch. He strode through the flat, talking at a fast pace, accompanying his words with chopping gestures with his right hand. 'When I lost my belief in God, the balance of my life changed. Before, life was weighted down by the prospect of eternity. Now the weight is removed and life flies upwards as free and shortlived as a balloon. Of course many men, if they don't believe in God believe in society instead, which amounts to much the same thing, as religious laws are generally only sensible social safeguards. So if he is a good member of society, he will continue to act in a moral manner. But that depends on his regarding society as a mutual help co-operative system. He may, on the other hand, regard it as a grabbing contest, and a survey of history and politics and business and crime will strengthen this view. In this case, he is free not only because he disbelieves the God myth, but because he is also sceptical of the social myth.' Beckett leapt in the air. 'For the duration of his short life he is completely free to do as he likes.'

'You're quite right,' Dyce said. Then he enquired: 'Are you on benze?'

'No,' Beckett said, wiping his damp forehead.

'Well you look ill, and you act like a madman.'

'I'm all right.'

When he left Grosvenor Court Gardens his fists were in his pockets, one holding the gun, the other clutching a wad of fifty pounds in notes. He felt an almost unbearable excitement, as if he was the electric circuit between the two objects.

His left hand caressed the notes in their elastic band. They were crisp and new, which added to his pleasure in them. This intense excitement could only be caused by ill-gotten notes; he had never experienced it with the earned money in his pay packets. He imagined that thieves and prostitutes must also feel this excitement from handling the money they gained.

He wondered what he had done tonight; he tried to discover the nature of his act. Moral links seemed severed, so that his action was irresponsible, airborne, out of moral context. He suspected that tomorrow, when he had recovered his sense of values, he would find the action to be wrong.

Through habit, he took a bus to Notting Hill Gate. When he got off, he decided that rather than take the trouble of finding a new room, he would put up at a small hotel for a few days. He walked in the direction of Queensway until he saw a neon hotel sign.

He felt trepidation at entering, because of his shabby appearance, the craziness that had thinned his face, his staring sleepless eyes, and the grey despair that had worked into his skin like grime. He was afraid that he would be refused admittance.

Behind the reception desk sat a faded woman in a hand-knitted jumper. Beckett explained that he wanted a room for a few days, that he had left his luggage at the station and would collect it tomorrow.

She did not query his explanation, but led the way up the stairs to a vacant room. She informed him about the times of meals if desired, the whereabouts of the bathrooms, gave him his keys and left him.

He woke to white walls and quiet. Like a patient emerging from anaesthetic, he had no idea of the time. It was broad daylight. He looked at his watch, but it had stopped.

From somewhere in the hotel a telephone rang three times and then stopped. He thought: Obviously people are up and about. It must be late.

The room smelled of closed windows and talcum powder. He rolled and lit a cigarette, then lay watching the silken floss of smoke that ravelled and unravelled in incense-blue threads.

The smoke worsened the used smell of the room. Inhaling made him dizzy. His headache was like a steel clamp round his brow, and his body prickled with hot and cold sweats.

He got up and opened the window. No air came in, the heavy net curtains did not stir. The street below was deserted. The tall white hotel opposite was the same as his own tall white hotel.

A young woman turned the corner and came down the street. The tap of her high heels was sometimes behind her, sometimes ahead of her. She had dark hair, a black low-necked sweater, and a flaring orange skirt.

She passed under his window, made squat by perspective, and he could see intimately her hair parting, her fat breasts and the junction of her several shoulder-straps.

It occurred to him that although he was living in a state of excitability he had not been troubled by desire for women lately. He wondered whether the Thyrodine pills dulled the sexual appetite.

Remembering the girl with pearly hair in the lift, he felt warm inside. He knew that every time he remembered her he would feel warm and happy inside in this way. The incident had been complete in itself; he had not wanted to spoil it by seeing her again. He knew that she, too, would occasionally remember the episode and feel happy about it. Poor kid, he thought, having to live with that fat slob and entertain his ghastly friends.

The dark woman and her footsteps had gone. The street was again deserted except by the heat. He turned back to the room.

There was an inverted toothglass on the ledge over the washbasin. He gulped down warmish water from the cold tap. Then he looked round the room. The paintwork was white like the walls. On the dressing-table were a crochet mat set, specks of face powder, and a few brown hairs.

He opened cupboards and drawers which were musty-smelling, lined with pages of *Woman's Own,* and biscuit-crumbed. The previous owner had left behind a wire coat-hanger, an empty Tampax carton, a bottle of auburn hair-tint, and a telephone number written in lipstick on a Senior Service packet.

He had to discover the time. He opened the door and looked down yards of silent carpet. The other doors were all shut, and there seemed to be nobody around. He went downstairs, suppressing a desire to do so on tiptoe.

In the hall, the grandfather clock, with courteous, old-world tick, was at ten past four. He had slept through the morning and most of the afternoon. The receptionist had left her knitting on her desk, but she herself was not there. There was a low murmur of voices from behind the television-lounge door.

Beckett returned to his room to wash and shave. The hotel had provided a laundry-stiff hand-towel which hung from the rail under the basin and a bar of hard cheap soap. When he was clean, he took the gun from his pocket. He balanced it on his palm and his hand turned to steel like the gun. The gun had the beauty of all efficient mechanisms, a high-powered beauty because its purpose was death. Beckett took the flowered cotton coverlet off the bed, and wrapped it round the gun. Then he put the bundle into a drawer. He peeled two pounds from the wad of notes and put the remainder in the drawer with the gun. He locked the drawer and pocketed the key.

At five-thirty he descended the stairs again and let himself out into the street. He went first to an off-licence, where he bought a bottle of Beaujolais and four packets of the most expensive cigarettes in stock. Then he went to the corner store and bought a large meat pie, a loaf of black-rye bread, butter, and cheese. The scent of fruit made him realize his craving for fruit. Oranges, apples, bananas, and apricots delighted his senses. He bought a pound of each, and left the shop with paper bags clasped to his chest. His last stop was at a newsagent's, where he bought *Reveille, Weekend,* and an *Astounding Science Fiction.*

When he got back to the room, he took off his shirt and socks and washed them with toilet soap in the basin. Then he hung them over the open window to dry.

He opened the bottle of wine by attacking the cork with his penknife. The cork went down suddenly, and wine spurted over his hand and bare chest. He licked his hand, then wiped his chest with his hand, then licked his hand again. His initial nausea overcome, he found that he was hungry. He tore off a hunk of bread, and buttered it with the penknife. There was a notice on the door forbidding eating in the bedrooms, but he had made the room his cave and did not want to dine with the other guests. His mouth full of bread-and-cheese, he swilled down wine, drinking straight from the bottle. Then he started on the pie, with its golden crust and juicy lumps of steak and kidney. When he had demolished most of the food, he started on the fruit. Soon the room was filled with the tang of oranges.

The breakdown of his moral system was still unrepaired. The links which normally bound behaviour into a certain pattern had gone. The murder seemed unrelated; there was no standard to measure it by. It was morally meaningless, having no good nor bad, just as an object outside gravity has no top nor bottom.

He tried to think of taking Dyce's money as bad, but could only see it as an action.

Water dripped off his nylon shirt on to the linoleum. From somewhere in the hotel he could hear music from a television cowboy serial. Behind the music was the distant sound of cars going somewhere else. He burped, and rubbed his stomach.

He thought: With me, everything is intellectual. I would even kill on an intellectual theory. I lack spontaneity.

He unlocked the drawer and removed the gun from its wrapping. For a while he fondled it, then reparcelled it in the flowered coverlet and returned it to the drawer.

He lay back on the bed to finish the wine and smoke cigarettes. There was an article in *Reveille* about Brigitte Bardot which he read.

Chapter 15

BECKETT GOT OFF the train at Sealing. He was ahead of schedule, because he wanted to arrive with the commuters on the city train in order to merge with the crowd. He walked towards the barrier, holding the black imitation-leather briefcase awkwardly under his arm. Irrationally, he feared that people were looking at him, that they knew the contents of his briefcase. It was a relief when he had got through the ticket barrier, and found himself in the High Street.

Sealing is a country town some twenty miles from London. Some of its inhabitants work locally, others in London. Trippers come down on cheap-day returns to picnic in its outlying beauty spots. There is a market in the square every Thursday.

Passing a Lyons teashop, he had an hallucination. He thought he saw Silent sitting at a table, with his plastic-surgery face and unmatching eyes, and his crutch propped against the table as it had been in Mick's Café.

The incident unnerved him. He had a sensation of horror. It was like the time when he had seen the baby's skull on the bed. There was no reason why he should imagine those particular things, the skull and Silent, but both images had been accompanied by the same sensation of horror.

He regained his grip on himself. He walked very straight, like a knife blade, along the centre of the pavement.

His thoughts turned to Dyce, weekending in Hampshire. He remembered that Dyce had recounted that he had once been lost in the jungle and had survived with no food and a minimum of water while searching for the path. If this story was true, it showed that Dyce had physical toughness and strong willpower. Dyce's only weakness was his desire for stimulating excitement, which might make him boast or deliberately throw out clues.

Beckett also thought that Dyce might try to swindle him out of his share of the money. Then he knew that the money was not greatly important to him. He had pretended that it was, because a money motive made his actions easier for both himself and Dyce to understand.

The entrance to the municipal gardens lay between the public library and the public conveniences. Beckett ran down the steps to the Gents and locked himself into a lavatory.

Here, in privacy, he opened the briefcase. He had bought it yesterday, secondhand. He checked the contents: the revolver, a pair of socks, a pair of gloves, a torch, a handkerchief, and a penknife. His hand closed round the gun, caressing it, as he listened to the footsteps on the pavement above his head. Then he locked the briefcase, violently pulled the lavatory chain, and left.

A snackbar was open, so he entered with the intention of having a coffee and sandwiches. Once inside, he knew that it would be impossible to stay in the café. He had to keep on the move. He asked for the sandwiches to be put in a paper bag to take away.

He returned to the municipal gardens. There was shorn grass and, as a centrepiece, a formal flower-bed in patriotic red, white, and blue. A few ducks swam on the artificial lake which was edged with crazy paving.

He sat down on the bench beside the lake. In the distance he heard the noise of children at play, a monotonous shout on one note only. He tore up the sandwiches and threw the pieces to the ducks. They made vee-shaped wakes as they swam for the bread. In the background the library building looked peaceful with the last sunlight on it. The scent of flowers fainted on the air.

He considered the difference between men and ducks. Men were political and had concepts of an improved future. To realize these concepts it was necessary to sacrifice human lives, like constructing a building and using individuals, willynilly, as bricks. Complete anarchy and individual freedom were impossible except in small political communities. There was a dialectic between the claims of individual freedom and social concepts. Yet the concept of a better society, a higher form of life, was humanity's greatness. These ducks had no such concepts. They had no wars, but no aspirations either.

The evening sky was coloured like plum juice and custard. When the sandwiches were finished, Beckett stood up and shook the crumbs from the bag into the water.

In the High Street he stood undecided, pressing the briefcase against his chest. He had time to kill and nowhere to go. Then he entered a pub. He saw himself approaching in the mirror over the bar, between the advertisement for Gordon's Gin and the electric light disguised as a bunch of glass grapes. He was a young man in a cheap suedette jacket, with an ill, rigid face and wariness behind the eyes. He leaned against the bar while he drank two double whiskies, and half-watched the other customers. Then he half-read an article in somebody's evening paper headed '*I Still Love Her*, Marquis says'. He stared around him and the pin chessmen rattled in his pocket. Some had escaped their box and he touched them with his fingertips.

The pub did not provide a resting place for long. He

left and, unable to think of anything else to do, went to the cinema. Here he sat through a comic film.

Upper Lane led from the outskirts of Sealing into the open country. There were a few isolated houses along it. The house, Woodstock, was easily recognizable because, as Dyce had explained, it was directly opposite a pillar box. Beckett pulled on the socks over his shoes, then put on the gloves.

Standing in the laurel-bush darkness, he flashed the torch on the back door. The missing pane had been replaced by brown paper. He carefully tore away the paper, inserted his gloved hand and unlocked the door.

Inside the kitchen, he shone his torch again. A cat woke from a bed of old cardigans and stalked towards him, its tail erect, meowing. When he opened the kitchen door, the cat tried to follow him, and he had to hold it back with his foot while he let himself out into the passage.

According to plan, his first task was to search the ground-floor rooms, taking anything of value as a burglar would do.

His torch beam travelled the dining-room, resting briefly on the heavy Victorian furniture, the bobble fringe of the tablecloth, stuffed birds under a glass dome, a television set, and various photographs in velvet frames. One of the photographs was evidently of Dyce, taken some twenty years ago. The young Dyce had a hard new face and Brylcreemed hair.

His immediate impression was that he would find nothing of great value here. The old woman was a miser who preferred to keep her money in the bank. His thorough, systematic search yielded nothing except for six pound notes hidden in a biscuit barrel. He also discovered a box which had been hidden behind the cushion of an armchair. When he opened the lid, he found a chiffon scarf, a packet of sweets, and a few Woolworth's trinkets. These things seemed new, and he guessed that they were the prizes of kleptomania.

A clock struck with sweet silver notes. The inside of his mouth was dry. He had to hurry.

He left the room and started to mount the stairs, keeping one hand on the wall to guide himself. The free hand clasped the briefcase and torch to his chest. Halfway up, he had a moment of panic. He could not move. He stood paralysed, with one foot advanced towards the next stair, frozen in the everlasting moment. His limbs were heavy, like the slow-motion attempts to escape in a nightmare. He closed his eyes, and breathed deeply. Then, with an effort of will, he continued to mount the stairs.

He reached the landing. The house was noisy with silence. He mentally reconstructed Dyce's plan, labelling each door. This was the door of the spare room. Down the passage were the bathroom and the companion's bedroom.

Now, at the last moment, he was perfectly cold and calm inside. He moved automatically. He wrapped his handkerchief round the torch, then silently opened the old woman's door.

Inside, he flattened himself against the wall. He heard her heavy breathing. He crossed the bedroom crabwise, keeping an eye on the bed. The woman slept on. Her breathing was regular except when it stumbled on a snore.

He turned and met three lights aimed at him. For an instant he was bewildered. Then he realized that it was the triple mirror of the dressing-table, reflecting his torch.

He was mirrored in triplicate as he approached; three men behind three butts of light. Three hands stretched towards the dressing-table.

On it was some jewellery, which he snatched into the briefcase. He opened the drawers, but found only underclothes, a photograph album, a felt rose on a safety-pin, and an enema appliance.

He had reached the hardest part of his task. He had to wake her, in order to complete the effect of a burglar disturbed in the act. He listened to her breathing. Reluctantly, he took out the revolver. He wanted to take the things and go; he did not want to kill her.

The woman turned over in her sleep, grunting. Beckett stiffened, willing her not to wake.

For a second, it was in the balance whether she would subside into sleep or surface to waking.

Then she sat up suddenly, uttering incoherent grunts at first and then words: 'Who is it? ... Margaret, is that you? ... Who is there? ...'

Beckett shone the torch full in her face, trying to dazzle her and pin her down with the beam while he made his escape.

For a moment the plan worked; she was blinded and immobilized. Then she ducked under the beam, slid out of bed and made for the door.

They were some twelve feet apart, facing each other, she in the doorway and he in the room.

He croaked hoarsely: 'No... No...'

She, seeing the gun, set up a hysterical jabber: 'No, no, no, no!'

Then they both dried up like actors who have forgotten the script, and looked at each other.

Beckett levelled the gun; an assertion of dominance.

She jabbered again: 'No, no, no!' Her silk dressing-gown was hanging from the door, and she reached to take it down.

Beckett stepped towards her.

When she fell, the heavy thud shook the floor. The

gown, dislodged from its hook, fell over her, its folds collapsing gently until it was still.

Beckett slapped her cheeks, felt for her heart and pulse, and held a mirror to her lips. Then, by the light of the torch, he inspected her face. It was the face of an ageing woman, shiny with cold cream. The hair, henna'd at the ends and grey at the roots, was twisted into metal curlers. It recalled, in a clear flash of visual memory, the face of the road-accident victim whom he and Dyce had seen; the dead man who had had blood twisted into his flesh like wire.

As before, the knowledge was there without question. This was a dead body.

Panic flooded him. He tried to reconstruct the moments before her fall, but there was only a blank. She had fallen with a crash. Had that crash also contained the report of his gun?

He inspected it. The six cartridges were unfired. He had not shot her, then. But she was dead. He fought back the reeling panic. Somewhere, out of the past a memory emerged. Dyce had said that she was supposed to have a weak heart.

He turned, and again saw his triple image in the mirrors. He raised his arm to break the glass with a blow from the gun. Just in time, he stopped himself, but the momentum of his athletic swing with his arm carried him forward so that he fell with his head on the dressing-table. For a while he stayed in that position, dizzy as a drunk, breathing in the dust of spilt face-powder.

Then he straightened up. He realized that the noise might have woken the companion, and that at any moment he might be discovered. He must leave immediately. The woman had fallen across the doorway, and the door could not be opened. He half-lifted her body and dragged it across the floor. As he did so, her metal hair-curlers made a scraping noise on the linoleum.

He opened the door and stepped out into the passage. The house was in silence. He groped his way down the stairs, his cars strained with the expectation of discovery.

When he gained the garden, he broke into spasms of shuddering. He wrenched open the briefcase and grabbed the jewellery, which he flung far into the bushes. Then he ran out into the road, not going down towards Sealing but uphill towards the open country.

He ran crouching, like a commando landing on a beach, with the arm holding the briefcase crippled against his chest. He remembered that he was still wearing the socks, and paused to drag them off and stuff them into his pocket. Then he was running again, up the steep hill, and gasping aloud: 'Oh God... Oh God... the curlers scraped when I dragged her over the floor... Oh God... Oh God... the curlers scraped on the floor...'

Finally, sheer exhaustion forced him to slacken pace. He walked until Upper Lane became a mud track, through a wood and out into the country. He blundered on without knowing where he was going, walking in order to shut out thought.

A fine rain started to fall. He was oblivious of it until it changed into a downpour. Then he broke into a run again.

His jacket was soaked and his shirt clung to his back. The rain flattened his hair and trickled in rills down his neck. His wet trousers clung to his knees, hampering his progress. Still he ran on, his throat raw with his rasping breaths. He felt as if he was outside his body, running beside himself.

Fields gleamed whitely beside the path. He shone his torch through the rain, and saw that they were cornfields. The corn had been cut and bundled into stooks.

He scrambled over a ditch and up a bank into the field. He lifted one of the stooks and set it down beside another, so that the two formed a tunnel. Then he lay down on his belly and inched his way into the tunnel. There was just enough room for him to lie, cramped and awkward, with the briefcase for a pillow, under the wigwam of corn.

For a while he lay immobile, while his mallet heart and the rawness of his throat gradually eased. He could hear the secret rustle of insects in the corn, and the noise of the rain outside. The corn smelt musty, like sacks in a damp shed.

As his physical condition improved, he could no longer keep himself from thinking. The crime, intended to dynamite the way to freedom, had instead been the ultimate unreality, the concentration of all the previous unreality into a sickening unreal nightmare. He had tried to commit an act of will, but instead events had been taken out of his control. The woman had lain on the floor, and he had not known whether he had killed her. That moment had been the ultimate unreality.

He had had to inspect the gun to find out whether he had fired it. He had not. But that discovery solved nothing. The responsibility for her death was his, although he had not actually killed her.

He did not even know whether, at the last moment, he had intended to kill her. He tried to think back, but his memory was blank. He remembered the events, but not his intention. Had his cry of 'No... no...' been a denial of intent to kill? He did not know.

He had pointed the gun. Had that been to fire, or merely to threaten? He did not know that, either. He would never know...

His thoughts kept returning to the sound of her curlers scraping the floor. That small incident had become the emblem of horror. It was linked in his mind with the image of the twisted wound on the face of the accident victim. He tried to erase the double image from his mind, but it persisted. He could not escape from it.

If only he knew whether he had intended to kill her. If only he knew why he had pointed the gun, why he had protested: 'No... no...'

Beckett was numb with cold and cramp. With his hands tucked under his armpits and the hard briefcase pillowing his head, he lay sleepless throughout the night.

It was daylight. He must have slept for a few hours. He crawled from the stooks and stood up. His clothes had dried stiffly and he was shuddering with cold. There was a pain in his right thigh because he had lain on it all night. He limped when he moved.

Around him the coarse white stubble of the corn smoked in the morning sun. A lark rose on rain-darkened wings, soaring higher and higher into the sky, showering its pure notes. Beckett was the only man on a countryside cold-washed by morning.

He limped across the field. His feet were numb and icy in shoes that had dried hard like wooden clogs. His steps bruised a dark trail across the field.

He found a footpath, which led to a main road with a signpost indicating twenty-three miles to London. He set off along the main road, and before long a car stopped for him, and the driver enquired whether he would like a lift.

Beckett assented, and got in.

The driver said that he was not going as far as London, but only to Sealing. Beckett was disappointed at this news, as he wanted to avoid Sealing if possible, but there seemed no alternative.

The driver was a prosperous-looking man, with a good breakfast in his stomach, and his jowls freshly shaven and spruce with after-shave lotion. He said that he was a commercial traveller dealing in novelty goods and ornaments, and indicated the boxes of samples on the back seat. He said that the secret of being a traveller was to like people. 'I sincerely like people,' he told Beckett. 'I think of my customers as my friends. That's the way to make them like me, and buy my goods. I stand them drinks, and remember where they spend their holidays so that I can ask whether they had a good time at so-and-so, and sincerely like them.' He then went on to talk of Sealing, and said the Dog and Duck did a good lunch, quite reasonable.

Beckett did not really listen, but he was grateful for the other's flow of talk, as it absolved him from talking himself. He offered the driver a cigarette from a squashed packet.

'No, thanks all the same,' the driver said. 'I've got my own.' He indicated three unopened packets wrapped in cellophane, which were in the glove-rack.

Beckett, with hand trembling with cold, held a cigarette that was stained yellow with damp. So far he had not spoken, but had only sat shuddering, subject to waves of nausea that had their source deep down in his physical centre of gravity.

Locked in his nightmare, he was hardly aware of the driver. He felt only a sort of incurious wonder at the plump, confident hands controlling the wheel, and the man's background of saloon bars and commercial hotels and shrewd-eyed laughter over light ales.

On the edge of the town the driver turned left into a car park. 'Well, this is as far as I go. I have some business in Hallidays, that shop over there. Must catch the buyer bright and early, before he disappears for his coffee-break.'

Beckett got out, and stood clutching his briefcase. He said: 'Thank you.'

The driver suddenly realized that this was the first time Beckett had spoken. The two men stood facing each other from opposite sides of the bonnet. The driver's face slackened with bewilderment.

The parking attendant came up, his ticket-puncher at the ready, but was unnoticed by both of them. Then Beckett turned and started to walk away.

The driver called after him: 'Here ... old chap ... half a mo...'

Beckett did not turn back. He walked away at an even pace. Inwardly, the incident had upset him. Why had the driver stared at him like that? Why had he called out? Was there something about him, Beckett, some mark of guilt that made people stare?

The rear of the large store, Hallidays, formed one of the walls of the car park. A trio of girls, arriving for work, gave him cool glances, their crisp summer frocks flouncing as they went in the staff entrance.

Beckett's panic increased. Everybody was staring at him.

The High Street was thronged with shoppers. He did not know which way to go. Women with shopping baskets jostled him as he stood undecided.

He was thus hesitating when he received a sharp blow on his ankle. He turned, and saw Silent, who had struck him with one of his crutches.

Beckett realized that this was no hallucination, but reality.

Silent said: 'I've got something to tell you.'

'What?'

The cripple leaned closer, and whispered with his mouth against Beckett's ear: 'Don't worry, this isn't the kiss of Judas.'

'What do you mean?'

'Hold this...' Silent gave him one of his crutches. Then he wound his free arm round Beckett's neck. In this manner, they started to walk together up the street.

Beckett said: 'I didn't know you lived in Sealing.'

'I don't. My sister does. I stay with her sometimes.'

Silent's arm was heavy. It was as if, with the crippling of the rest of his body, all his strength had gone into his arms and hands. His hands had the sensitivity of a blind man's. Beckett had seen him, in the past, gauge minute differences in the weight and balance of objects by holding them on his palms. His arms had strength and reach, like an ape's. Now the muscles of his upper arm were pressing into the side of Beckett's neck. It only needed the curving of his arm and a bit more pressure to be a strangle grip. As they progressed up the street, Beckett thought of the words 'the kiss of Judas'. At the edge of his mind was the premonition of betrayal and disaster. He already knew that Silent would betray him. He compared himself to Sinbad who was forced to carry on his shoulders the Old Man of the Sea, who was throttling him.

He could have asked Silent to slacken his grip. But somehow it had become a point of honour not to. There was an undeclared duel between them. Silent was trying to make Beckett admit defeat and ask for mercy. Beckett was determined that Silent should waste his strength and temper, for nothing. Silent supplemented his weapons with an unpleasant, mocking laugh at intervals.

They turned up a side road, and stopped outside a small terrace house in a row of its identicals. The front door was ajar.

Inside was a gong, which Silent struck with his crutch. There was no response. 'My sister has gone out. Good.'

In the kitchen, they sat on either side of a table covered with a plastic cloth. The radio on the dresser, turned low, was playing *Housewives' Choice*.

To Beckett, accustomed to seeing Silent in the Soho café world, the setting seemed strange. Silent also appeared embarrassed by the neat domesticity.

Beckett said: 'I want a drink. Is there any?'

'Bottom of the larder. Brandy. She keeps it for medicinal purposes.'

Beckett poured brandy into two daffodil-patterned glasses. When he drank, he knew that he had been cold and exhausted and was now better. The brandy went down and formed a centre of heat inside him. It was warm in the kitchen. Condensation had formed on the window behind the check curtains.

Silent enquired: 'Got your portable chess?'

'I don't want to play now.'

'Lend it to me for a moment.'

Beckett took the cardboard box from his pocket.

Silent removed the elastic band that secured the battered lid and set out the pieces. One of the white bishops was missing; the broken one.

Beckett poked in his pockets but could not find the missing piece. 'Never mind; use a match.'

'When did you lose that piece?'

'I have no idea. Use a match.' Then something in Silent's voice made Beckett look up sharply. He met the gaze of the unmatching eyes and suddenly realized that he was dealing with an extremely clever man.

Silent said: 'You are a fool. You drop things.' His voice had become curt, rapping out words; the voice of authority. Then he raised his glass and said: 'Your health.' The box had been broken for a long time. The loose piece could have fallen out anywhere. Beckett tried to reconstruct his movements of last night. Had there been any time when the piece could have dropped out of his pocket?

'Nothing personal,' Silent said. 'I don't care for anyone; they can all go and stuff themselves as far as I'm concerned. Most people are stupid, and humanity would be no worse off without them. But the ones who do care, the ones who like or dislike their fellow men, seem to think that you're a decent enough bloke. So it's nothing personal. I buy goods and sell information; I am a businessman. The people concerned don't interest me.'

'What do you mean?'

'Precisely this. First of all, I saw you in the High Street last night. I spun the memory machine and what emerged was this: Dick Dyce has got an elderly relative living in Sealing. Joe Beckett is in Sealing. Conclusion, Joe is probably here in connection with Dick. Right?'

Beckett said nothing.

'Now, when somebody wants to find out something, they ask me. Because I am a very informed man. So I wasn't particularly surprised when two gentlemen called here early this morning, and asked if I knew anything of a person named Mrs Kathleen Dyce Grantley.'

'Police?'

'They hadn't come to read the gas meter. It appears that Mrs Grantley had been found in a condition that most people try to avoid. I mean dead.'

Beckett, determined to avoid committing himself, got up and looked out of the window. There was a row of back gardens, and a woman was hanging up washing in one of them.

Silent continued: 'The man who did it must have been an amateur, because he threw away the jewellery he had stolen. Threw it into the bushes. Also he dropped something in the bedroom, beside the dressing-table. A small object of white plastic imitation ivory.'

234

'Did the police know what it was?'

'No. But they showed it to me. And I knew.' Silent tapped his forehead. 'There's a computer in here, you know. I keep facts in my brain.'

Beckett exclaimed angrily: 'Why did you bring me here?'

'Because I'm a cripple, of course, and needed somebody to help me home. Your support served as well as anybody's. Besides, it might not have occurred to you, but the police are looking for you. So why not stop here, instead of wandering in the streets?"

'No. I'm going.'

'You can't leave by the station.'

'Why not?'

'Because, of course, the police will try to intercept you there. What a hopeless amateur you are!' Then Silent began to gasp, and flopped back in his chair. 'Oh, I'm exhausted. I've been subjecting myself to too much exertion. First there was the excitement of the police calling, and the identification of the chess-piece. And after that, patrolling Sealing in search of you. That walk back from the High Street has finished me. You must help me upstairs to bed.'

'All right. Put your arm round my shoulder again.

Beckett helped Silent up the stairs. This time, the cripple's weight was the heaviness of exhaustion rather than active pressure.

'My sister... bloody inconsiderate bitch... why does she give me a room upstairs instead of downstairs?...'

Beckett panted with the physical effort. He managed to get Silent to the top of the flight. In the bedroom, he helped the cripple on to the bed.

Silent collapsed. He looked as useless as a wreck on the shore.

Beckett commented: 'You're clever, aren't you? You keep in with the Mick's Café set of pilferers on small deals. And work for the police on big ones.'

That's business.' Then Silent added: 'I'm not a pretty sight. I can't get a woman. Even a noisy little nobody, a jumped-up little chit like Ilsa Barnes, can laugh at me. But when it comes to brains, then I have the laugh on them.'

Beckett realized that Silent, who despised and insulted everybody in Mick's, loved Ilsa.

'You sleep with her, don't you? You're her lover.'

Beckett did not reply. He collected his briefcase from the kitchen and left the house.

Chapter 16

IN THE TELEPHONE kiosk, he asked for the weekend number that Dyce had given him. There was a delay while one exchange contacted the other. He heard a snatch of popular song on the line, then silence. He clutched the briefcase, willing the operator to hurry.

A woman's voice answered the phone. He asked for Captain Dyce. There was another delay while Dyce was called.

Finally Dyce's voice said: 'Hello? Yes?'

They had prearranged a code whereby Beckett could communicate his success or failure. Now he found that he could not remember the code-words. His mind was blank.

Dyce repeated: 'Hello?'

'I had to phone you. I've bungled it.'

There was silence. Beckett thought: Why doesn't he say something? He said: 'Are you there?'

'Yes, I'm here. What's happened?'

'I went through with it all right. But I've been found out. They're after me.'

'Christ, no!'

He could hear his own breathing and Dyce's. Looking through the glass wall of the kiosk, he noticed that the market clock-tower was ornamented with Gothic spires and that the time was five-to-ten.

'No, Christ almighty! How on earth could you have gone wrong? What happened? Have you done for both of us?'

'Not for you.'

Sharply: 'What?'

Beckett stopped looking at the clock-tower. He said: 'You're not necessarily done for. You can keep out of the

237

whole thing. I was broke. I knew your aunt had money and jewellery on her premises. I decided to burgle her house, so I stole your service revolvers without your knowledge. Etc.'

'Are you on the level?'

'There's no point in two people getting done for one crime.'

'No,' Dyce said quickly. 'Of course not.'

'All right then.'

'Listen, this phone is in the dining-room. Someone might come in.'

'All right. Well, goodbye.'

'Wait...'

'What?'

'Wait... No, nothing.' Dyce said: 'Joe?'

'I'm here.'

'I mean, you can take care of yourself all right, can't you?'

Beckett smiled. He replaced the receiver and left the kiosk. As Silent had warned him about the station, he decided that his best plan would be to walk to the next town, Horsley, from where he could take a Green Line bus to Victoria.

Sealing and Horsley are both situated in valleys, separated by a high sandstone ridge. The ridge is so high that, on fine days, one can see three counties. Or perhaps it is five. He could not remember.

He climbed the steep lane. The hedgerow had a country smell like brown bread, and the odour of wet earth stirred secretly.

When he reached the heights, a sailor gale hit him. The road lay along the spine of the ridge, flanked by steep drops on either side, and formed a target for bad weather.

The gale buffeted him so that it was difficult to stand upright. Trees, uprooted by last night's storm, had fallen across the road and torn leaves hung from the telegraph wires. He was alone on the high altitude. He flung himself into the gale like a swimmer into the sea and gulped down draughts of cold air. Unlike town air, which only reaches the edge of the nostrils, country air fills the lungs. Beckett felt drunk with it. The exhilaration was so great that he could hardly hold it. He started to run, with his head back and his arms outflung, in order to work off some of the joy that threatened to explode inside him.

As he ran, he shouted aloud into the deafening wind: 'Glory... glory... glory!...'

Then he pulled up, and stood, with the wind outlining him coldly, like a god surveying the countryside arrayed below him.

A fine drizzle fell, and there were different diffusions of light. Milk white, electric light, foggy purple, the acid-thinned grey of morning mists, curdled light, veils of black crepe, water-colour washes, choking industrial black and sulphur, intensities of lemon, gold and silver radiance — all were choral like the ranks of angels, cherubim and seraphim.

Since he had left Silent, his tyrannical will had abdicated, his stubborn mind had stopped forcing matters, and he had abandoned hope. Having made these rejections, he received, like grace, an insight that was more potent than formal knowledge. Blessed, he gave praise and blessing to all creation. Previously, he had felt paralysed in a world without meaning. Now he experienced the polar opposite state; he was strong and had potentialities, and he affirmed everything.

He had lived in a negative hell that was absence of God. His present vision was that God was the common force manifested in all nature and in the conscious receptacle of his own soul. This force was at high tide

in his soul. It was vital and yet peaceful, like exulta-
tion. It gave him back his lost sense of meaning.

Meaning confers freedom from paralysis. Beckett recognized that his newfound freedom entailed the
responsibility of retaining and increasing it. Accordingly,
he made various resolutions.

He resolved to make his experience on this hill the
centre of his life, and to try to re-attain its ecstasy. He
resolved to realize his potentialities, by study, work,
and living, and, to fight against sliding back into the
trough of boredom and lethargy. He finally resolved to
undergo whatever sentence he received for his crime of
manslaughter without complaint, and without being
broken by it.

It occurred to him that although he was an agnostic
he had used religious terminology best to express his
inexpressible experience. The concepts God, hell, and
rebirth were all religious. This led to the conclusion
that religion was rooted in subjective experience, which
accounted for the success of religion. It seemed to him
that religious doctrines were formal projections of
human experience and paradox. He was glad that he
had arrived at this idea, as it cured his bitterness
against his Catholic upbringing.

He left the road and descended to Horsley by way of
a track down the sharp flank of the ridge. He moved in
leaps and bounds; loose scree spurted from his heels.
His momentum prevented a fall; after a perilous leap
he went straight on to the next before he had time to
fall.

He took the coach to Victoria, then the bus to Notting
Hill. He had decided to go to the police station and give
himself up. He chose the local police station because he
wanted to complete his circuit; to return to the district
where he had fought the looming walls of his bedsitter,

where the air had swollen heavy and oppressive with the vitality it had drained from him, where he had lain sick with accidie, like a python, crushing his chest and coiled round his immobilized limbs.

There was something dashing and daring in his decision to return. He wanted to show that he could get back to base before voluntarily giving himself up. He had caused a death, and would suffer for it. It seemed to him that these two facts were on the heroic level. They had an order, an expensive tragedy, which was absent from the haphazard trivialities that dotted the lives of most people.

Near Tewkesbury Road, a woman spoke to him. Momentarily, he did not recognize her. She was a housewife, drearily clothed, holding a shopping-bag of groceries. Then he realized that she was Gash's landlady.

She said: 'I thought you should know the bad news. It was such a shock.'

'News?'

'Poor Mr Gash passed away last night.'

He looked at her, frowning. Then he looked at the pavement. Then at her again. He said: 'No. No, that's terrible.'

'I didn't know he was so ill. I mean, he hadn't ever told me about it. He hadn't ever seen a doctor. All the time he was having these attacks of asthma, but he never complained. But I mean, he should have gone to a specialist about it, shouldn't he?'

'Yes.'

'A lady I knew had this asthma, and she went to a specialist and had injections. She had to keep off things, various things to eat, as well. But poor Mr Gash didn't take care of himself at all. He was all for the spirit and never mind the body. Well, that doesn't do any good, does it?'

He agreed absentmindedly. 'No.' Then he said: 'Asthma?'

'Yes. That's what the doctor said, when he came this morning. I found him this morning, you see. I could tell he was dead, and I called the doctor.'

'Poor Gash, dying alone.'

'I went into his room this morning, you see, to ask him, if he'd like a cup of tea as we were making one for ourselves. And when he didn't answer me, I thought at first that he was just in one of his far-away states. Then I asked him again: "How about a nice cuppa tea, Mr Gash?" And he still didn't answer.'

Beckett rubbed his fist between his brows.

She said: 'He's been lodging with me for years now, and I'd sort of got fond of him, in spite of his odd habits. I mean, there wasn't any harm in him, was there? A bit cranky, but a kind old bird."

He tried to think of something to say. He repeated: 'It's terrible.'

'Anyway, I've phoned his daughter, and she'll be coming up to take care of the arrangements. She'll let you know about the funeral and everything.'

'Thanks.'

'Well, I thought you should know. You were the only person who ever visited him. His only friend, so to speak.'

They parted. When Beckett reached Gash's house, he paused to notice the closed curtains. Inside, the body of Gash would be laid out on his pile of blankets on the floor, with death drawn down over the eyes. He wondered whether his own belongings were still in the corner where he had left them. The thought of Gash dead, Dyce's aunt dead, and his mother dying, produced a sharp lurch of delight in being alive himself.

He noticed that, opposite his old lodging, a man was sauntering with hands in pockets. The man stopped and looked up at the windows. Then he started to cross the road towards the house.

Beckett was sure that the man was a policeman. He broke out in a sweat of shock. His brain was confused, and he could only stand and gape at the policeman. Then, from the confusion of his brain, the dominant impulse emerged: to run. He wanted to run and escape while there was still time.

At that moment the front door opened, and Ilsa walked out.

The policeman saw her, and gave her a quick, hard glance, noting her description.

She walked down the street towards Beckett. She had not seen him yet.

Beckett stood as if frozen. He could not run now, for that would attract her attention, which would in turn attract the attention of the policeman. He kept still, just inside Gash's gate. Ilsa was on the other side of the street, and might not notice him.

She was wearing her slim white dress with the gold belt. She paused to light a cigarette, screening the match with the open flap of her handbag, and he saw the thin awkward angle of her arm as she fumbled the match.

The policeman also watched her.

Then she saw Beckett, and shouted to him across the street: 'Joe-Joe!' She ran towards him, teetering, in her tight dress and high heels, in an odd Charleston run as if her knees were tied together. As she ran, she waved enthusiastically, and screamed in her strident voice: 'Honey! I went to your house and the old bitch told me you'd left! Told me you'd done a flit!'

Then she was in his arms, and he said with automatic affection: 'Ilsa, Ilsa, Ilsa.'

'I get so choked with anybody else but you.' She buried her face in the shoulder of his zipper jacket.

As he held her, he thought, ironically, that it was typical that he should be betrayed by this girl for whom he felt the unreal parallels of love and indifference. She had prevented his heroic gesture of giving himself up and had subjected him to the humiliation of capture.

In the end the lie had won. He was speaking the easy words of love: 'Ilsa, darling Ilsa,' although dissociation was like a cold stone in his mind.

He accepted that he was like that. With people, he would never get farther than a kindness born of basic indifference. He would always live behind a glass wall. But although he was condemned to live in unreality, he had been given, as recompense, the power to experience ultra-reality. He had been equipped to receive experiences like his vision on the hill. This equipment, built into his brain, was his recompense for his difference from other people. He decided that it was worth the price.

Over Ilsa's blonde head he met the eyes of the policeman, who was watching with folded arms and a tight smile of satisfaction.

Beckett held the girl, but was already alone as the policeman started to walk towards him.

The children were wheeling and shouting as always; their screams ricocheted from the buildings. Two women walked along the pavement, pushing their shopping in wheeled baskets. A front door banged, a radio played. The sky was London grey over Tewkesbury Road on a Saturday morning.

About the Author

Laura Del-Rivo was born in 1934 to middle-class Catholic parents in Cheam, Surrey. Her father worked in a bank. She was educated at Holy Cross Convent, New Malden, and left school at sixteen. She had various unremarkable jobs and went to Soho cafés after work. She lived in furnished rooms before she joined a house of writers and painters in Chepstow Villas, Notting Hill. Laura Del-Rivo was part of a loose group of writers which included Colin Wilson. She was photographed by Ida Kar and recently appeared in Kar's retrospective at the National Portrait Gallery.

The Furnished Room was released as a film, *West 11*, starring Alfred Lynch, Eric Portman, Kathleen Breck and Diana Dors, in 1963.

Laura Del-Rivo became, and remains, a Portobello Road market trader. Her most recent novel is *Speedy and Queen Kong*, published by Paupers' Press. She is still writing.

Available from New London Editions

Available from bookshops or www.fiveleaves.co.uk